COME ALIVE

EXPERIMENT IN TERROR #7

KARINA HALLE

1

So fucking horny.

    I know that was a crude thing to think after a day of assisting the police with the gruesome search for Mitch and decapitated llamas, plus taking Perry to the local hospital to get her injuries looked over, but I gave up on censoring myself from myself a long ass time ago.

Besides, wouldn't you be horny as fuck when the woman of your dreams was sitting beside you in your car for eight damn hours, wearing a low-sliced top that did nothing to cover up her amazing tits that jostled with every turn? Every time we hit a bump in the road I nearly came in my fucking pants.

Yeah, fuck seemed to be my word of the day. But Perry brought that on herself when she crawled into my room last night like something out of my most depraved and desperate dreams. I still felt like pinching myself to make sure what happened was real and not one of my ghosts. If only pinching didn't turn me on.

When we had sat in the motel hot tub for longer than doctors would recommend, we both went back to our rooms, our stupid separate rooms. The last thing I wanted after nearly dying in the mountains at the hands of a lunatic and the teeth of a motherfucking Sasquatch was to have her out of my sight. I wanted her in my bed, in my arms. Screw the formalities, screw whatever had happened between us —I needed her like I'd never needed anything and I could swear that she needed me too.

But she told me to sleep well and retreated to her room, the one next door, closing it between us. I felt like she shut the door on everything that was and could ever be. It was like a guillotine blade on my future, *our* future.

I tried to make peace with it, just lying there on the sketchy motel sheets, working over the scenarios in my head, the ways I could cope. I could turn off my heart as I had done so many times before, but the funny thing was for once I was afraid I wouldn't be able to turn it on again. It was like if I gave up on Perry then I was giving up on love forever. Dramatic, yes. But I was Dex Foray and "dramatic" was my middle name, along with "The Fuckmaster" and "Pierre."

I stewed on it for a while, wondering if Perry was going to follow through with her threat of moving out as soon as we got back home. I'd do anything to make her stay, I just couldn't figure out what I had to do. She knew how I felt. I couldn't have been more honest, more clear out there in the forest with her, essentially handing over my heart. She had it and it just seemed like she didn't want it. I couldn't blame her but I also couldn't give up; I'd given up on so much before. I was afraid that I'd drive her away if I didn't give her space, if I didn't let things be. She'd told me that maybe we were only meant to be friends and though I couldn't have disagreed more, if it meant having her as a friend or having nothing at all, I'd have her. I'd always have her, in any form I could get.

Getting nowhere, feeling her presence in the other room and wishing I could pick up on snippets of her dream like I had sometimes gotten from her thoughts, I'd gotten up to use the bathroom. It was when I was glancing at myself in the mirror, seeing my reflection in the darkness, that I swore I saw another person in the room with me. It was just for a split second but it was one second too much. I had a feeling I knew who it was, too.

After that, I left the bathroom light on. I didn't care if that made me a pussy. I'd rather have a vagina than see my dead mother again, and if I felt leaving the light on helped, so be it. But like the most beautiful of ghosts, soon Perry appeared at the foot of my bed, her spirit shattering my fear, her body shattering my resolve.

She came toward me, half lit by the bathroom light and I couldn't even believe what happened next. She stripped down until she was naked as all hell, all fucking woman to the max—the wide curve of her hips, the small of her waist, her fat, heavy breasts that begged me to weigh them in my hands. To say I was hard was an understatement. I was made of steel, the only solid thing in this sea of bewilderment I was drowning in. Like, what the actual fuck was going on?

It wasn't too long before I figured it out. She crawled on top of my body, hands all over, breasts pressed against my chest, and took me all in. She gave herself over and took me with her and I couldn't have asked for more. I mean, I guess I could have asked for a blow job before the morning sun reared her ugly head, but I was fast asleep with Perry in my arms, holding her like I'd never let her go.

And then, before we could even wake up slowly, warm

skin to warm skin, before I could relish in the morning after that we'd never been granted before, there was a ridiculous ruckus outside.

"Dex Foray!" someone bellowed as they pounded on the door. I jolted up, almost forgetting who was in my bed with me. I looked down at Perry, who was both wide-eyed and annoyed. Still fucking beautiful.

I looked over at the clock. It was 7:30 AM. The asshole bird got the worm. I gave Perry a sympathetic look and quickly slipped on my jeans and checked through the peep-hole. Three cops were outside. I was right about the asshole thing.

Apparently they hadn't been up into the mountains yet and were relying on us to show them the scene of the Twat-waffle massacre. Fair enough, I suppose, but don't you think they'd let two foreigners who'd nearly been eaten alive in their primitive Canadian woods sleep in for a little bit?

No such luck. Captain Asshole was the officer who had been drilling us the most the night before, and he barked at me to be ready in five minutes. Then he went to the next room to do the same to Perry and I had to gleefully inform them that she was in my room with me already. They didn't care, which was too bad because I thought *everyone* should care that I fucked Perry last night and fucked her good. Perhaps I needed to get an airplane to write that in the sky. I knew an auburn-haired snatchslinger who needed to see it.

Because we were forced to get ready for the latest episode of *M.O.U.N.T.I.E.S: Canucks on Patrol,* Perry and I didn't have any time to discuss what the previous night meant. Not that I was one for having relationship talks so soon after sex, but I would like to have at least some idea of what was going on between us now that it was the light of day and our hormones were no longer at the wheel.

Although, mine were always driving me—Perry had turned me on even when she came out of her room with no makeup on her face, dressed in jeans and a bulky sweatshirt. You see, it's what's underneath that counts.

We climbed into the back seat of Captain Asshole's squad SUV and listened to him drone on about the dangers of the woods and how Rigby's llama trekking expedition was always a little suspect, and how his daughter Christina had been caught smoking pot once behind the 7-Eleven. Only I wasn't listening to him, I was listening to Perry.

And she wasn't listening to him either. She was thinking and thinking hard, nodding her head only so often to let the cops think she was paying attention, but I could tell from the way her brows came to meet each other above her bunny nose that it was all for show. Plus, you know, I heard her thoughts.

All right, so I had only heard two of them, but it was enough to make me want to open up her head and stay a while.

One thought was the more harmless, "*I just want to go home*," which I assumed she meant was our home in Seattle. But maybe it wasn't. Because did she consider that her home or did she mean her home, her parents' place in Portland? After all, that whole "I'm moving out" thing was still on the table and I couldn't be sure that a night of hot sex would eradicate that.

The other thought that blasted its way into my head, like I couldn't have kept it out even if I tried, was a lot more loaded: "*This is so fucking weird.*"

The minute I heard that, I had to bite my actual tongue to keep from asking what was so weird. Not only did I not want the cops to think we were nutty telepaths, but I didn't want to put Perry on the spot. She knew I could read her thoughts on occasion, but the less I drew attention to it, the better. I never censored myself but I knew Perry would, especially when it came to us. I was fortunate enough that she was sitting there and thinking away without shooting me nervous looks.

Not to say that she didn't look a bit uptight, rubbing her lips together like she was on the receiving end of never-ending Chap Stick. She kept staring out the window, at the endless rows of trees as the cop car climbed higher and higher into drama llama land. There were so many fucking things I wanted to say to her, to do to her. And no, not just bending her over, but holding her hand, putting my arm around her. But maybe that's just what was *so fucking weird*. Maybe it's that things between us were so unresolved and we couldn't even have a moment to resolve them.

I waited until we pulled up to Rigby's to finally reach out to her.

"You doing okay, kiddo?" I asked before she stepped out of the vehicle, putting my hand on her knee.

She gave me a small smile and I was relieved that she didn't flinch from my touch.

"Just tired," she said.

I couldn't hide my smart-ass grin. "It was worth it though."

She nodded, her cheeks going pink. Score one for me.

I applied pressure to my grip and leaned in closer. "There's more of that where that came from. We'll just do what we can this morning, then get you to the hospital—"

"Dex, I'm fine."

"And after we get you checked up at the hospital," I went on, voice harder, "to make sure nothing gnarly happened to you yesterday—"

"You're the one who should get checked out. You were

buried under a ton of rubble when the cliff collapsed beneath you."

"Yeah, but I'm clearly fine." And that was my own thing that was so fucking weird, every day finding out that I wasn't quite the man I used to be. "And I'm sure you're fine too, but I'm being more careful with you from now on."

She rolled her eyes.

I continued, giving her knee a final squeeze. "And then we are high-tailing it the fuck back to Seattle."

Captain Asshole chose that moment to rap loudly on the hood of the car.

"Are you coming or what?" he said, opening Perry's door.

I leaned across her and looked up at him. "I thought Canadians were supposed to be polite."

"Not when Americans are wasting our time," he said. "Now please, if you will, let's get this thing over with."

Clearly they still didn't believe in the whole Sasquatch thing, even when we handed them what evidence we had. They wanted to write Mitch and Twatwaffle off like the victims of a mangy bear and move on. For once, I was totally cool with them not believing us. It would make things move a lot faster.

"Can you give us a moment?" I asked, and then reached for the door handle and shut it on him before he could answer.

My face was just inches from hers, and if this was weird, it wasn't coming through. She just looked scared, like a baby deer. A totally fuckable baby deer.

Jesus, Dex, I told myself. *Get a grip before you start imagining her on Animal Planet.*

"Perry," I said softly, my mouth too close to hers. Could I kiss her? Should I kiss her? Would she want me to? Did that belong only in the bedroom? Did it belong to only last night?

When would I know?

She swallowed, her delicate throat moving, and I had to fight the urge to run my tongue up it. I focused on those big blue eyes instead.

"I think maybe you should stay here in the car," I told her. She twitched, shocked.

"Why?"

I shot Captain Asshole a quick glance before coming back to her. I was totally aware that I was leaning over her, encroaching in her space, but I didn't care— she was going to have to get used to it.

"I know you don't want to go back out there, and frankly I don't either, but I'll do it. They don't need two of us to be the tour guide for the Snowcrest Llama Massacre. Besides," I lowered my voice, "I want to get out of here. You stay here because of your injuries and then I can at least insist that they take us back to town early to get you checked out."

She didn't seem to think that would work—and probably didn't appreciate me using her injuries as an excuse— but I knew she was grateful to stay behind in the car, even if the cops were a bit reluctant to leave her there alone.

Luckily, the plan did end up saving us a lot of time. Rigby came out of his house, still shell-shocked it seemed, and together we led the cops over the snowy ridge and to that damn cabin. I explained again what had happened to us over the last few days, Rigby piping up now and then to back me up. The cops were still set on the whole mangy bear idea, and if they weren't so close-minded I would have felt sorry for them. I mean, I don't know about you, but personally I'd want to know if some monster was lurking in the woods, ready to rip your arm off.

Speaking of mutilated corpses, the decapitated Twat-waffle was evidence enough for them that this was the work of a crazy animal. They wanted me to lead them into the woods and show them where Mitch was, but I just scribbled it down on the map, staunchly refusing to go myself. The cabin was hard enough to revisit, the horror that we experienced just waiting to relive itself in my brain. There was no way I'd be taking them into Mitch corpse territory, and especially when Rigby and I both knew that the beast could still be out there, perhaps dead or perhaps merely wounded by his shotgun. Either way, I used the opportunity to remind them that I needed to get Perry to the hospital, and one of the officers agreed to take us back to town, especially since they had to organize a bigger search party.

Perry was napping by the time we got back to the car. I was torn beside sitting in the backseat with her and riding shotgun. I decided to ride in the front because it made me behave.

On the way back down the mountain, I'd be lying if I wasn't trying to read her thoughts again, waiting for some clarity to make sense of what I heard earlier. No such luck. I couldn't pick up on anything, not when we pulled into town, not when the doctor looked her over and proclaimed her fine (despite slathering her scratches in antiseptic), not when we hurried back to the motel and checked out before the suspicious front desk lady tossed our luggage in the hot tub.

And certainly not during the ass-numbing drive back to Seattle. Oh, Perry and I talked when we weren't listening to our ever expanding playlist. But our topics were safe—wondering about if we'd get in trouble for making a run for the border without checking in with Rigby or the cops, or what Jimmy was going to say when we told him we didn't have any footage and how he needs to trim his nosehairs. I wanted to ask her a million questions and talk about a million other things—big things, meaningful things—but every time I opened my mouth to do so, I was met with fear.

I remembered what she said last night: "You are a part of me, Dex. You're every part of me. Always have been. Always will be." I remembered clinging to those words as I fell asleep. And I remembered the things that she didn't say. That I'd told her I loved her and never heard a thing in return. I had never told her just so she could say it back, but the silence was...nerve-wracking.

WHICH MADE the fact that I was unbearably horny even worse. Dex with blue balls was one thing, but when I was anxious as well, it made for a capricious situation. So I did my best to keep my eyes on the road, wishing she'd put her bulky sweatshirt back on, and got us home as quickly as I could.

It was around 11PM when I pulled the Highlander into the underground garage and parked it in my space. I switched off the engine and twisted in my seat to face her. Her eyes twinkled in the dim light but I couldn't read her expression.

"So," I said, trying to ignore the awkwardness that seemed to be building up in the car by the second.

She gave me a small smile and placed her hands in her lap. "So."

Oh Jesus. Why did it feel like I was back in high school, trying to score with Cindy Brown in my beat-up Civic? Granted I ended up getting a wicked handjob, but the moments leading up to it were like pulling teeth. And I wasn't even trying to get a handjob here, I'd just forgotten how to talk to Perry.

I bit the bullet. "Are you happy to be home?"

She nodded. "Fuck yeah."

I held myself in check. I lowered my voice and leaned in closer. "Do you consider this to be your home now?"

My eyes searched hers, my brain concentrating, trying to hear anything, see anything, to get the truth from her.

"Seattle?" she asked cautiously. She looked down at her hands and tilted her head. "Yeah. I think I do."

I should have accepted that. That should have been good enough. But it wasn't good enough.

"I mean with me. Am I your home?"

She rubbed her lips together as the pressure in the car increased. The waiting, the tension, was unbearable. On the plus side, I didn't have an erection anymore.

"Dex..." she started. "I'm still a bit confused over everything. Things have changed so fast...I just need time to get used to it, that's all. I haven't been able to think about much other than not dying. You know?"

I stared at her intensely and put my hand on her cheek, relishing the warmth of her skin, that incurable softness. "You're my home, Perry. And I *will* be yours."

I leaned over and kissed her softly, just a taste of her lips and what she could promise me. I pulled away and her eyes fluttered open, her lips still parted.

Swallowing hard, I gave her a quick smile and said, "Let's get our things upstairs."

We got our gear out of the car and embarked on a short but awkward elevator ride up to the second floor where my —our—apartment was. I started thinking that perhaps I'd been a little too presumptuous telling her I wanted to make her my home and that I would be hers. Then I realized I'd been nothing but presumptuous with her from the very start, from that very moment she made me pie. There was no point in stopping now, no matter how heavy my legs felt as we walked down the hall to our door, no matter how sweaty the back of my neck was, no matter how badly my mind wanted to analyze the moment. There was no stopping this—us.

I paused in front of the door, my keys out, and took in a deep breath. Then I turned to look at her. She stared back at me in anticipation neither of us could ignore any longer.

I cleared my throat. "I just thought I should warn you that the second we walk into the apartment, I am going to maul the fuck out of you. I don't care if you're tired or bruised or scratched. You'll just be more so when I'm finished."

I didn't think it was possible for her eyes to get wider. But they did. Hey, at least she now knew what was coming.

Both of us.

I opened the door and stepped into the apartment which smelled slightly musty. Damn Seattle dampness got into everything. I expected Perry to hesitate after what I'd just told her, but she marched right on in after me. Her confidence was a surprise. My hard-on was back in full swing.

I dropped my bag then grabbed her, slamming the door shut by slamming her up against it. She let out a cry, but it had a throatiness to it, the kind that reached into my gut and stroked my balls and made me want to unleash everything on her that I'd kept to myself all day.

I devoured her lips with mine, wanting so much of her, all of her, always wanting more. She tasted sweeter than she did back in the car, wetter, more open, more giving. Our tongues entwined in the heat and I pressed hard against her, wanting to consume her in every way possible. One hand was lost in the silkiness of her thick hair, tugging on it lightly, the other was jerking up her shirt, soaking in the feeling of her skin.

My lips pulled away and went to her ear where I licked up the rim, feeling her shiver under my tastebuds.

"I want to put my tongue so deep inside you," I moaned.

She let out a breathy laugh. "I think you just did."

I smiled as my lips trailed down her neck. "That was nothing."

I pulled her shirt over her head and unclasped her bra until her heavy breasts bounced free. I dipped my head and sucked hard on one nipple, making it pucker delicately in my mouth. Perry's breath hitched sharply and I knew I was on the right track. Last night she was in charge, but now, now we were on my turf and I was going to fuck her senseless.

When a groan escaped from her sugary mouth, I started undoing her jeans and slid my fingers into her fine hair, nearly losing it when I discovered how goddamn slick she was. She was practically melting into my touch.

Once she began panting, I dropped to my knees, keeping her pressed back against the door, and yanked down her jeans and underwear until they were on the floor. I brought one of her legs up, hooking it over my shoulder, then left soft, wet kisses from the side of her knee all the way up her inner thigh. Her body tensed and relaxed from my touch, and I grabbed her ass, hard, bringing her into my face. My lips met her swollen ones and I teased her clit with the tip of my nose before sliding my tongue along her cleft and plunging it inside her.

Oh god, nothing tasted better, felt better, than this. She gripped the top of my head, nearly pulling out my hair, and

I knew I was blowing her mind. She was sinking into me, hips rocking for pressure, and I was an insatiable beast who still wanted more, more, more. I wanted to be inside her in every way I could. I wanted to stay there and leave my mark, make her feel me, make her never forget.

She came hard into my mouth, her clit pulsing beneath my lips, her fold blossoming open, and I drank her all in, keeping her coming until she was moaning for me to stop.

I pulled my head away and looked up at her exquisitely pleasured face, wiping my lips with the back of my hand.

"Welcome home," I said with a grin. Then I helped her shaking legs step out of the rest of her jeans and led her to the bedroom.

My turn.

2

There's sleeping in and then there's *sleeping in*. We did the latter, burrowing into my bed like we were hibernating for the winter. Her soft skin, my comfy duvet—it's all I ever needed. I could die there, death by relaxation, preceded by death by pussy.

"You've always belonged in my bed," I whispered into her ear as I pulled out of her and wrapped my arms around her chest. That was orgasm number a billion for the both of us, which explained why it was so hard to get out of bed. After I followed through with my promise to fuck her sense-less last night, I added a 3AM session (blowjob, finally), and two rounds in our warm, half-asleep state.

She snuggled into my arms and I could hear the smile in her voice when she said, "I guess Fatty Rab will have to make room for me then."

"There's no way that dog is sharing a room with us. You only get one dog in your bed, baby, and that's me." I had half a mind to call up Rebecca and beg her to take care of Fat Rabbit for a few days more, giving Perry and I plenty of time in this faux-honeymoon period, but I knew I'd start missing the stinky bastard sooner or later.

"And you're one bad dog," she teased.

"Woof, woof. Give a dog a boner."

She giggled and smacked my arm. And that's why I loved this woman. She let me say the stupidest shit, and on occasion, actually found it funny.

There it was again. That word, that feeling of sinking, falling, drowning. Good, wonderful, delicious, scary. I was going to have to get used to it. I was going to have to start being okay with being in love and hope to hell she'd start to catch up with me.

"Hey, Perry," I said, kissing the top of her head. Fuck she smelled amazing, like sex and vanilla.

"Mmmm?"

"What are you doing tonight?"

She turned her head and smiled up at me.

"Besides you?"

I grinned. "Baby, doing me is always and forever a given. It's like Newton's law of gravity, or Amazon taking over the world."

She pursed her lips playfully, as if she had no other option, as if she'd ever turn down my cock again. "Good to know. Then I don't know what else I'm doing tonight. I was thinking about unpacking..."

"Unpacking here, right?" I didn't know if it was a stupid question or not, so I had to ask.

She stared at me for a few beats. "Yes, I'm unpacking here."

"And here, in this room, our room...not the den?"

She nodded. "If you'd like."

I sat up and adjusted myself so I could look at her better. "Perry...you know what I'd like, what I want. I want you to stay here permanently. I wasn't joking with that making me your home business. As cheesy as it sounded, I fucking meant it."

"I know," she said, her eyes softening, sky blue in the morning light.

"I don't want you in the den. I want you in this bed, forever. I want to be with you. Not just as a partner, not just as a friend. I want us to be together, to be one, to be...I don't know, a fucking couple."

She rubbed her lips and I had the urge to kiss her hard enough to make her see just how I felt. Finally she said, "I want those things too, Dex, I do. I just...I want to take it a bit slow. I'm just..." She trailed off and exhaled loudly. I could see the worry on her brow and knew I was coming on too strong for her right now. Perry had other things to consider instead of just me. She was my everything at the moment, a challenge to overcome. But she'd just been uprooted from the only home she'd ever known, been ostracized from her family on account of me, and was dealing with the ever-looming threat of becoming someone like her grandmother. In my impatience, I had forgotten all that.

"I'm sorry," I whispered, stroking her head. "I'm getting ahead of myself. Seriously. I know you're going through so much shit right now, and if I could carry all of it for you, baby, you know I would. Take all the time you need. You know I'll be here."

She gripped my arm hard and looked up at me with questioning eyes, as if she didn't really believe that.

"It's fine," I reassured her. "Let's just start with you, right here with me, and go from there."

A smile slowly spread across her lips, her eyelids lowering seductively.

"I'll go first," she said. What a fucking little horndog she turned out to be. She started running her hands down my chest and stomach, marveling at my muscles, before groping my dick. "You're hard again."

"I'm always hard," I told her, leaning back and closing my eyes, succumbing to her touch. "Another constant you'll have to get used to."

She began stroking me back and forth, her grip enticingly firm. If she wanted to take it slow, I could think of a million ways to make the time pass.

～

IT WAS around noon when we finally dragged ourselves out of bed. We showered together, another slippery session that had me coming in her mouth, before she booted me out, telling me she had to beautify herself. When I was with Jenn, the beautification process usually took half the day—shaving, waxing, scrubbing, sanding, welding—so I let Perry be and went about tidying up the apartment.

There was a knock at the door that had me puzzled. I knew Perry and I could be pretty vocal, so I hoped it wasn't a prudish neighbor, irate that I was getting some and they weren't. But then I heard a snuffle and a scratch at the door and knew the person on the other side was the opposite of a prude.

I opened it and saw Rebecca in the hallway as a white devil darted through my legs and scampered into the apartment, his claws scratching up the hardwood floors.

"Hey sweetheart," I told her with a grin as Fat Rabbit tore about the living room in circles.

She smiled tightly, looking a bit off. Oh, she looked as fucktastic as she usually did—tight dress, fishnets, Betty Boop shoes, a Louise Brooks bob. But she wasn't wearing her trademark red lipstick, and that was strangely troubling. It was like seeing Homer Simpson without those two squiggly lines on the top of his head.

"I've been trying to call you," she said, her English accent sounding clipped, and stepped in and walked past me. She heard the shower running and raised her brow. "Perry's still here?"

I looked at her askew. "Why wouldn't she be?"

She shrugged. "So I guess everything went fine in Canada?"

"Yes...kind of. Sorry I didn't call you, I didn't have time to recharge my phone yet."

"When did you get back?"

"Late last night..."

Her eyes drifted to the shower again. "Everything okay between you guys now?"

I folded my arms as Fat Rabbit sniffed around my ankles. "What's with the one hundred and one questions, Miss Rebecca?"

She rubbed underneath her eyes and it was then that I noticed her black as death eyeliner was gone too. Who was this imposter?

"Are you okay?" I asked.

"Are *you* okay?" she asked right back.

We stared at each other. Fat Rabbit flopped down to the floor, bored with us.

I said, "I told Perry I loved her" at the same time that she said, "'Em and I broke up."

Then she smiled and I frowned. "Shit, I'm sorry."

"You told her you loved her?"

I waved my hand. "We can talk about that later. What happened?"

She exhaled loudly and walked over to the couch, sitting down in a similarly dejected pose like the dog.

"She wanted different things than me," she mumbled, her face in her hands. "And I knew, I knew this day was coming. I knew I'd have to choose what I wanted over her, even though, fuck Dex, all I ever wanted *was* her."

I bit my lip, unsure of how to comfort her. I'd never seen Rebecca rattled before. "I'm sorry. You wanted to get married, didn't you?"

She nodded. "Yes. I mean, I wasn't pressuring her, at least I don't think I was. But I feel like I drove her away. We could have compromised...maybe I could have been more understanding. But you know, I wanted to adopt children one day, blimey, maybe even have one myself. I wanted a family and she...she doesn't. I knew from the start that she wouldn't come around, I knew we were going to crash and burn. The last year I just let myself keep falling for her, tricking myself, like a bloody tailspin and there's that little voice telling you to 'pull up, pull up' and I didn't."

She was making airplane analogies. This really wasn't good. I came over to her and sat beside her, putting my hand on her shoulder. It was bonier than I remembered and I wondered if she'd stopped eating.

"I wish I knew what to say," I said, feeling stupid. Usually I had tons of shit to spew, but this, what she was telling me, was hitting a little too close to home. In some ways, I knew how she felt. The need to start a family, to finally have a fucking family, was something slowly creeping up on me, day by day. I wondered if that's why I'd been coming on too strong with Perry, if instinctually I wanted to get started on something that I'd secretly wanted for a very long time.

And then the thought of Perry's miscarriage hit me in

the gut and I swallowed away the pain, trying to focus on Rebecca.

"I know," she said. She lifted her head and wiped away a tear. "There's nothing anyone can say because there's no good and bad or right and wrong here. It's just bloody life and it really, really sucks sometimes." She shot me an apologetic look. "Sorry, Dex, I know you know that more than anyone."

I smiled gently. "True. But it doesn't mean it won't suck for anyone else."

The shower turned off and I heard Perry sliding back the curtain. Rebecca straightened up and plastered a smile on her face. "So tell me about Perry before she comes out here and we have to speak in code."

I grinned and got up, fishing a handful of Kleenex out of the box on the coffee table and handing it to her.

"I'm pretty sure Perry would break that code," I told her, my voice a bit lower.

"Let's try," she said, and after dabbing at her tears, she made an "O" with one hand and jabbed her other finger in and out of it. "Any of this?"

I laughed. "Oh, there's been plenty of that."

She smiled, no longer fake, her eyes looking brighter. "That's excellent! And you told her you loved her. That's so...I'm so proud of you, Dex. Finally. So what did she say?"

I raised my brows. "Uh, well, here's the thing..."

"Rebecca!" Perry exclaimed. Our heads swiveled over to the bathroom where she was stepping out with soaking wet hair, her towel barely covering her breasts, and looking shocked.

"Hi, Perry," Rebecca said, tearing her eyes away from mine. I couldn't have been interrupted at a better time.

Perry grinned uncomfortably. "Let me go change before I flash you."

"That wouldn't be a problem," Rebecca said, just as I was thinking it.

I cocked a brow at her. "You perv."

She shrugged as Perry disappeared into the bedroom. "I've been hanging out with you too long, Dex."

"Well, now that you're a single woman, I'm sure we could make room for you in bed," I said teasingly, a depraved part of me kind of hoping she'd say yes. But then her face fell at the mention of her newfound singledom and I felt like a complete asshole.

"Dex," she said, sounding disgusted.

"Sorry. I guess I should keep my threesome fantasies to myself, huh?"

She gave me a small smile. "Just pick your timing better." Then she put her hand on my knee and squeezed it. "Glad to see you're still a bit of a jerk, though. I was worried there for a second."

"Ladies love the assholes, don't they?"

Her eyes drifted to the closed bedroom door. "For your sake, I hope they do."

I nodded and went back to chewing on my lip. I didn't have to tell Rebecca about Perry, she already sussed it out.

A few seconds later, Perry came back out of the bedroom. Her face was fresh-faced and sexy, her body still mouthwatering in a long Pink Floyd tee-shirt and leggings.

Rebecca got up and hugged her tightly and I tried to get my head out of the gutter. I looked over at Fat Rabbit instead who was watching Perry carefully.

"Fatty Rab," I exclaimed. "Where's your greeting for the lady of the house?"

The dog looked at me then closed his eyes. Disrespectful fucker.

"How are you?" Perry asked Rebecca, and I wondered if she was picking up on the same vibe that I had been. Although the bloodshot and puffy eyes were a bit of a giveaway.

Rebecca twisted her mouth. "You know. I've been better. Em and I broke up."

"Oh shit, I'm so sorry," Perry told her. "We should get a coffee or something like that and talk."

I coughed and both of them looked at me. I wasn't sure what they were going to talk about exactly, but I was pretty sure half of their conversation would be about me. Not because the world revolved around me but...I don't know, some of their world had to.

"Just make sure you're back by seven," I said, looking at Perry.

She frowned. "Why?"

"Well, remember when I asked you what you were doing tonight? And you said you were doing me?"

Perry's eyes widened and she looked at Rebecca in embarrassment.

"Oh, don't worry about her, she already knows you're doing me," I added.

"Dex!" Perry cried out.

Rebecca rolled her eyes. "So much for speaking in code."

"Hey, we're all adults here. Except maybe Perry. You *are* dangerously close to being underage."

"Dex," Perry said again, her tone harder.

I reeled it back with a playful grin. "Anyway, I'm taking you out tonight."

"Out?" she asked.

Rebecca put her hands on her hips and watched our exchange with amusement. I had hoped to ask Perry out on our first date without an audience, but oh well, too late for that.

"Yeah. You know, outside? There's a great pizza place around the corner. I'd buy you dinner. Some drinks. Get laid after. You know...a date."

She blinked a few times but finally smiled. "Are you seriously asking me out on a date?"

"Am I not being clear enough? Yes. Perry Palomino, will you go out with me?"

She looked over at Rebecca who threw up her hands and said, "Hey, if Dex is paying..."

Perry looked back at me, trying to hide her smile now. But I saw it. It made my heart want to fucking burst. "Okay, Dex Foray, I'll go out with you."

I couldn't stop grinning. I thought my head was going to split open.

Rebecca shook her head. "I never thought I'd see the day. Are you sure I'm not making things awkward by standing here and watching all of this? Perhaps you'd like some pre-date privacy?"

"Nah, we're a good threesome," I told her with a wink.

She glared back at me. "Anyway, there was a reason for me coming over here other than returning your fartin' mutt and telling you my sob story. Jimmy."

"What about Jimmy?" It was hard to concentrate on work matters when Perry had just said she'd go out with me. I know it was reducing me to a thirteen-year-old kid all over again, but I didn't care. I felt like running down the halls of my old high school and yelling it to the world.

Rebecca's stern look reminded me that I was living in an adult world. "He's been trying to get a hold of you too, and when he couldn't reach you yesterday, he started harassing me. Seems a police officer from wherever you were in Canada called him wanting to confirm that both you guys did in fact work for him."

I wiggled my jaw back and forth. "Huh. Was that it?"

She looked at me dryly. "Was that it? It was kind of distressing to learn that you guys were involved in some police matter. Some local man was killed by an animal."

"Sasquatch," I corrected her.

"Right. Sasquatch. Of course."

"We're serious," Perry said. "It was Sasquatch. Or some terrible missing link. Definitely not a mangy bear."

I could tell that even Sasquatch was a stretch for the usually open-minded Rebecca. "Either way, it freaked Jimmy out and then it freaked me out. And then he started barking at me, like I had something to do with it. Apparently the police confiscated your footage?"

I was starting to get the feeling that perhaps Jimmy wouldn't be as understanding over the whole thing as I had thought.

"They did, for evidence," Perry explained. "And anyway, it wouldn't have been right to air what we shot. A man seriously died."

A man that probably deserved to die, I thought, feeling all the anger coming back over catching Mitch trying to rape Perry. But even with that fact, I knew that not showing the footage was the right thing to do. Whether he deserved it or not, death was death and his death must have been a terrible one.

"I understand," Rebecca said sympathetically. "But I would not count on Jimmy feeling the same way. He was throwing around the words 'fire' and 'cancellation.'"

"Oh come on," I said. "He can't seriously consider cancelling us again. We've barely been back!"

She shrugged. "You know how he is."

I groaned in frustration, rubbing my forehead. "Can't we just have one day of peace before we get shit on?"

"You do get one day," she said. "He told me to tell you to come to his office tomorrow, both of you, at two. Until then, go back to...what was it, *doing* each other?"

Perry's cheeks flushed adorably at that. She cleared her throat and looked at her feet. "So, Rebecca, did you want to get that cup of coffee now? Leave Dex here with his dog?"

She agreed and soon they were leaving the apartment for Top Shop Donuts, promising to bring me back a double chocolate artery-clogger. Whatever they ended up talking about, I hoped a skittish new lover and a jaded lesbian would take it easy on me.

~

"I'M GOING to go powder my nose," Perry told me, and I instinctively reached across the table and tapped her on the end of hers. My sexy bunny.

She slid out from the booth and made her way to the washroom. She was wearing a low-cut, bright blue dress that hugged her in all the right fucking places. Watching her walk away was dessert before dinner.

After she came back with Rebecca, she didn't seem any worse off than she was before. She seemed pretty normal actually, and from the way she yammered on about poor Rebecca and her break-up, I could tell that maybe they didn't spend much time discussing our relationship at all. Maybe there was no relationship to discuss. I still had a hard time with that one.

There was one thing that was off, however. Despite my smooth moves (which, honestly, was just feeling her up in the kitchen), Perry didn't succumb to my advances and more or less brushed me off from our sex session, saying she needed to go for a run to clear her mind. Okay, so maybe she and Rebecca did discuss me.

And, keeping in mind what Rebecca had told me, her fears that she pressured Emily too much and drove her away, I quickly removed my hands and told her to go get some fresh air, that jogging was a good way to get to know the city, and other such bullshit that covered up the fact that I wanted to stick my dick in her, make her scream my name, and fuck her until she felt something for me.

When Perry returned from her run, she looked a lot calmer, more pliable. I kept my distance a bit, getting sucked into yet another *Mythbusters* marathon with Fatty Rab, while she showered yet again and then joined me on the couch.

The interesting thing was that she sat on the other side of the dog. The farty little thing was being used as a goddamn buffer!

"You know," I said, turning to face her, "when you sit over there, it makes it a lot harder to put my arm around you."

I knew I was putting her on the spot. Didn't care. I wasn't too proud to admit that Dex Foray needed cuddles. Just because we were fucking each other didn't mean I'd stop being affectionate after the last drop was milked out of me.

She looked at the dog shyly, her hair falling in her face. I reached over and tucked it behind her ear.

"What is it?" I asked and took my hand back.

She fidgeted in her seat, still avoiding my eyes. "Don't you find this a bit weird?"

"Weird?"

"Yeah." Her eyes darted to mine. "You and I. Together like this. Suddenly."

My heart thumped like it took a hit of crack. Now I was really starting to worry about what her and Rebecca talked about. Becs had always been on my side, but chicks before dicks and all that. And in her case, it really *was* chicks before dicks.

I licked my lips, trying to be careful. "I don't find this very sudden, Perry. And I don't find this weird. I'm a bit weird, you're certainly weird, but this? This is the opposite of weird."

She smiled. "So it's normal?"

It's destiny, I thought. I leaned over and kissed her softly. When I pulled away I said, "Whatever it is, it's good. It's very, very good."

And then I picked up the dog and tossed him to the ground and put my arm around my motherfucking woman.

The pizza place I took Perry to, Zeke's, was just down the block from the apartment, along the monorail tracks and close to the Space Needle. We got a small booth by the window and put an order in for our pizzas and beer.

I could tell she was nervous by the way she downed her beer and kept playing with her hair. It was pretty damn cute. It was also refreshing, considering I used to make her nervous for different reasons.

While she was in the bathroom powdering her nose or whatever, our server came back over. His name was Marcus and I'd gotten to know him pretty well over the years. He was a good looking guy for what it's worth, one of those Italian types with black curls the ladies seemed to go gaga over and really hairy arms, like his testosterone needed a place to go.

"How are things?" he asked, loitering around the table,

hands folded behind his back. He was also really tall, which I hated. I could obviously take him in a fight though and I was certain my dick was larger.

"Fine," I told him, eyeing him inquisitively. "I mean, the beer's fine, if that's what you're asking."

He smiled and jerked his head to Perry's empty seat. "Who's the chick?"

I frowned. Look, I've called every woman a chick, from the old lady at the post office to my teacher back in university. But it didn't sit right to hear it from another guy when talking about Perry, not in the tone that he was taking, anyway.

"The woman, you mean?" I asked slowly. "Her name is Perry."

"Nice," Marcus said with a grin. "Two women at the same time? I promise not to tell." He made a crossing motion over his heart.

I was a tad confused. "Two women? I don't have two women."

"What happened to the super hot Maxim babe? Your girlfriend?"

"Jenn?" I asked. "We broke up."

He shook his head. "I swore I just saw you guys in here."

"It's mid-March, Marcus. That was back in December. We broke up. I'm with Perry now." I felt like I was talking to a two-year-old.

He stared at me like he didn't quite believe me. "And," I added, feeling defensive, "Perry's also a super hot babe. She just wasn't in Maxim. Because it's a shitty publication."

Marcus nodded, his eyes going over to the other side of the restaurant where Perry was coming out of the washroom area. "She is pretty hot, I'll give you that. You lucky bastard.

Her breasts are so much better than the other ones. Gotta get them when they're young, am I right?"

"Hey," I growled at him. "That's my girlfriend you're talking about."

And there it was. I had just said the G-word. I had just publicly announced Perry as my girlfriend. Thank god she was too far away to hear it.

"Now, if you don't mind, we'd like another round of beer, stat," I said to him, watching her come closer. She was turning a few heads as she walked and I was met with this strange combination of worry and pride.

"Gotcha," Marcus said, firing his hand at me like a gun. He walked past Perry, ogling her bouncing breasts like I wasn't there. I gripped the edge of the table and tried to keep Hulk Dex at bay. Now wasn't the time. In the middle of the Canadian Rockies was, but in the middle of Zeke's Pizza in Belltown wasn't.

"I ordered you another beer!" I told her, smiling too much.

"Uh, thank you," she said, taking her seat. She moved her purse to the corner and gave me a funny look. "You okay?"

"Great," I said, my voice unnaturally high. I needed to calm the fuck down. What the hell was wrong with me?

She pursed her lips, studying me. I felt like she was looking into every crevice. I busied myself with a beer, wishing Marcus would bring back a pitcher instead.

"You're nervous," she observed.

I almost choked on my beer. "No, you're nervous!"

"Yeah, I am, Dex. But you know what? I think that's okay now. I think we should be nervous. I don't think we ever gave us this chance."

She put her soft hand on mine, milky white against light tan.

"I'm pretty sure I used to make you nervous," I told her. "When you first met me. You looked like you were about to run away every five minutes. Every time you were in the car with me it was like you were being trapped with a mental patient. Which, I mean, was a fairly accurate assessment."

She smiled and squeezed my hand and the affection was doing weird twirly, tingly, unmanly things around my heart. "You did make me nervous. You make a lot of people nervous, Dex."

"Cause I'm too awesome for them to handle."

"Yes, well, that's also true. But I was nervous because I didn't know you...I didn't know how you thought. I didn't know what you thought of me."

"And now?"

"Now I know you. I'm starting to know how you think. And I think I know what you think of me. I'm nervous for a whole new set of reasons. Because I'm...scared. And I'm excited. This, this *us*, this is totally new for me."

We stared at each other and I felt blessed with her bout of honesty. "It's new for me too. But new can be good."

Marcus came by with the new beers and the pizza and he escaped with only a death glare. As I munched away at my prosciutto pie, I found my mind wandering to the time I first met her, that fucked up night in the lighthouse. I'd felt something at that moment for her, whether it was lust or a certain connection, I couldn't be too sure. I had no idea I'd be lucky enough to have her sitting across from me at Zeke's as something more than a stranger. I had no idea that this tiny little woman with all her insecurities and bravery would become my *everything*.

"What are you thinking about?" she asked after she drank a healthy swig of her beer.

"About the first time we met."

"In Oregon?"

"In the lighthouse. You ran into me. Remember?"

"That's something you can never forget."

"So what was it like for you?"

She put down her beer and stared out the window. Fat raindrops began to fall, hitting the glass with the gusts of wind that were whipping up. Looked like a stormy night, much like the one that brought us together.

"I thought you were..."

"Nuts?"

She let out a laugh. "Well that was a given, considering you were in an abandoned lighthouse, alone, and trying to capture a ghost on film. Seriously, if that's not nuts, I don't know what is."

I finished my beer and wiped my mouth, leaning back in my seat. "Oh, I don't know, Miss Pot Calling the Sexy Kettle Black, how about a girl who decided to go off by herself in the darkness to explore said lighthouse, just for, what was it again? Kicks?"

"I don't do anything for kicks."

"Well you kicked in the window with your weird ninja moves."

"At least I wasn't trespassing," she shot back, as if it all happened just yesterday.

"Trespassing gets you everywhere. If I hadn't broken in and explored that lighthouse, I wouldn't be exploring you right now."

She rolled her eyes. If she hadn't seemed so nervy I would have joked about the futility of a *Keep Out* sign on her vagina.

"So that's it," I pressed. "You thought I was nuts? Nothing else?"

"Obviously I thought you were cute."

"Just cute?"

"Hey, you think *I'm* cute."

I shook my head. "I think you're cute and sexy and gorgeous and outstandingly fuckable. You meet all the requirements for one infuriatingly hot piece of ass, an ass that I'd love to shoot hot—"

She shot me a warning look. The mother of a family of four across from us was giving me the stinkeye. Whoops.

"I'm sorry," I apologized to the mother. "It's our first date."

"And will probably be your last," she muttered to herself and turned back to her kids. One was still staring at me with a frightened expression. I'd forgotten I had that effect on children.

"I get it," Perry said quickly, bringing my attention back to her. "Though I have to say your wooing skills need some work."

"These are my wooing skills," I said, raising my hands and wiggling my fingers, "and from what I can tell, they work just fine."

"Dex."

"Miss Palomino."

We watched each other for a few moments before breaking out into simultaneous grins. For a first date it was going pretty well. For Perry and I, getting to know each other on another level, it was going spectacularly.

And we hadn't even gotten to dessert yet.

3

I woke up in the middle of the night noticing two strange things while my brain struggled to catch up. One was that the clock radio was flashing at 3AM, as if the power went out at that time, bathing the bedroom in sporadic hits of red. The other was Perry sitting on the edge of the bed.

I blinked hard and eased myself back on my elbows. My mouth was dry. "Baby? Are you okay?"

She didn't move. Her long dark hair covered her back and she was facing away from me, her face obscured. She was wearing a long white nightgown that had frills at the wrists. It was weirdly familiar but I knew she hadn't gone to sleep wearing it.

My chest started to feel tight.

"Perry?"

I didn't want to reach over for her. I was too afraid of what I might find.

"Answer me, please," I said, my voice shaking. I sat up straighter and stuck out my hand, reaching very slowly for her shoulder.

She felt like ice. I tightened my grip.

"Perry?"

She twitched. I held my breath.

Then she turned around.

It was the face of my mother.

"Declan," she said in an inhuman voice.

I screamed and screamed and screamed.

Everything went black.

Then I was waking up again in my bed. The clock wasn't blinking and I was alone in the room. My mother wasn't at the end of the bed anymore but Perry wasn't next to me either. I looked at the clock. It was 3AM.

I touched my forehead and found it was wet with sweat. I exhaled slowly, gathering my strength and wits, then got out of bed. I slept bare-ass naked so I slipped on a pair of boxer briefs that were lying on the floor and went out into the apartment. The bathroom was empty.

"Perry?" I asked quietly. Fat Rabbit looked up from the couch, his white head glowing in the darkness, then went back to sleep. I moved closer to the kitchen and saw the balcony door was open a crack, cold air flowing into the room.

I opened it and poked my head outside. Perry was sitting on a chair on my small rounded balcony, bundled in my house robe, staring at nothing. She was smoking a cigarette, her hair being whipped around by the wind.

"What are you doing?" I asked, more horrified that she was smoking than anything else.

She gave me a tired smile. "I just needed to clear my head."

"Well, clear it inside where it's not freezing cold," I admonished her, motioning for her to come in.

"It's almost Spring."

I shook my head at that. "Why are you smoking? Where did you get that anyway?"

"Sorry. You had a whole stash hidden in the den in one of your hollowed out books."

"Ah fuck. Well...please come inside, I'm worried about you." I stepped out and reached for her arm, ignoring the split second hesitation, the fear that she might turn into my mother. But that was a dream. This was real.

And she felt like Perry, warm and solid underneath my robe. She got up, stubbing out the cigarette on the railing and flicked it over the edge. I didn't like this one fucking bit. Not just the smoking itself but that it was so unlike her to smoke.

I ushered her inside and brought her over to the couch and took her hands in mine.

"Now talk," I told her, her face dimly lit by the streetlights outside.

Her eyes darted to my crotch. And no, this time I did not have a boner. I'm not an animal.

"It's hard to talk to you when you're in just your underwear. Makes me want to do things to you."

And shit. My dick twitched.

No, no, no, focus, she's just trying to distract you with sex, I told myself. I shook my head vigorously and squeezed her hands.

"Later, Perry. I want to know what's wrong first. Why are you sitting on the balcony at three in the morning smoking? I've never seen you smoke before. And why were you going through my books?"

She shrugged but looked slightly chagrined. "I knew that's where you used to keep your pills. I thought that's where your pot was too. Didn't find that either, so I went for the smokes. I don't know, it calmed me down."

"Calmed you down from what?"

She sighed and laced her fingers through mine. "I'm just sad, that's all."

For a second there I thought she was going to tell me she saw my dead mother too, but this was much worse. It broke my heart in two to hear her say that. And, selflessly, it stung a bit, because if she was sad, it meant I wasn't making her happy.

I chewed on my lip before asking, "Is it because you're homesick?"

She nodded, her eyes shining. "Yeah. I guess I am. I just miss...I don't even know what I miss. I miss Ada. I miss the way my parents used to be around me. I'm..." She sighed loudly, looking up at the ceiling. "I hate that I can't have everything. I hate that I can't have both you and them."

Ugh. It felt like my gut was being filled with rocks. I found myself asking a question that was probably better left unasked. "Would you rather go back to them and leave me behind?"

She looked at me sharply, a pained expression on her brow. "No. No, Dex, I chose you because I...I know you'd never make me choose. And my parents, well, they made it pretty clear what they think of you, think of me, and think of us together. And hell, even if they didn't have a problem with you, I'd still have a problem with them. As long as I'm seeing ghosts and acting like Pippa, my mother is always going to be afraid of me, a hair-trigger away from trying to get me help. It's just...it's not fair. I want that normal life and to be treated normally and to be loved."

"I love you," I said quietly, blurting it out more than anything. I remembered what I'd told myself about not scaring her or pressuring her, but fuck, the words kept wanting to come out all the time. It was taking over me.

She swallowed. "Oh, Dex." I could tell she was fumbling for words, searching for something to say that would placate me but nothing else would do. We both knew it.

"It's okay," I told her, bringing her hand up to my lips and kissing along her knuckles. "I just want you to know that I'm here for you. And I will do what I can to give you a normal life here."

"Thank you," she said softly. Then she smiled. "Though I don't think normal is in the cards for us."

I got up and loomed over her. "That's true. But do you know what *is* in the cards for us?"

I stripped off my underwear and threw them across the apartment. From serious to hard-on in zero point five seconds flat.

I reached down and scooped her up in my arms. She squealed with delight, scaring the crap out of Fat Rabbit, and I carried her over to our bedroom.

∽

NORMAL DEFINITELY WASN'T in the cards for us. Not when you went to a meeting with your boss and he was trying to tear you a new asshole because your footage of Sasquatch had been confiscated by Canadian authorities.

"You seriously fucked up this time!" Jimmy barked at us from behind his desk, his face red and contorted. We'd only been in his office for two minutes before the obscenities started flying out of his mouth.

I looked over at Perry who was wringing her hands together, looking wary of the big bad Korean man who only recently begged her to come back to *Experiment in Terror*. What a fickle fuckhead.

"Hey, Jimmy, hey," I said, jerking my head at Perry. "How about toning it down a bit in front of the lady?"

Jimmy looked at me as if I had a cock growing out of my head. "Tone it down? Christ, Dex, the girl works with you. Or she did." He glared at the two of us and leaned across his glass desk. "You can't possibly think that going all the way to BC on the company dime and not coming back with an episode is okay."

"We didn't think it was *okay,* but—" Perry started.

He raised his hand. "Stop. I don't care about your excuses. For once you actually had something—evidence—and it was taken away."

"Oh fuck that," I exclaimed. "It was the police, it was evidence of a fucking murder."

"Murder?" Jimmy scoffed.

"I don't know, maybe not murder, but the thing was definitely related to us in some X-Men mutant type of way. Whatever. An attack. The man died. Of course the damn cops are going to confiscate it."

He narrowed his eyes at me. "You should have lied. You should have said you didn't have any evidence."

I glared right back him. Jimmy had always been a bit of a dick, but this level of dickishness was new.

"Well, maybe, Jimmy, we thought it was in bad taste to air the episode anyway."

"That is not your call," he seethed. Then he straightened up and walked over to the window with its view of Elliott Bay. It was overcast and blustery but the rain had held off today. He clasped his hands behind his back and rocked back and forth on his heels.

"The economy still hasn't picked up yet," he said to the window. "And I'm having to take a long hard look at the lineup and figure out what's worth it. Some shows are doing really well with hits, others are tanking. You guys were doing really well but I don't think I can rely on you anymore."

"With all due respect, sir," Perry said rather snidely. "This show was dead and buried. *You* resurrected it."

"I assumed you wouldn't be wasting my money. Obviously I was a moron and now I'm in the hole because there's no show to air. So the resurrection is on hold until I figure out what to do with you." He finally turned around and eyed us over his glasses. "This isn't the first time you've nearly gotten hurt or lost most of your footage. What you do is entertaining, even when you have nothing to show for it, but it can't survive in the long run. I was this close to getting a big fucking sponsor for you guys, I was counting on it. It would have meant better pay, better technology. But you two just aren't professional enough."

I felt my blood begin to boil. "You hired us because we aren't professional. I recall you throwing around words like real and believable."

"No, Dex. That's what you said. That's what you wanted. If we'd done it my way, it would have been Hollywoodized."

"And shitty."

He raised his shoulders. "Perhaps. But people like shit if it's shiny and covered with glitter."

I sighed, feeling like we were on the short end of the stick here. How many times had Perry and I had this same damn conversation with Jimmy? To be honest, I was getting kind of sick of it. Obviously I needed to talk to Perry about our strategy, but I felt like things were finally coming to a head. That said, like fuck I was about to bow out on account of Jimmy Kwan. He and Shownet could go fuck themselves. They weren't telling us what we could and couldn't do.

"All right, well how about we compromise?" I suggested.

Jimmy laughed unkindly. "Right. You, compromise."

"Hey, I compromise a lot." I could have gone on but I shut my mouth right on time.

He sat back down, leaning back in his seat, and studied me.

"Do tell, Dex, what is your compromise?"

I exchanged a quick look with Perry to make sure we were on the right track before I said, "Give us one more chance."

"No."

"Just hear me out. Give us one more chance. We'll pay for the whole thing out of our own pocket." Perry stiffened beside me at that. "We'll arrange everything. We'll shoot the episode and we'll get that sponsor. If the sponsor doesn't come on board, then we quit. We're done."

I could feel Perry's eyes on me. I knew she was going to flip out over the whole paying for it thing. She had no money anymore, not really. Jimmy had been her only source of income and it was a shitty income at that. But I had money, money from my inheritance, money I'd been smart with over the years, and I'd take care of everything for her. If she'd let me.

Jimmy pursed his lips then said, "This sounds promising, Dex. But I have to think about it."

I groaned, exasperated. "Why? It's all on my head here, I'll carry the whole thing. What do you have to lose?"

He gave me a pointed look. "A lot. Even if it does work out and la di da we have an episode, and the sponsors come on board, how are you going to keep it up? The two of you together are trouble."

I heard Perry snort from beside me but kept my eyes on Jimmy.

He went on. "You understand me? There's no guarantee

what we'll get from you in the future. Unless the format changes in some way."

"Look…"

"Dex, I said I'll think about it. Give me twenty-four hours or less to let it stew. Then I'll come back to you."

Damn. Somehow he was still calling all the shots. I hated having a boss.

He dismissed us with a tired wave, and Perry and I left the office just as my man Seb was coming in.

"Dex," Seb said. "Dude, it's been like forever."

I did one of those bro hugs with him: hand clasp, slap on back, no eye contact.

"Seb, you have no concept of time," I told him. He was quite the stoner but his brain-dead antics kept me entertained during the whole Perry and I debacle.

"Maybe time has no concept of me," he said, tapping his head where his disheveled ponytail was coming loose. It was only then that he noticed Perry. "Hey…Perry, right?"

"Yes. Hi, Seb," she said with a smirk on her face.

"Cool. Well I better go in and see what Jimbo wants."

"You have a meeting too?" I asked. Seb had a show with my friend Dean called *Gamers*, where they just basically acted like fucktards and played video games. It was pretty popular, considering, but maybe not as lucrative as I thought.

He shrugged. "I guess so. Hey, I'll see you tonight, right?"

I frowned. "What's tonight?"

"Nothing, just me and Dean feel like getting shitfaced. I let Rebecca know too. We'll be at the Spelling Bee.'"

The Spelling Bee was one of those divey on purpose type bars that served overpriced drinks over on 2nd, not too far from the apartment. I wished him luck and told him we'd hopefully see him there. To be honest, I felt like getting a little loose tonight and even more than that, I felt like showing Perry off.

"Do you feel like going out tonight?" I asked her as we got in the elevator.

"I'm up for anything."

"Oh really?"

I whipped around and pulled out the elevator's STOP button. The elevator lurched then went still.

"What are you doing?" she screeched, wild-eyed.

"Nothing you need to worry about, baby," I told her, placing both hands on either side of her head and kissing her hard, hard enough that she was flattened against the wall. We didn't discuss it, but we naturally played our relationship cool in front of Jimmy. Now I was making up for lost time.

I bit her lower lip, pulling it between my teeth. She moaned and I smiled.

"You ever had sex in an elevator?" I asked, taking my mouth to her sweet neck and alternating between wet licks and fierce sucks. I didn't care if she ended up with a million hickeys. The more the better.

"No."

"Anywhere in public?"

"Does a Canadian national park count?" she whispered, sounding both turned on and uneasy.

"No, it doesn't," I murmured, my hands cupping her breasts. "Sounds like something we have to fix, doesn't it?"

"Isn't this illegal?"

I pulled away and looked at her. "Elevator malfunction. Living it up while I'm going down."

She smiled and then arched her back to give me more access to her fantastic breasts. "You can't use Aerosmith as an excuse."

"I can do anything I want," I grunted, pressing my erection into her hip.

"My goodness," she exclaimed at the pressure.

I grinned, my hands folding down her bra and rolling her nipples between my fingers.

"I told you. I'm always hard for you, I'm just good at hiding it. Which, actually, isn't easy when your dick is the size of your leg."

She laughed and lowered my head to her breasts, my mouth yearning, searching.

"Hello?" a voice said from behind me.

Startled, I turned around, expecting someone to be in the elevator with us. I was probably expecting it to be inhuman as well.

But the voice repeated, "Hello? Are you okay? Is this car two? I have reports you have stopped."

Shit. It was security on the speaker. In some elevators, pulling out the stop button just stops the elevator. I guess in this one it alerted security. Cockblockers!

I sighed and looked up, just now becoming aware of the camera in the corner of the elevator. I gave it a wave.

"We're fine. False alarm."

"That's what I thought. We're starting the car again," the voice said.

The elevator groaned and began to move. I quickly reached over and pulled up the neck of Perry's shirt just as the car stopped and the doors opened. We both smiled innocently at the two business men who came in. The younger one smirked at me. Oh, he knew. Guys always knew when another guy was trying to get elevator tail.

"Maybe later," I whispered into her ear, my hand going down to her ass for a discrete feel. Now that I had that gorgeous booty in my possession, I was going to take full advantage of it.

She shifted away from me but that only made me smile. Perry was a funny little thing. She could be outstandingly horny in private (and who could blame her, I mean aside from being with me, the poor girl had only slept with some college chump and the douchenugget, he-who-shall-not-be-named), but in public she was still so unsure of herself, of her body, of me. It was going to take me some time to marry the two sides of her together, but damn, I was going to make her my sex queen whether she liked it or not. And fuck, she *was* going to like it.

4

Aside from the elevator incident, which did lead to more bedroom antics back at the apartment, Perry did feel like going out. I was almost giddy at the prospect of taking her out with my friends. Well, giddy was a pretty girly term, but I did catch myself singing into my comb while I was grooming myself in the bathroom. But I was singing to Dillinger Escape Plan, which negated all girlyness. It's true, look it up.

Perry wore a simple, long black tank top, ass-tight jeans, and looked absolutely beautiful, no surprise there. Every moment I was around her I was absolutely floored by her. Maybe that's what every guy in love says, but what really got me, what *always* got me, was that she didn't see it herself. No, she wasn't as thin as a lot of women, she didn't eat only raw foods or do drugs or workout every day. But just because she wasn't toned on every part of her body didn't mean I wasn't hard 24/7. I'd slept with all sorts of women, big, small, fat, skinny. It didn't really matter. If I found a woman attractive, then I found her attractive, and sticking her in a box didn't matter. Women are women are women and they all have parts I love.

And Perry, well she was just perfect for me. She had curves, curves that melted into my hands, into my skin, more than other women I'd been with. Her body molded to mine, soft, sensual, nurturing. It sounded archaic, but she just oozed fertility, and with that fertility came a power that she had no idea about. She looked at herself and hated what she saw, and I was going to do my best to show her that she was beyond beautiful to me. And aside from hers, my opinion was the only one that should matter. Not what other women thought or other men thought and definitely not what Cosmo thought.

Sir Mix-A-Lot and I had a lot of things in common.

"You look stunning," I said as she slipped on her boots in the hallway.

She blushed. "Really, Dex."

"Hey," I said, my voice deepening. I grabbed the house keys off the kitchen table and stopped right in front of her. "I warned you once about learning to accept a compliment. You better start accepting mine."

She swung her thick, shiny hair off her shoulders and rivaled any shampoo commercial. "Sorry. I'm just not used to all the compliments like you are."

I smiled. "Kiddo, I rarely get compliments. So I just decide to compliment myself instead. You should try it sometime."

It only took us about ten minutes to find the bar on 2nd avenue. It was a Thursday night but Thursday was the new Friday and all that bullshit, and the place looked like it was going to get really busy soon. Luckily it was only 7PM for us and we beat most of the crowd.

Everyone was already there, and by everyone I meant

Seb, Dean, Rebecca, and a young Asian couple I didn't recognize. Judging from their nerd shirts that said PWND and I Love Commander Shepard, I assumed they were friends of Seb and Dean.

Rebecca clapped her hands together excitedly as we approached them. They managed to snag a booth near the front of the bar, and judging by Rebecca's over-excitedness and the range of drinks in front of them, it looked like they'd been sitting there and drinking for quite some time. I didn't go out all that often, but when I did, things got pretty messy. I made a mental note to try and behave myself, but I couldn't promise anything. I hoped Perry wouldn't mind getting groped by Drunk Dex.

We squeezed in the booth with Perry on the outside (I didn't want her to next to Seb since he also got a bit "ass and tit ogly" when he got drunk), and Rebecca ordered another pitcher while Dean introduced us to his friends Janet and Justin.

"So, it's nice to see you two here together," Dean said with a smile, looking between the two of us. I placed my elbows on the table and stared at him curiously. Dean was one of my good friends, if not the best. It didn't mean we braided each other's hair and had sleepovers, but he knew me pretty damn well. He was also a bit of a smartass, so I couldn't figure out if he knew something about Perry and I or not. I eyed Rebecca who seemed preoccupied with her beer. No martinis and fancy drinks for her tonight—the world must have been ending.

"Uh huh," I said, while Dean continued to grin at us and adjust his glasses. "Nice to see you too, Dean."

He looked at Perry directly. "How are you liking your new roommate?"

She shrugged and put on a face. "He's alright, I guess."

Dean laughed. "I couldn't imagine living with Dex. I think he'd drive me nuts. No offense, man."

"None taken. It's not like I could live with a guy who plays Halo until four in the morning. I'd feel guilty for being the only guy in the house that gets laid."

"Oh, like you're getting laid now," Seb interjected with a lazy laugh. "Didn't you and Jenn break up?"

I felt Perry stiffen up beside me, and I glared at Seb while I kicked him in the ankle. "Very astute, Seb. Have you even been conscious for the last couple of months?" I asked snidely.

"Ow, dude," he exclaimed, leaning over to rub his leg. "I can't pay attention to all the gossip."

I rolled my eyes. Seb had been there with me while I tried to get over Jenn, when I started to turn over a new leaf. Fuckhead.

I shot Perry a quick glance to see how she was faring. She was sitting there quietly, her eyes sweeping the bar as if she was looking for someone.

"You okay, kiddo?" I whispered.

It took her a few seconds to bring her attention back over to me. "Yeah, I'm fine," she said in a small voice. "Just thought I saw something."

"A ghost?"

Seb snorted from beside me and I kicked him again. Meanwhile, Justin and Janet looked puzzled at the sincerity of my question. I sometimes forgot that seeing ghosts and hunting them for a YouTube show wasn't the most natural thing in the world.

Perry shook her head and shot me a tight smile. Maybe all of these questions were bothering her. I wanted to tell Seb that I was getting laid, and by the woman next to me,

but I wasn't sure how she'd feel about that. And I didn't want
to rock the boat.

"So," Dean said again, "I hope Dex has been putting the
sock on the door when he brings a lady home."

Good fucking god!

"Dean, shut the fuck up," I snarled at him, and it barely
erased the smile from his face. He knew how in love with
Perry I was, and now I definitely knew that he knew about
Perry and I; he was just trying to be a legitimate shitburger.

"Actually, we haven't worked out that system yet," Perry
said smoothly. "Dex is more fond of leaving the door open.
Scares the poor dog half to death."

Well, she was certainly handling the awkwardness with
ease. I reached under the table and squeezed her knee, smiling
at her. She smiled back, but still a little timid. This wouldn't do.

"Do you wanna do a shot with me?" I asked her.

She nodded enthusiastically. We got out of the booth
and made our way through the crowd that was growing
larger by the minute.

Once at the bar, while we waited for the bartender to
notice us, I put my arm around her waist and pulled her to
me. I kissed her long and hard, not caring who saw it.

She kissed me back, hot and wet, before the bartender
cleared his throat, wanting our attention. I smiled like a
jackass and ordered us two shots each of Jameson.

"Was that okay that I did that?" I asked, brushing her
hair behind her ear, staring at those sweet little lips.

"Kissed me?" she asked.

"Yeah, like this," I leaned and kissed her again, my
tongue slipping along her lower lip, my hand holding her
firmly in place at the back of her head.

I pulled away reluctantly when I heard the bartender

again. I slammed down a fifty without even looking at him, saying "keep the change."

"I don't think I could ever object to you kissing me. Except my knees are a lot weaker and I suddenly wish the bar was empty so I could ride you right here."

She smacked the bar top and my dick strained against my pants.

"You are a fucking naughty girl," I told her.

"Or just a naughty girl you're fucking," she said and picked up one of the shots.

You're so much more than that, I thought. But I picked up the shot and raised it at her. "Bottoms up for now. Your bottom's up later when I smack the shit out of it."

She grinned and we downed the shots, then the other. I pushed them toward the bartender and gave him a look that said, *how did I get so lucky?*

We walked a few steps, the crowd between us and the booth, and I grabbed her arm, pulling her close.

"Do you mind if I do that in public...you know, in front of my friends?" I don't know when the fuck I had become so respectful and how long it could last, but the threat of scaring her off was ever so imminent.

She bit her lip and looked around. "I don't know..."

"Okay, I understand," I told her. "No public displays of erection in front of my friends."

She grinned. "God, Dex, I hope not." Her eyes darted over to the bathroom. "If the waitress comes by, can you order me a glass of Chardonnay? Too much beer already. I'll be right back."

I nodded and watched her go and tried to steady my racing heart. I didn't know why this kind of talk made me nervous but it did. All I wanted was to just call her my girlfriend and let everyone know, but it just didn't seem like she was there yet. Motherfucking baby steps.

I straightened out my tee-shirt (it was black and a little on the small side, but hey it showed off the goods) and took a deep breath. I pushed my way through the crowd, and was almost at the table when I saw an anomaly.

And by anomaly, I mean a fucking terrible thing that wasn't there before and should never be there ever, shouldn't even exist.

She was standing in front of the booth, talking to Seb or maybe just talking at him. He had a stupid goofy grin on his face while Dean and Rebecca looked pissed off and all cagey. Her hair was honey gold and really long, like to her ass, and quite obviously fake. Figured she'd put in hair extensions, probably chopped off some virgin Russian's head and sold it for pennies. Other than that, she still looked pretty good from behind—your quintessential "hot girl" body in booty shorts and a sparkly tank top. But I knew the person the body housed and she was rotten to the core. And probably freezing.

I wiggled my jaw back and forth, trying to reduce the strain, and straightened up, shaking out my shoulders. I refused to let my ex-girlfriend, Jennifer "Brad Banger" Rodriguez, intimidate me.

I walked toward them, feeling the tension in the air thicken as I got closer, and stopped right behind her. I caught a whiff of the expensive perfume she always doused herself in and fought the urge to sneeze.

Too late. I sneezed, horribly loud, and she whipped around to see me.

We eyed each other like two territorial wolves, only my eyes were watering as I fought another sneeze.

"Dex," she said rather brightly, and I sneezed again. I guess it took me this long to find out I was allergic to skank.

"Jenn," I said, once I composed myself, not really sure what else I could say. Everything else seemed terribly inappropriate. I moved past her and sat down in the booth beside Seb and looked up at her expectantly. "Well, to what do we owe the honor of your presence?" I asked snidely. National Slut Convention next door? Twatwaffles Anoymous?

Her eyes narrowed at me briefly. And then her eyes narrowed in on my arms, my chest, my shoulders, and her expression changed. She liked the new Dex, liked him very much. Figured. Too bad this was all for Perry now and not her.

Perry. My eyes darted over to the washroom. She was still in there. I knew how awkward she'd feel if she came out right now, and I hoped Jenn would move her miniscule ass away from our table.

She smiled at me and I couldn't remember the last time I'd seen her smile. "I'm here with some friends of mine and we were just looking for a place to sit. All the tables are taken."

I eyed Rebecca, who was staring at me and giving me a no-fucking-way look, and obviously I couldn't agree more. But then Seb spoke up and said, "You can sit with us, we don't mind. Look, there's space beside Dex."

"No there's not," I snapped at Seb and made a move to kick him again. The stoned little bastard was surprisingly quick this time and moved out of the way.

"I can move over," Janet said sweetly, obviously having no idea what was going on and far too socially inept to pick up on it. I couldn't help but roll my eyes and sigh, but she didn't notice and Jenn sat down next to her, full of unearned pride.

Great.

"Dex, you look fantastic," Jenn said, leaning on her elbows, her breasts pressed together. Nice try honey, but that ain't cleavage.

"Thank you. I feel like a new man," I said matter-of-factly. As in, I am much better off without you.

"Well, it looks good on you," she said, then fluffed up her hair. I knew what she was doing—flirting with me—but I didn't really know why. I didn't like it.

"How's Sir Swagger Douchington the Fuck?"

She frowned. "Who?"

"Bradley. How's your boyfriend doing?"

Her face fell for a second then morphed into her puffy-lipped robot expression. "We broke up," she said like she didn't care, but I could tell she did.

"Awwww, what a shame!" I exclaimed. "That must just plain suck for you." Okay, so I was a bit over the top, but come on.

She glared at me, and I remembered how hot I used to find her when she was angry, and how grateful I was that I wasn't turned on in the slightest anymore.

The waitress chose to interrupt Jenn's awkward moment by asking us if we wanted more drinks. While everyone else got two more pitchers, I ordered a Jack and Coke for myself and "a glass of chardonnay for my girlfriend."

The waitress nodded and took off, not at all noticing the very gigantic bomb I had just dropped at the table. The bomb that had everyone—aside from Janet and Justin—with their jaws on the floor. Rebecca gave a little yelp of drunken delight, Dean leaned back in his seat and said,

"You dog," and Seb and Jenn both asked in unison, "Girlfriend?"

And just like that, as if the fates of karma were on our side tonight, Perry appeared at the table. She didn't notice Jenn at first, was just smiling at me, cute and refreshed as fuck, but then she noticed the silence around her and the fact that everyone was staring at her. Including Jenn.

I felt kinda bad for her; I mean Jenn was my ex, so it was way more awkward for me, but Perry looked like she'd just seen a ghost. She wasn't quite surprised as she was just...horrified.

"Just ordered you a drink, baby," I said, smiling as charmingly as possible, and patted the seat next to me.

She sat down carefully, her eyes downcast, avoiding Jenn who was full-on hate glaring at her now.

"*This* is your girlfriend?" Jenn asked, pointing at Perry with a long purple-painted talon. "Ghost girl?"

Perry looked at me, wide-eyed. I didn't know if she was angry that I called her my girlfriend in public like that or what. But hell, if there was any time she'd be happy to be announced as my girlfriend, it was probably with Jennifer staring across at her, utterly dumbfounded.

"Yes," I said, putting my arm around Perry and holding her to me. "Perry is my girlfriend." I grinned at Jenn, watching her squirm and enjoying it far, far too much. I tilted my head toward Seb. "And as you can see, I'm very much getting laid."

Seb chuckled and Jenn nearly jumped out of her seat.

"Nice, Dex," she sneered. "You couldn't wait to get in her pants, could you? You're a pig."

"And you're the shit this pig used to roll around in."

Jenn's mouth dropped open, and she spun around on her heel and walked her skanky ass back into the crowd. It was amazing to think that I'd spent three years of my life with her, but I'd found a lot of true colors and feelings came out when they became your ex. They seemed a lot more skanky.

I looked over at Justin and Janet who were watching me, absolutely flabbergasted. "Sorry," I apologized to them. "That was my ex-girlfriend. This is my new girlfriend. You know how it goes."

"I knew it," Dean cried out. "I knew you guys were together."

"Because Rebecca can't keep her mouth shut," I said, staring at her pointedly.

She smiled but didn't say anything. She became strangely mute when drunk.

"Well, man, congratulations," Dean said sincerely. "Both of you. Although to you, Perry, I'd say good luck."

I looked down at Perry who was nestled under my arm. Well, she wasn't exactly nestled as she was sitting straight up and rigid as I held her body to my side. I wanted her to loosen up and get used to this, to own it, to be proud.

"I hope I didn't embarrass you," I said, lowering my voice and face to hers.

She looked shy. "You didn't, I was just shocked. I mean, I thought I saw the she-beast earlier and I just assumed I was being paranoid...I didn't know I was your girlfriend."

I looked up, wondering if we needed to continue the conversation outside, but upon meeting my eyes, everyone else at the table started chatting loudly with each other on cue.

I turned back to Perry. "Well, you're more than a girl-friend. Girlfriend is such a juvenile term, and as juvenile as I am, that's not the way I feel about you. You're a partner, a lover, a friend, and so much more than that. Sorry if I put you on the spot."

"No," she said, smiling. I wanted to kiss her nose. "It's okay. I'm glad you did it. I'm sorry I'm being such a weirdo about all of this. It's just hard to believe how far we've come, you know? My brain is just catching up now."

"So you're okay with me being your boyfriend? I'll treat you real nice. We can go steady and you can wear my letterman jacket."

"Ooooh, maybe," she said playfully. "What letter is on it?"

"No letter, just a picture of a cock."

She snorted. "Of course there is."

"It's a rooster, you pervert."

She eyed me dryly. "Oh yeah? Why a rooster?"

"It symbolizes my cock. Can't love me without loving cock."

I heard someone cough. I looked up and Janet was staring at me, her thin brows raised to the ceiling, but Justin was giving me the "dude, I know" head nod.

I felt Perry tense up slightly and wondered if I took things too far. Wouldn't be the first time. Then I wondered if it was because I threw the "love" word out there. Wouldn't be the first time for that either.

Luckily our drinks came just then, and I quickly ordered two rounds of shots for everyone at the table. The evening was turning out to be all sorts of weird and unknown territory, and getting drunk was the quickest way through it. Pretty soon everyone was getting sloppy. Having a good time, but sloppy nonetheless. Rebecca kept looking like she was about to face plant into the table, Dean and Justin were engrossed in game talk, Janet was drunk and in a mad texting war with someone overseas, and Seb kept going out to smoke a joint until he just never came back.

And Perry and I? Well, the alcohol and the whole "we are now a couple" speech swirled around to make our own personal concoction of lust and longing. I tried to behave myself, I really did, but my tongue was down her throat, my hands were down her pants, and I was one soft moan away from blowing my load all over Janet's shoes. Okay, well in my defense, "behaving myself" meant I wasn't undressing Perry in public, though that was starting to become an option.

I kissed down her neck, biting along the way and murmured, "Remember what we tried to do in the elevator?"

"I have a vague recollection," she said, her voice all airy and enthralled. Such a turn-on.

"How about you go to the ladies' washroom and I meet you there in a minute. It has a lock on the door, right?"

She placed her hand on my chest and pushed me back to look me in the eye. "Are you serious? The women's washroom?"

"Baby, I'm always serious when it comes to getting you off. You should know this by now." I pulled her to me and sucked hard on her delicate earlobe. "Besides, I can feel how wet you are. Would be a real shame to waste that." I pressed my fingers into her until she twitched.

She straightened up in her seat and brushed her hair back, gathering it at the nape of her neck, her eyes searching the table and bar to see if anyone was paying attention to our antics. No one was. Satisfied, she gave me a loaded look and then walked off to the washrooms. Hot damn. Hate to have you go but love to watch you leave.

I finished the rest of my drink, waiting a few beats, kinda

hoping that someone *would* notice what we were about to do, but no one did. Dean and Justin were now talking to Janet about something heated, and Rebecca was passed out on the table. We'd have to take her home soon, but I knew we wouldn't be in the bathroom all that long, not at the rate I was jacked up.

I got up and moved through the crowd to the washrooms. There was no line outside the women's, which was good, only problem was there were two of them and I didn't know which one Perry was in. I knocked on the first door, just a quick rap, and heard someone yell, "Occupied!" as if her life depended on it. Sheesh, women were uptight about pissing.

I went to the next one, knocked softly and said, "Perry?" and it opened a crack, showing just half of her face. She looked so damn nervous and shy that I pushed the rest of the door open and went inside, quickly locking the door behind me. The need to drive my cock inside her suddenly overpowered me, and I grabbed her face, kissing her hard, my hands moving down into her hair, down her back to her ass where I got a good meaty hold and squeezed hard. She let out a cry of pain, but it was good pain from the way she attacked me, hands, lips, teeth, everywhere.

I quickly pulled her leggings and thong off, and then whirled her around and pinned her up against the wall. She wrapped her bare legs around my waist and held me close to her as I fumbled with my fly. Once my cock was free, my jeans dropping to my ankles, I wasted no time in guiding the tip into her, just teasing her cleft with her own wetness.

"Fuck me, Dex," she cried out, her head back, her hips trying to thrust closer, to get purchase. Her nails dug into my back.

"Tell me how much you want it," I groaned, feeling her expanding for my tip, so needy.

"I want it, I want you. I need you inside me."

Oh god, please keep talking, I thought. My heart was competing now with my dick.

"Tell me how much."

"So much. Please, I need you inside me, please thrust inside me, please."

Her cries were my undoing. I thrust into her, feeling her expand around me, so slick, so tight, so, so beautiful. It was a space meant for me, only for me, a place I'd spent my life looking for, a home inside a woman who was my home. There was no place I'd rather be. Fuck.

I started off slow, relaxing into the rhythm, trying to hold myself in check. She felt so good and I started rubbing her clit to ensure I felt the same way for her. She started panting, squirming, wanting more.

"Harder," she pleaded. "Take me harder."

I licked her neck. "Aren't you a demanding one." I kept going slow and steady, not ready to give her everything just yet. I was amazed I was able to hold her up like this, and when I pulled my head away I noticed she was watching my clenching ass in the bathroom mirror as I pushed into her.

"Do you like what you see?" I whispered, delighting in the primal lust in her glazed eyes. "Those muscles are all for you. I was born to fuck you, baby."

I thrust into her deeper, faster, finally giving us what we both wanted. She held me tighter, dug her nails in harder, bit down on my shoulder as I pounded her, keeping my fingers quick and steady. Her legs began to loosen as she approached climax.

"That's my girl, that's my girl, that's my girl," I grunted as the pressure reached the breaking point. Everything tightened before the damn was unleashed and I poured into her, wanting my seed to go further, to implant itself somewhere deep inside her where a part of me would never, ever leave.

She cried out as she came, whimpering, moaning, then tried to muffle it once she realized where we were. I couldn't care less. I wanted the whole bar to know.

I breathed into the hollow of her neck, swimming in her smell, the feeling of her as she came for me, the sweetness of vulnerability in the moments after. This was heaven, this was priceless, this was everything.

"Wow," she said, catching her breath. Her legs started shaking around me, tired from the strain. I grabbed hold of her thighs and gently pried her off of me, lowering her. "Wow."

"Now you can cross that off your list," I told her, handing over her leggings and pulling up my jeans.

She put them on and looked herself over in the mirror, her face flush, her hair messed. "What else is on this list of yours?"

"You'll find out," I said, "and you'll like it."

Even though we were a bit disheveled, I unlocked the door and opened it, expecting to see an impatient woman on the other side of it, waiting for the bathroom.

I was right. But it wasn't any woman. It was Jenn.

"Whoops, sorry to keep you waiting," I said to her with a shit-eating grin.

Jenn's jaw dropped as she looked at us both. I looked down at Perry, wondering if she was going to bolt or be embarrassed. But Perry had time to recover from the first meeting, she was high on orgasm endorphins, and the steady look on her face told me she hadn't forgotten who Miss Anonymous was. This was her moment. This was her payback.

She smiled at Jenn, all confidence with a hint of smugness. "So sorry about Bradley." She reached over and tapped Jenn's shoulder sympathetically. "Don't worry, you'll meet someone one day. Just keep on truckin'."

Then she walked away, head held high, hair still messy from sex. I waggled my brows at Jenn and hurried on after her. My woman was changing before my eyes and I was loving it.

5

The next morning Perry and I both felt like death. I don't know what it is about draft beer, but it gets you every damn time. Well, draft beer and copious amounts of Jack Daniels and Irish whiskey.

We woke up around ten when Fat Rabbit demanded to be walked or he'd piss all over the house, and because it was my dog and I was a gentleman, I got up and took him for a quick walk in just striped pajama pants and a stained white tee, ignoring the nipple-tweaking wind. The fresh morning air did perk me up and when I got back inside, and I told Perry, who was still huddled under the covers and craving grease and water, that I'd be taking her out on her second date: Pike Place Market.

Yes, it's the quintessential tourist trap of Seattle, but fuck if the market didn't have good shit. Besides, now that we were living together and Perry wasn't moving out, we needed to get some good grub for the place. We couldn't survive on my famous macaroni and hot dogs forever.

It took a little coaxing to get her out of bed, even after making her bacon and eggs, but soon we were heading out the door and walking down the street toward the water. I grabbed her hand, already cold from the wind that wouldn't quite latch on to Spring, and held it tight. This was nice. This was right.

"So what do you think Jimmy is going to say?" she asked as we turned left onto First Avenue.

"I really don't know," I admitted. "Are you nervous?"

"Kind of. What if he cancels the show?"

I took in a deep breath. I'd been trying not to think about it for the last twenty-four hours. After Perry quit the show, I was a complete and utter Cheetos-covered mess. That was due to her absence, of course, but I think not having the show messed me up a bit too. Like her, it had given me a new purpose, and a life without the show seemed odd and meandering.

"I know I was hesitant about getting you back on the show," I told her, "but I was more concerned about your safety than anything else."

"I suppose you had a right to be," she said under her breath. She cleared her throat. "That...beast was..."

Yeah. That was bad judgement for both of us, thinking that Sasquatch wasn't real. We should have known better than that.

"But even so," I went on, "I do like doing the show with you. I feel like it's something that makes sense of who we are and what we see. It gives meaning in a way...I just wonder if maybe there's a better way of doing this. Not ghost hunting but...well, I don't know, this sound ridiculous, but maybe there is something to ghost whispering. We've already confirmed that you have the breasts for it."

She smacked my chest. "I'm more than my boobs."

"Yes you are, but they certainly help," I said. "But I'm serious too. If Jimmy does cancel the show, maybe there is something else we can do—together—to make sense of what we have. I don't think we need him like he wants us to believe we do."

"But a sponsor would make things so much easier. I could actually bring in an income that counts."

"Hey, kiddo, you know you don't have to worry about that stuff with me."

She stopped in her tracks, pulling me back a bit. Her expression was grave. "Dex, earning an income is important to me. I know you have your inheritance, how else could you afford a new Highlander and a nice apartment, but that doesn't mean I want to be taken care of."

"It bothers you, huh?" I asked.

She nodded. "Well, yeah. My parents always treated me like a freeloader and I just don't want you to think I am too."

I played with her hand. "Perry, I don't think that of you at all. I *want* to take care of you. I've never been able to take care of anyone in my whole life. I'm more than happy to do it."

She seemed to consider that. I pulled gently at her. "Come on, let's go get some fish thrown at you."

I led her down the road until it turned to brick. We ducked into the market, and despite it being a weekday and off-season, it was still packed full of people. Luckily they were locals who didn't gawk and shuffle along like they'd never seen fresh food before. We pressed past vendors selling jewelry, farmers with their rows of green vegetables, a woman yelling at us to buy chocolate fettuccini. Perry looked adorably wide-eyed, and once we got to the main attraction—the fish people—I got one of them to toss a salmon right at her. To her credit, she actually caught it and instinctively tossed it to someone else. They didn't work at the market but it was still pretty impressive.

I grabbed us both a fresh crab cocktail, which worked surprisingly well for hangovers, and we were munching on it outside the bronze pig statue when Jimmy called.

I handed her my cocktail and said, "Here we go, kiddo," while answering my cell. "Jimmy."

"Okay, I've had time to think about it," he said.

"Twenty-two hours exactly," I told him.

"Yes, well I had some things to figure out. Anyway, I have a proposition for you, Dex."

"And Perry."

"Yes, both of you."

"You know I'm not a fan of being propositioned, Jimmy, unless it's by a very breasty woman."

I winked at Perry, who was watching me stone-faced, oblivious to the people all around her, fighting to touch the pig.

"This is how it is," Jimmy went on with a sigh, clearly as sick of dealing with me as I was with him. "And there are no other options. You got that? It's this or it's nothing. Either you do it my way or it's the highway. It's this or nothing. Do you understand?"

"Yes," I hissed into the phone, grabbing Perry by the elbow and leading her away from the crowd. Satisfied we had some privacy, I eyed her and said, "Jimmy says he has an option for us, just the one option. If we don't take it, we don't have a show."

She nodded, grim but curious. "Okay, what is it?"

"Lay it on us," I said to Jimmy.

"I have someone I want to add to the show."

The fuck? No. And I almost said no flat-out, but I wanted to make sure I wasn't screwing myself over by being so impulsive.

"Go on," I said tersely.

"Dex, you and Perry, to put it mildly, cannot be trusted. You can't be trusted with delivering a good show, let alone a show in general. You keep screwing up or acting unprofessional. I mean, how many cameras and phones have you two lost so far?"

"No more than the average person."

"Right. And I think you know what I'm talking about, too. You just don't have a leg to stand on at the moment, and if I trusted you enough to let you go on as is, you'd just disappoint me all over again."

That would have hurt if it wasn't Jimmy who was saying it. I hated the idea of having someone else work with us; it'd totally ruin our dynamic. We worked fast and on the fly, we took risks and chances that sometimes didn't pay off but sometimes did. Adding an extra person to the pot could make the job more dangerous than it already was.

"So, Dex," Jimmy continued, "if you two agree to work with this person, then you'd have the sponsorship. Naturally it means that you'd be working a threesome for the near future until an alternative is brought up."

"Naturally. So what, is this person going to be our babysitter? A host? What?"

"For now he would just be a supervisor. He would pick and plan where you go next—and he already has something lined up as it so happens—he would make all the arrangements, he would make sure everything is running smoothly, he would help you whenever you needed help, and this is crucial, when you think you don't need help but actually do. I know you, Dex, you're one stubborn son-of-a-bitch. You need help more than you know."

"Thanks for your wonderful vote of confidence. So it's a he then. Who is this guy?"

"You already know him."

And at that, everything around me began to spin and swirl: Perry, the pig, the tourists, the brick road, the Starbucks up on 1st, as a heavy hunk of lead settled in my stomach. It wasn't the crab, it was that I knew who he was talking about, and that the person was also standing across the road from me, staring at me above the crowd of people and passing cars.

One ginger fucking head.

I dropped the phone and it clattered to my feet. Perry let out a little cry, trying to go for it while juggling the crab cocktails. I didn't know if it was yet another phone broke and I didn't really care. Because I was locked in a surreal staring match with someone I had hoped to never see again.

Maximus was outside of a bookstore, rain jacket on, white and orange plaid shirt peeking out underneath. He smiled at me, at the dumb fucking expression that must have been on my face, and started to cross the street.

"Oh good, it's not broken," Perry said, straightening up and peering at my phone, shaking it. "I think you lost Jimmy though. Dex?"

"We've got bad news," I managed to say, still staring at Maximus as he sauntered over.

"What did Jimmy propose?" she asked. "What was the... the *fuck* is he doing here?"

Yup. She saw him too. I reached for her hand, as if we were preparing to meet a ghost head-on, but no ghosts deserved a punch to the nuts as much as this vag-burglar did.

"Howdy, Dex," he said in his stupid drawl with his stupid lopsided grin. He nodded chivalrously at Perry. "Little lady."

"Little lady? Who the fuck are you, John Wayne?" I sneered.

"Here to save the day," he said, his legs wide apart, arms folded across his chest.

"The hell you are."

"So Jimmy already told you, has he?"

"Told him what?" Perry asked. "What the hell are you doing here anyway? How did you find us?"

He shrugged with one shoulder. "It's a small city."

I narrowed my eyes at him, this feeling of unease spreading through me. It wasn't just the unease of him here, of Jimmy proposing that we work with him, but that he had just found us here, randomly and at the right moment, which seemed to make it not random at all. Suddenly, it occurred to me that nothing with Maximus was random, and I had to bury that little insight away so I could concentrate on the greater threat.

"Dex, what's going on?" Perry asked.

I shot her a quick look. "Jimmy was about to tell me that we can get the sponsorship if we add a third person to our party. Him." I jerked my head in his direction.

Her eyes got big like saucers. It was a relief to know she felt the same way I did. Now that I knew that Perry and Maximus had slept together while we were...well, not talking...a part of me wondered if she still harbored feelings for him. And when I was feeling really insecure, I wondered if her reluctance to be with me was a cause of that. Even if she didn't have feelings for him, his dick had been inside of her, and that made me want to go on a killing spree every time I was reminded of it. Such as now.

"You can't be serious!" she exclaimed, looking horrified. That's my girl. Keep at it, kiddo.

"Oh, I'm afraid Jimmy is very serious," Maximus said. "And you two don't have much of a choice. You either bring me on board or you're out of a job."

Perry shook her head. "No. This is ridiculous. Dex, Jimmy is always saying shit like this and it doesn't stick."

I sighed loudly, running a hand through my hair. Oxygen seemed rare at the moment and solid thought was escaping me. The universe was conspiring to bring Maximus Jacobs back into my life, and I couldn't figure out why, other than that the universe had a shitty sense of humor and liked fucking me up the ass. Horny bastard.

"This time it's sticking, honey," Maximus said.

"Don't call me that," Perry sniped.

I glared at him too. "Don't you act like you know shit all, dickweed, because you don't know shit. I've been working with Jimmy for the past three years."

"And yet here I am, brought in to be your saving grace."

"How much did you bribe him to get the job?" I asked, not holding back. "How much?"

He rolled his eyes. "Right, because this is my dream job, chaperoning you two."

"You aren't chaperoning anything! Perry and I have agreed to nothing, and like hell if we'll let you be a part of what we started." My phone chose that moment to ring. I eyed it. Jimmy. Fuck.

"What?" I yelled into it.

"You hung up on me."

"I dropped my phone. It doesn't matter. I know what you were going to say. He's right here. Somehow." I squinted at Maximus over that last part. He smiled back at me. It was so fucking hard to get to him and so damn easy for him to get to me.

"So then you know. So what do you guys say?"

"I say you can shove this idea—"

"Dex!" Perry interjected, grabbing my arm. "How about discussing it with me first before you screw us both over."

My mouth flapped open. "You can't be seriously considering this!"

She looked at Maximus and back to me and nodded at the phone. "Jimmy said we have no choice. It's either this or nothing at all."

"She's right, Dex," Jimmy said in my ear. "This is your option. You either bring Mr. Jacobs on board as your, I don't know, let's call him a production manager, or you don't have *Experiment in Terror* anymore. One choice gives you security and a sponsorship. The other choice gives you nothing. Or you can keep being a stubborn ass and screw your partner out of something good just because you and your ex-buddy have some old beef to deal with. What do you say?"

I say fuck you. I say no way. I say I'd rather cut off my balls and I *love* my fucking balls. But I looked at Perry, and even though I knew how much it would bother her to do this with Maximus, I also knew she needed hope in her future. I saw how desperate she was for that, how badly she needed something solid in her life right now, something more than just me. She wanted to have something be a constant when everything with her family and her mental health and her income was up in the air. She wanted something she could count on and I didn't even have to hear her thoughts to know that.

I took the phone away from my ear and looked at her. "So what do you want to do? You know what I want to do."

She frowned. "Quit? Just like that?"

"Always a quitter," Maximus murmured under his breath.

I spun around and slammed my fist into his chest, sending him stumbling off the curb while Perry cried out in surprise. I hadn't meant to do that, the dude was usually as solid as a tree, but then I remembered the new dynamic. I felt almost bad, but that didn't stop me from spewing, "What the hell did you mean by that?"

Maximus rubbed at his chest, his chin dipping, eyes becoming green slits. I rarely saw him mad and it was kind of scary, I had to admit.

"I mean," he said carefully, "just because I'm involved, your first reaction is to quit. That's how much you can't handle being around me. I didn't think I got to you that badly, Dex, really."

I knew what the asswipe was doing and damn it was working. My ego never went down without a fight.

"Hey, I can handle being around you, I just prefer not to work with douchenozzles, that's all. You're only going to get in the way. You don't know what the hell you're doing."

He stepped back on the curb, towering over me. "Oh, and you do? I can see how well you've done so far."

"Dex? Dex?" Jimmy's tinny voice came through the phone in my hand. I forgot he was still there.

I lifted it to my ear. "Yes, Jimmy, sorry, working out the kinks here."

"I can hear that. If you want a minute to discuss it with Perry, I can wait. I'd try and leave your feelings toward Maximus out of it."

"Fine. I'll call you back in a few," I told him and hung up. I felt like tossing the phone as far as I could, but I reigned in Hulk Dex and tried to think about Perry.

I exhaled sharply and cracked my head back and forth before turning to her and said, "So what do you want to do? We've got a few minutes to decide."

"Well obviously you just want to say no and shut this whole thing down," she said, sounding annoyed.

"Look, just a few minutes ago you were horrified at the idea of bringing him on board."

She pulled at her hair hard, looking frustrated. "Well yeah, I am. The three of us can't even have a conversation without a fight breaking out."

"That wasn't a fight," Maximus piped up cockily.

She glared at him. "You, shut up." She then looked at me. "I think it's a bad idea, but I think right now, at this very moment in time, the other option is even worse."

I took a step toward her, reaching for her hand, and lowered my voice as I gazed at her. "Baby, I told you I would take care of you."

She smiled and laced her fingers into mine, which was doubly nice considering who we were in front of. I could *feel* him frowning at us behind me. "I know you can take care of me. But I have to try and take care of myself too. Let's just give this a shot. If it doesn't work, then we can still quit and do our own thing. But if it does work, this could change a lot of things for us. I would...I would just feel a lot better knowing I had a solid job to rely on."

My heart felt like it had been stabbed with a very fine needle and I fought hard to keep it showing on my face. I hated, hated, hated that I wasn't enough for her at the moment. It was stupid and selfish and immature to think I should be her world and her only world, the only thing she needed, but damn. I needed that from her like I never needed anything before.

I smiled at her, hiding everything, and said, "Fair enough. If that's what you want, then that's what we'll do." I really, really hoped I wouldn't start resenting that.

I turned around and looked at Maximus. He was eyeing our hand-holding with puzzlement, and I couldn't wait to rub this shit in his face but now wasn't the time. "Fine. Perry says yes. I guess that means I'll just have to suck it up and deal with your ginger-ass ruining everything."

He looked my way, observing me like only he knew how to do, like he was on the inside of a joke I knew nothing about. "This is really going to tear you up inside, isn't it?"

I forced myself to shrug nonchalantly. "Well, I got through college with you following me around like a lost pooch, so I suppose I can get through this too."

He raised a brow but didn't say anything. I knew what he was going to say too, that I didn't actually get through college, that Abby started showing up and ruining everything, that he stopped being my friend, that I was locked away and everything was taken from me. But I suppose even he knew when to keep his mouth shut.

"You better call Jimmy," he said, turning his attention to the market and the people going to and fro with bags of specialty olive oil and dried peppers.

And ginger-douche bossing me around had begun. I exchanged a tepid glance with Perry then dialed Jimmy's number.

"Well," he answered. "I don't have all day."

I took in a deep breath, looking deep into Perry's baby blues. She was hopeful. That was all I needed. "We'll do it. I suppose we don't get to negotiate this a bit further."

"Nope. From now on, you're the cameraman and editor, same as ever. Perry is the host. Other than that, Maximus Jacobs is in charge of absolutely everything."

"Fucking fantastic."

"Thought you'd agree," he said. "Now the best part of this whole arrangement is that I don't have to deal with you and you don't have to deal with me. Everything will be dealt with through him."

"Where did we go wrong, Jimmy? Don't the good times count for anything?" I pleaded mockingly.

"Things went wrong the day I met you. Take care, Dex. Watch out for Perry. And listen to the redhead."

He hung up and I stared at the phone dejectedly before shoving it in my cargo jacket. Well, that was that.

I looked at Maximus, who was grinning to himself and pretending to not pay attention.

"I feel like I just signed a deal with the devil," I said.

He grinned wider and eyed me briefly. "Oh, Dex, didn't you know? I'm one of the good guys."

6

I saw my mother again. Well, I didn't see her, but I could *feel* her and that was more than enough.

I woke up in the middle of the night, 3AM, right on the fucking dot, and had to piss like a racehorse. Perry was snoozing beside me, beautiful and peaceful in the dim, and I was careful not to wake her.

I didn't feel that anything was wrong at first, in fact I didn't even turn on the light, keeping the door open and using the hazy glow from the hallway to illuminate the bathroom. It wasn't until I was pissing away, when I heard the door slowly shut behind me. The bathroom grew very cold, very suddenly, and I knew that it wasn't caused by some random breeze.

I shook the last drops off my dick and was about to get out of there when the door clicked fully shut. I tried to swallow my panic and fumbled for the knob. When I found it, it wouldn't open. It was locked. I was trapped. Oh my shit.

I put my hands along the wall, feeling for the light switch, debating how long I had before I started screaming for Perry to come help me, when I felt it. Hot breath on my neck. The presence behind me was nearly indescribable, both familiar and malevolent. I knew it had come from the mirror.

Then the light turned on by itself and I knew I could turn around and see cold, dead eyes staring right at me. I could come face to face with the oldest of my demons. But I didn't. It took all my courage to keep staring at the door, to put my hand back on the doorknob and force it to turn with all my might.

And turn it did, like it hadn't been locked at all. I bolted out of the bathroom, not daring to look behind me, not even checking to see if she was following me to the bedroom or not. God, I hoped not. I had no idea what would happen if Perry got involved.

I closed the bedroom door behind me and locked it, as if that would do any good. The bathroom light spilled in from underneath the door frame, a reminder of what was out there.

I crawled into bed, spooning Perry and pulling the covers over my head. I didn't sleep until the dawn broke through the clearing sky.

~

"You look tired," Perry said to me as the cab rattled along the I-5.

I gave her a dry look and squeezed her close to me. "Thanks. How would you like it if I said you looked tired?"

"Do I?"

I shook my head and kissed her forehead. "No, you look beautiful as always and supremely asstastic."

The cab driver eyed me in the mirror and I merely smiled at him. We were heading toward the airport, Maximus having wasted no time in getting us on our next shoot. I barely had time to convince Rebecca to look after Fat Rabbit again.

Our destination: New Orleans. To be honest, I was pretty excited since I'd never been to NOLA before, or Louisiana. Unfortunately, Maximus was from the state, and his knowledge of the land would ensure that neither Perry nor I would have much say in anything.

Maximus had told us that NOLA was just swimming in haunted houses and estates, which was common knowledge, I mean even I knew that. But he said that there was one old mansion that had been flooded during Hurricane Katrina. Ever since then, the paranormal activity levels had been off the chart. A few ghost hunters had already been there and weren't able to walk away with much evidence aside from the usual orbs and cold spots, but he figured with our "abilities" we would have a much better chance of capturing something. He said he had a contact in NOLA that would help us find something worth filming, even if that house fell through. Which, in other words, meant the three of us were staying in the Big Easy for as long as it took to come back with a show.

"I thought I heard you get up last night," Perry said, bringing me back to the moment. "But when I looked at the time on my phone, it was like 4AM and you still weren't back in bed. What were you doing?"

I froze—my blood, my veins, everything was ice.

"What?" I asked, barely able to pronounce the words. "What...you said I didn't come to bed until 4AM?"

"Until at least 4AM. That's when I fell back asleep," she said.

I rubbed at my face, squeezing my chin. The fuck? I got up at 3AM, and I wasn't in the bathroom for more than two minutes...was I?

"What were you doing?" she continued.

"I, uh, couldn't sleep. I was watching TV with Fatty Rab. Infomercials."

She raised her head and studied me. The thing was, I knew I sounded like someone in a horror movie, when there's obviously something very wrong going on and the person stupidly says "I'm fine" when they clearly aren't. I knew that's what was happening here but I couldn't help it. "Baby," I said to her, "I'm fine. Just couldn't sleep. I get insomnia sometimes. Get used to it. Just a roommate quirk, like how you put empty cartons of milk back in the fridge."

It's funny how I was able to tell her about the time I saw my mother in the motel in Snowcrest. But now, to tell her again, would make something out of something that I desperately wanted to go away. My mother wanted attention, she always did. I wouldn't give her that. She would be my secret for as long as I could keep it.

I suppose it didn't matter, because I could tell that Perry didn't believe me. I could see the doubt in her eyes, but I could also see the respect she had, the respect she'd followed from the day she first met me. Perry had already sussed out so many of my terrible secrets from the very beginning, if not knowing exactly what they were, knowing that something was wrong. She was devastatingly perceptive.

"All right," she said, settling back in the seat and ignoring the dig about the milk cartons. Seriously though, that was annoying.

We got to the airport a little bit early, hoping to beat Maximus so we could get our seats next to each other and away from him, but the flame-haired bastard was already there and waiting at the checkout for us, carry-on in hand.

"About time you two showed up, I was getting worried," he said in all seriousness.

"It's like ninety minutes before our flight," I protested.

He shrugged and I felt like kicking him in the knees. This was going to be a hell of a long trip.

He handed us our tickets. "No worries."

I glanced at the ticket. I had an aisle seat. I tore Perry's out of her hands and peered at it. Window.

"You ass," I said. "Where are you sitting?"

He smiled. "I took one for the team. Middle seat. Between you guys."

Right. If he really took one for the team he would jump out of the airplane.

"How considerate," Perry said, her eyes full of disdain. She glanced at me and sighed. "Okay, well let's get through security then so we don't have to worry."

I've been in a lot of awkward moments in my life, and most of the time, I actually enjoy them. I don't know if it means I'm a sociopath or what, but I just don't feel awkward or self-conscious when I know I should. But lately, I'd been feeling that tinge of heavy air, things unsaid, especially around Perry. Being with Maximus and her was no exception. With him there, I felt like a spotlight was being shined on every single move, every shot I did at the bar pre-flight (whatever, there's no judgement in alcohol after 11AM), or magazine I rifled through at the gift shop, every glance Perry and I shared. Suddenly everything was everyone's business and I didn't even know what the goddamn business was.

The flight was much, much worse. I had strategically planned to get to the seats before Maximus, so that at least I could get the middle and sit beside Perry, but the cock-blocker was quicker and pushed past us when it was time to board. Apparently he was a "gold club member" and we weren't. By the time we got to our seats, he was already in his, looking up at us smugly.

"Do you mind at least moving so I can get to my seat?" Perry asked after shoving her carry-on in the overhead compartment.

"You can squeeze through," he said, wagging his brows and insinuating that her ass was going to be pressed against his freckled knees.

"Ugh," she said in frustration, and squeezed past him. I kept my eyes on him, daring him to try anything, just try. I didn't care if it got me kicked off the plane; I would make a scene.

To his credit he stared right back at me, even moving back in the seat to let her go through.

"Now you," I said to him, tapping the aisle seat, "you sit here and let me sit next to Perry."

He shook his head in amusement. "This is my seat."

"Yeah, yeah, took one for the team. But I would like the middle seat, so get out." I motioned for him to get out quick.

"Dex, just sit down," he said, nodding at the rest of the plane. "People here need to get to their seats, buddy."

It was true, I was preventing a whole line of people from moving down the aisle, and hell hath no fury like people once they are on an airplane. It's like the minute everyone's in this giant Tylenol-shaped contraption, their patience threshold changes dramatically. The baby boomer woman closest to me was turning red, a vein popping out on her harried face.

"Fine, you leave me no choice," I said to no one in particular. I moved into the aisle seat and kept going. I plunked myself down right on the giant ginger's lap.

"The hell are you doing?" he yelled, trying to get me off of him, but I just pressed myself down into him harder, one leg wedged against the seat in front of me, the other pushing off the aisle seat arm rest.

The passengers in the aisle shot us uncomfortable looks, as if Maximus and I were involved in some lazy, clothed version of the mile high club.

"Dex, get the hell off me," Maximus grunted in my ear.

"Oh yeah, you like that don't you, baby," I said with a grin. I knew his Southern sensibilities were being tested; poor guy couldn't handle anything even remotely homoerotic.

"Is there a problem here?" A flight attendant suddenly appeared. She could barely hide the disgust on her face; I'm not sure if it was because I was acting like a child or that we were getting loosey goosey. Either way, her bun was tied way too tight, pulling back every feature on her face.

"No, we're good," I said at the same time Maximus said, "Obviously there is a problem."

"Sir," she said, glaring at me. Boy, how the friendly skies had changed. "Can I see your ticket?"

I handed her my ticket, and she pursed her lips while reading it over. "Mr. Foray, your seat is the aisle seat not the middle. Now if you don't get off this man's lap, I'm going to have you removed from the plane."

"Dex, just sit in your seat," Perry said beside me. I glanced at her. She was pressed up against the window and looking at us with a mix of revulsion and embarrassment.

"Fine," I said, and quickly climbed off of him, settling down in my seat and fastening the belt. "Just trying to take one for the team."

The stewardess watched me for a few beats, giving me one last evil eye, before she moved down the aisle.

"Dex, you are something else," Maximus said to me, looking a bit shaken. Perfect.

"Once you have a Dex in your lap, you can't go back," I said. I looked over at Perry. "Ain't that right, kiddo?"

"No comment," she said, and pulled out the in-flight magazine. Yup. Fun trip ahead of us.

After that risqué start, the rest of the flight was fairly uneventful. I started calling Maximus "Vegetable Lasagna", a *Seinfeld* reference that was obviously over his head, and did my best to talk to Perry when I could. Too bad the oaf didn't leave his seat once, not even to go to the bathroom. The rest of the time I just sat back and listened to the new Slayer album, feeling more connected to Perry by listening to her favorite music.

My luck changed once we switched planes in Houston. Maximus was sitting further up on that plane, while Perry and I got two seats together at the back. The flight was quick, too quick to convince Perry to join the mile-high club with me in the bathroom, but long enough to drink a few Bloody Marys in preparation for the Big Easy. Again, I was getting a bit excited at the idea of going to New Orleans and started wishing that it was just Perry and I there, taking the sights in as tourists. Man, what I'd give to go on an actual vacation with the woman. No ghosts, no work—just us, booze, and sex.

"How you doing?" I asked her as the plane began its descent. It was already dark outside, the city a mystery beneath us. I wasn't a nervous flier but I guess she was because she grabbed on to my hand and squeezed it hard. I squeezed it right back.

"I'm okay," she said. "Kind of excited."

"Me too."

"Nervous."

"Fear of flying?"

"Yeah, I mean I'm okay, it's just not my favorite thing in the world. But I'm also nervous about the next few days...or week...or however long we'll be here."

I peered at her closely. "Bad feeling?"

She managed a smile. "Well, I never have good feelings before we do a show. I don't know, I guess I just don't like how Maximus is involved. I don't trust him."

"That makes me ridiculously happy to hear you say that."

"You don't trust him either, I know that much."

I laughed dryly. "I've never trusted him. But I gotta tell ya, I was worried about you."

She gave me an odd look as the plane rumbled, landing gear coming down. "Worried how?"

I chewed on my lip, knowing I'd gone too far to hold anything back but the truth. I turned my attention to the runway lights outside the window.

"I know what's done is done but the fact that you and Maximus...that he..."

"You know I wasn't even myself when that happened."

Right. She'd said that several times, but that didn't stop it from hurting; it didn't erase that it happened.

"Anyway, I guess I worry that you might still have feelings for him." There. I said it.

She squeezed my hand again, and this time I couldn't tell if she was trying to assure me or herself as the plane made contact with the ground, bouncing us along before the brakes were applied with urgency.

"Dex, I don't have feelings for the man. Especially not

after what he did to me. He turned on me when I needed him the most and I'm not going to forget that."

"He has his excuses though, about why he did what he did," I pointed out, playing devil's advocate for some reason.

"I still don't know what they are. He said he was trying to help me in the end, but he nearly got me carted off to the hospital. It was because of him that the whole mental thing started with my parents, that was what put the idea in their heads."

I wasn't too sure about that part. As much as I hated Maximus and loved to blame him for everything, I knew Perry's parents were against her from the moment I first met them. I didn't mean that they wished her harm, that they didn't love her. But they didn't understand her and they were afraid of her and that made them dangerous.

"So you think he's going to do something like that again? Because baby, you know I am not going to let a single thing happen to you. I'm going to be with you, be in you, as much as I can."

We deplaned fairly quickly and met Maximus out at the gate. I looked around the airport, a lot smaller than I thought it would be, with all of the stores closed. When we stepped outside to line up for a cab, I was met with the unmistakable smell of swamp—musty, damp, and earthy.

Maximus smiled to himself. "My Lord, is it good to be back home." He breathed in deeply and for a moment I was almost happy for him. Almost. I wasn't. It just reminded me again that we were on his home turf and he was the one calling the shots. But I refused to let his love for his state cloud my own opinion of it.

We got in the cab and had one hell of a chatty driver who talked to Maximus like they were old buddies. The Senegalese cabbie moved to the city just after Katrina blew through, attracted by the cheap housing and the underdog spirit of the rebuilt city. Maximus hadn't been back in the city since right before Katrina hit. Apparently after we cut ties in college, he had come to NOLA and lived there for three years, just working at a bar. That's what he'd told the cabbie, anyway.

The cabbie dropped us off on a narrow, bumpy street in the French Quarter, telling Maximus that some districts had gotten worse post-Katrina and warned us to stay out of them like our lives depended on it. He said he wouldn't even drive through certain areas, no matter how much the fare was.

We thanked him for his warning, pulled our bags out of the cab, and looked up at our accommodations. Perry and I had been flying blind so far but Maximus did alright in this department. We were staying in an old three-story house with a wide front porch, gas lamps and wrought iron balconies. It looked straight out of a plantation or perhaps just straight out of the French Quarter itself. That was the thing I'd instantly discovered about the city—it looked exactly as you'd imagined it. I looked behind me at the flickering lanterns that lined the street, the brightly painted houses beside quaint bars where I was immediately tempted to drink my face off, the hidden courtyards; it was like stepping into a movie.

"I feel like I'm in Disneyland," Perry said, looking up at the house with a big kid smile on her face.

"You, missy, have to stop being so damn cute," I told her, bringing her to me and kissing her on the lips.

Maximus cleared his throat. "Glad you guys like it, it's a bed and breakfast with the tastiest beignets you'll find in the city. Well, aside from Café Du Monde, if it's still there."

I pulled away from Perry and eyed him. He didn't look too pleased at our PDA, and I was wondering when he'd start questioning what was happening in our relationship. Obviously he knew that we were together now, and judging from the beady look in his eyes, he obviously didn't like it. Tough tits, ginger.

The look got even worse when we went to check in and I told the pucker-faced, extremely spritely receptionist that we would only need two rooms, not three.

"I see," she said, studying Perry and I. "I wasn't aware that there was a couple staying here."

"Neither was I," Maximus said under his breath.

"Sorry," I told her, jerking my head in his direction, "this one here made the booking without consulting us first."

She adjusted her glasses. "Yes, well, since it was such a last minute reservation, I'll just cancel the room without penalty. Probably better that way anyway—it is the haunted room."

"Haunted room?" Perry spoke up, looking frazzled.

The woman smiled. "It's just George, the resident ghost. He's a friendly one, don't worry."

"Friendly, sure, I've heard that before," I said. She gave me an odd look and I didn't bother trying to explain myself. The day I met a friendly ghost was the day I came up with better analogies.

Both of our rooms were on the third floor, overlooking the street, with a shared balcony connecting us through French doors.

Perry and I tossed our bags on the bed and surveyed the quaint room. It was a little too old lady-ish for my liking, like the receptionist decorated it, but Perry seemed absolutely enthralled. I guess there was a romantic, girly-girl some-where beneath that Mastodon t-shirt.

"I guess the bastard wants to keep an eye on us," I told her.

"I heard that," came his muffled voice through the wall. Oh great, and the walls were paper-thin too. Though that made me extremely glad that I'd remembered to pack something.

"What's so funny?" Perry asked.

I wiped the smile off my face. "Nothing, just trying to look on the bright side. Shall we unpack?"

"No time," Maximus said from the doorway. Shit, he was just everywhere, wasn't he?

"Can't you just give us a few minutes alone?" I asked.

"Sorry I'm such a cockblocker—"

"At least you're apologizing this time."

"—but there's someone I want you to meet and I'm not sure if we'll miss her or not."

I raised my brow. "A...a her? You've had contact with the female species? I don't believe it."

He pointed at Perry. "I've had intimate contact with this one."

"You son of a bitch," I snarled, ready to jump him.

"Guys!" Perry yelled, putting her arm out in front of me. "Dex, calm down. You, ginger balls, you shut the fuck up."

I laughed. "Ginger balls, that's my girl!"

He smiled venomously at her. "The very balls you—"

Before I had a chance to knock his face in, Perry was there first, kicking him right in the shin with her Doc Martens. Her violence surprised even me, and I stood there, shocked and impressed. And maybe a bit scared.

Maximus was shocked too, groaning and rubbing his leg. "Have you gone fucking crazy, Perry?"

She put her hands on her hips. "Maybe I have. If you say another fucking thing about what happened between me and you, I'm going to show you what else I can do to your balls, you hear me?"

"Jesus," he swore, straightening up, "all right, all right. You're not much of a little lady after all, are you?"

"I never was. Now tell us where the hell you want us to go and who the hell you want us to meet and why."

Maximus looked at me and I shrugged. I was going to let Perry do her thing. This inner bitch of hers was giving me a hard-on.

"All right," he said, wincing a bit as he shook out his leg. "There's a girl I used to know, our contact. I want to see if she still works at the bar, the one I used to work at. It's just here in the Quarter on Royal Street."

"So let me get this straight," she said slowly, "this girl is our contact and you don't even know if she still works at the same place. Haven't you been in contact with her?"

"Not since I left."

I frowned at him. "Maximus, you do know what the term 'contact' means, don't you? It generally means you've been in contact with the person."

"Yeah, well I reckoned there wasn't time. Besides, we don't need her, we can investigate the haunted house on our own. I just thought we should get her involved."

"Why?" Perry asked, leaning back on one leg, full of attitude.

He slowly tilted his head back and forth, considering the question. Finally he said, "Because she's a lot like you guys."

"What do you mean like us?" I asked warily.

"She sees ghosts, too. She's...pretty special."

"And what's her name?" Perry asked. "This special ghost girl?"

"Rose," he said, almost sadly. "Her name is Rose."

And with that, he turned and left the room, heading down the staircase. I had a feeling that Rose was more than just a contact to him. How much more, well I guess that was something we were about to find out.

I nodded at Perry. "Grab your purse. At least we're going to a bar."

I think we were all going to need a drink at this point.

7

We got to the bar by walking down Bourbon Street for a bit, just to get a feel for the place. Perry and I stopped at one of the bars that were open to the street and ordered two sickly sweet Hand Grenades to go, sucking back on that antifreeze while we navigated the early crowds and puking frat boys who'd probably been drunk all day. And how could you not be? I mean booze to-go? Public drinking was encouraged? Suddenly every bad vice I had was begging to come back.

Rose's bar on Royal Street was further away from the touristy crowds, a large place filled with live jazz, crazy cheap drink specials, and locals having a good time. I was in heaven, especially with the hot woman at my side.

"Do you see her?" I asked Maximus as we stood in the doorway, surveying the room. Most people were sitting near the jazz band, though a few of them were playing pool, and a handful were sitting at one of the two bars.

He shook his head.

"What's the name of this place?" Perry asked.

"It's nameless," he said absently, walking toward the jazz

set-up, searching the seats in front of it. A lanky woman with giant breasts and an afro to match was singing sweet sadness, while two old hep cats played easy drums and mellow bass.

"Ugh, this makes me want to play," I mumbled to myself, feeling the energy of the music seeping through my bones, revving my engines.

"The bar has no name?" Perry went on, still stuck on it.

I nodded to a coaster on the closest table. "Nameless is the name."

"What happened to your hand grenade?" she asked, noting my empty hands.

"I drank it." I turned to her. "Do you think they'd mind if I went up there and sang?"

She frowned at me. "Don't you dare."

"Hey, I know you find my voice sexy."

"Dex, you're one of the best singers I know and I'd love more than anything if you were to sing for me. But please don't go tossing that woman out of the way. Let's not get ourselves kicked out when we just got here." She appraised me more closely. "You're in a real shit disturber mood today."

I couldn't argue with that. "Maybe the drummer would let me take over. He's got to be what, ninety-years-old? If he keeps playing, he could *die*."

"Dex," she warned. "Come on, let's get you another drink while he looks for her."

"Yes, a drink oughta have me thinking clearly."

We went to the closest bar and took a seat. There was no bartender, so I leaned over to the man next to me, an old grizzled thing with a beard that reached the table and said, "So if there's no bartender, do we just help ourselves?" I reached over the bar in jest when suddenly I was face to face with a woman.

"You touch any of my booze and I'm putting this shotgun under your chin," she said, her voice sounding as sweet as she looked, contrasting with her threat. She was around my age, maybe a bit younger, late twenties, and slender with a wide, tanned forehead, grey-blue eyes and curly, white-blonde hair that frizzed a bit at the ends. Pretty thing.

I grinned at her and raised my hands. "I don't see a shotgun."

"It's under the bar, aimed at your gut."

I cocked my head at her. "Are all bartenders this paranoid in the Big Easy?"

"Sugar, this is *my* bar and I'm as paranoid as I need to be."

The bearded man next to me snorted. "He's a tourist, Rose, just let him pass a good time and charge him the tourist price for drinks."

I exchanged a glance with Perry. So this was Rose. Well, well, well. I felt a bit smug knowing that we'd found her before Maximus did.

"*You're* Rose?" Perry asked.

"Tourist price?" I added.

"Yeah I'm Rose," she said, folding her arms. "What's it to y'all?"

My, she was a prickly little thing wasn't she.

"Oh, well, we're here with a friend that says he used to know you. Wasn't sure if you still worked here or not," I explained.

She squinted at me. "Work here? I own the place now. Have for the last four years. Who is your friend?"

Oddly enough, I didn't find it was my place to say. Either that, or I wanted to see what her reaction would be to seeing him, not just hearing about it. Was she going to jump across the bar and beat him up (cuz she seemed like the type to put those ginger balls in a vice), or would she act like she'd never seen him before? I didn't know what their history was, and guessing was half the fun, especially when it came to bodily harm inflicted on him.

I was about to look behind me and see if I could spot him in the depths of the place, but she let out a small gasp and I knew she saw him.

Her eyes went wide, her hand went to her chest, and she said, "My sweet Lord." I looked over and saw Maximus, halfway across the room, just staring at her, like he was frozen in a dream. I turned back to Rose and saw a wash of sadness come over her brow. Sorrow and regret.

Ah fuck, I couldn't take any pleasure in this; this was ending up being a lot more sensitive a thing than I had originally thought.

"Max," she said in barely a whisper, her eyes still glued to his. I looked down at Perry beside me, and she raised her brows and put her hand on my knee. She didn't know what to make of it either, but suddenly it felt like we were intruding on a very private moment in a very public place.

Still, I had to say, "Oh, he doesn't like to be called Max anymore. It's Maximus. Yeah, I think it's pompous too."

Suddenly she was looking at me, a weird understanding in her eyes. "You're Dex."

It sounded like an accusation. "Uh, I am. How do you know my name?"

"I'd heard a lot about his asshole friend from college," she said, and before I could say anything to that, she walked out around the bar, stopping just a few feet away from Maximus, hands fidgeting at her waist.

"Was I being an asshole just then?" I whispered to Perry.

She patted my knee. "I didn't think so, but then again, I'm used to it."

"You are getting a spanking later," I warned her, then turned my attention to their awkward reunion. Unfortunately it didn't last long. Maximus motioned to the outside and Rose followed him out onto the street.

Great. Now we really were in the dark and our bartender was gone. I looked at grizzled Beard Man. "Now what?"

He just shook his head and drank his beer. Luckily, Rose and Max didn't take forever outside. He came back and sat down next to Perry, and Rose went behind the bar and made three mint juleps for us, extra strong.

"Remember to charge them tourist prices," Beard Man said.

She nodded at me. "Unfortunately they're friends of an old friend, so it's on the house."

"Woo hoo," I said. "Everything's coming up Milhouse."

"Everything would come up green if you kept drinking those hand grenades," she said, eyeing the empty one that Perry had finished earlier. "So, Max...sorry, Maximus."

"It's Max to you, darlin'," he said.

She smiled tightly, unsure of herself and quite the change from earlier. "Max. Have you told them about my... uh, ability?"

I looked at Beard Man beside me for his reaction, since talking about "abilities" and stuff in public wasn't usually kosher. But he just drank his beer, indifferent.

"Don't worry, he can't hear me," she said. I looked at her. She was pouring herself a drink.

"Can't..." I started.

"Yes, I told them," he interjected. "Well, I told them you were like them."

She eyed me and Perry warily. "Is that so? So you guys can see the afterlife too, is that it?"

Again, I looked at Beard Man and gave her the 'are you crazy talking about this so casually' look, but again she said, "I'm serious, he can't hear me right now. I guess you *don't* have all the same abilities, do you?"

"Either way," Maximus said, raising his voice before I could say something, "they understand. And that's why we're here. We want to investigate the haunted house in the Desire Area. We need a solid episode, and these two can turn up the goings on that the other teams missed before."

She sighed and finished the rest of her drink. A couple appeared at the end of the table, waving for her attention but she blatantly ignored them. "I suppose I can help you with that, although I think if you're wanting to go after something really interesting, you'll want to talk with Mambo Maryse."

"My Mambo?" he asked. "Why? I didn't even think she was still alive."

"She is, she's just very sick. But something weird has been happening with the Voodoo crowd lately and I think she'd be the best person to talk to about it."

"What's happening?" he asked.

"What is a Mambo?" I asked. My mind was going back to the fruit chew candies I had as a child. Suddenly I really, really wanted one.

Rose addressed me first. "A Mambo is a Voodoo priestess. And I don't really know what's happening, there's just been some rumors of...uh...zombies in the ninth ward and surrounds."

At that, I choked on a mint leaf. Perry pounded on my back until I finished coughing and then said what I wanted to say. "Zombies? There are no such things as zombies."

"And technically there are no such things as ghosts either," Rose argued, "but you and I know better than that."

I looked at Maximus. "Seriously, zombies?"

He shrugged. "It's a thing. But not in the way you think. Plus, documented cases are few and far between."

Rose nodded. "He's right. This isn't your Hollywood version. These are still people and they aren't really dead. They've just been buried alive, fished out of the grave, and given damaging amounts of mind control drugs."

I eyed my drink, careful not to suck up a leaf again. "Oh, well that sounds so simple."

"And this has been going on here? People are seeing zombies? What are the zombies doing?" Perry asked, leaning forward and obviously intrigued.

Rose leaned toward us, elbows on the bar. The couple at the end of it gave up and went over to the other bartender closest to the jazz band.

"This is just all hearsay, of course. But it's been reported in Treme, Lower Nine, Florida Area, all the places you don't want to go. Apparently people are being attacked, at night and in broad daylight."

"But that happens all the time," Maximus said.

"Yes, it does. But usually people don't try and eat each other. And then there's the fact that the people who are attacked report that they were attacked by someone they know is dead, well that's a little suspect too, don't you reckon?"

Maximus shrugged. "Ghetto kids on bath salts then."

She shook her head. "That's what everyone is passing it off as. But I've heard there've been at least twenty attacks."

"Twenty attacks?" I asked. "Why isn't this on the news?"

"Because President Bush don't care about black people," she deadpanned in a Kanye West impression. Then she raised her hand. "And yes, Obama is in office but that hasn't really changed anything here. So many of the areas, especially after Katrina, have turned a little Wild West, more than they used to be. And we all know how corrupt the PD is here. So what if twenty black thugs are attacked? Like anyone is going to do anything. Even if this became an epidemic, so long as it doesn't start involving white folk, then no one really gives a shit. It's sad."

"So why are you giving a shit?" I asked.

She pursed her lips, running a strand of frizzy hair behind her ear. "Because it ain't right. This ain't a matter of bath salts. Someone is out there controlling these people and making them do this. It's horrifying, it's sick, and if we don't stop it, it's only going to get worse."

"If we don't stop it?" Maximus repeated, his red brow raised. "Look, darlin', we just came here to film the good shit. We didn't come here to start killing zombies."

"I second that," I spoke up. "I don't even have a crossbow, and my redneck impression needs some work."

She rolled her eyes before her fine features became serious. "We...I...wouldn't be killing them. They're still people. I just want to stop whoever is doing this."

"But New Orleans has got to be full of these Voodoo people, right? Where would you even start?" Perry asked.

She shook her head. "Many people here practice Voodoo, but Voodoo is about spirituality. The worship comes from a good place. The ones who use Voodoo for bad, for evil, those are few and far between. In order to be one of those, you have to be a Bokor, be in both worlds." She looked at all of us in the eye and then sighed. "Tomorrow, come back here at noon and I'll take you to see the Mambo. She'll help us."

Help you, I thought.

Maximus seemed to have the same thought because he said, "And the haunted house. That's why we're here, Rose."

He said it as if she'd already gotten the wrong idea and she flinched slightly at his words. But she patted the table. "I'll help you with that too. I have to go."

Then she was gone, disappearing into the back room.

I looked over at Beard Man who was staring blankly ahead of him. I nudged his arm. "You catch all of that?"

I expected him to tell us we were all nuts, but instead he said, "Sorry what? I drifted off there."

He looked genuinely lost. I smiled at him. "No worries. Just wondering if there was another bar around here that you could recommend."

He smiled, glad to either help or to be rid of us, and told us there was a place called Speakeasy down the street. Maximus said he knew where it was and took us there. This spot was much smaller than Rose's Nameless. We slipped into a dark booth in the corner, and after ordering a round of shots and hurricanes, some fried oysters and gumbo (*the best in town!* they said) from the waitress, we got to drinking and talking.

I slammed back a shot and banged the table with my hand as it burned down. "Hooooo eeeeee! That takes the edge off." I wiped my mouth and looked Maximus square in the eye, his features hazy in the darkness of the bar. "So, I think you have some 'splaining to do, friendo."

"Yeah," Perry piped up from beside me. "What happened between you and Rose?"

"Nothing."

I snorted. "Right, like you two didn't hump like bunnies."

He cocked his head. "You mean, like you two are so obviously humping like bunnies?"

"What does that have to do with anything?" Perry asked snidely.

He shrugged with one shoulder. "How long has this been going on?"

"None of your business," Perry said.

"Since Canada," I answered. Proudly.

Perry kicked me under the table and I shot her a surprised look. "What? It has. There's no point hiding it, I mean we're sharing a bed and everything. It's kind of obvious."

"Does Jimmy know?" he asked.

I didn't like where this was going. "No. He doesn't. Now that is none of *his* business."

"Don't you have a habit of sleeping with the women you're filming?"

"Don't you have a habit of being an asshole?"

"Asshole? I expected something more original from you, Dex."

"I'm running out of names. There aren't that many vile things on this earth that can describe what a cum dumpster you are."

He ignored that. "I'm just saying, since you slept with Jenn and then had to bail from *Wine Babes*, don't you think Jimmy might disapprove of this little tryst you two are having?"

I ticked off one finger, inches from his face. "One, Jimmy doesn't have to know shit, and two," I ticked off the other, "this isn't some little tryst. She lives with me. She's my girlfriend."

"She's right here," she said, raising her hand, looking annoyed that I was talking about her like she didn't have a say. "And Jimmy doesn't have to know anything. Not that I ever saw a rule against interpersonal dating when I signed my contract, but if no one tells him, there's nothing to worry about. Which, then, begs the question whether you're going to tell him or not. Because, and maybe I'm just biased, but I get the impression that you're a bit of a snitch."

"I just think this is a terrible idea, for you guys to work together and—"

"Fuck each other?" I interrupted. "You can say it. I'm sorry you miss out on the verb all the time. Must be hard having a fire crotch."

He opened his mouth to say something, and I knew what too, but Perry was quick and leaned toward him. "My foot is aimed at that same shin, so you better watch it."

He sighed and leaned back in his chair, running his oversized hand through the red sea on his head. "When did the two of you become so volatile?"

"When you started insinuating shit and threatening to tell Jimmy that Perry and I are together. When did you start caring so much about what we do?"

"When I had to work with you."

I narrowed my gaze at him. There was something hesitant in his eyes, the twitch of his brows. There was something else but I wouldn't get at it tonight.

"Anyway," I went on. "So what is the deal with Rose? You banged her and then what? Banged someone else? She banged someone else? She was your one and only unrequited love?"

His eyes darkened over that last part and I admit I felt a little bad. It was enough to shut me up.

He licked his lips. "We dated and we broke up. It didn't end well."

"Who broke up with who?" Perry asked.

"Does it matter? What's done is done."

I felt like asking the serious question. "Are you still in love with her?"

He gave me a wry look. "What do you think? No. I got over that shit a long time ago. I had to. It's just a bit weird to be back here and back with her. She's changed, too."

The waitress brought over our food and I doused my crispy oysters with Louisiana hot sauce before asking, "How so?"

"She's harder. That's all."

"So she wasn't always the type to want to blow my head off with a shotgun?"

He smiled, close-lipped. "I reckon not." His smile faded and he paid attention to his food. "But I guess I've changed too."

"Well you've obviously upped your jackass levels."

"Yeah. I guess this is just what people call the human experience," he said before shoving a large shrimp po-boy in his mouth. He took a huge bite and sighed happily. "Now this tastes like home."

But with cryptic comments like that, sometimes I had to wonder where exactly Maximus's home really was.

∾

By the time the three of us returned to the bed and breakfast, I was three sheets to the wind. Not stumbly drunk, but horny, loud, enthusiastic and hyper drunk. I kept wanting to drag Maximus and Perry into bar after bar in secret hopes of climbing on stage and taking over—it seemed like every single bar in the French Quarter had live music of the highest quality. But Perry was onto my scheme and the two of them basically forced me back to my room.

We quickly said goodbye to Maximus and I was eager to

attack the living shit out of Perry behind closed doors. All that urge for music and no release meant I had extra energy in my blood, my dick hard as a rock and ready to go.

I also had my plan. Which was an incredibly immature plan, but a plan. And even though part of me felt for Maximus at times, his sob story over Rose wasn't enough to eradicate that he slept with Perry when she was possessed, manhandled his way on to our show, and had some major problem with Perry and I screwing each other's brains out.

So I decided to emphasize that very point. The walls between our rooms were paper thin and I was about to take Perry to whole new levels of orgasm. I was going to fuck her like she'd never been fucked before, and I was going to make sure Maximus could hear every single one of her moans.

I quickly locked the door behind me and started pulling off my clothes.

Perry smiled, blushing. "Dex, at least let me close the curtains."

I nodded at them. "Close them then. Then get back here and start stripping for me."

She frowned good-naturedly. "You're certainly bossy tonight."

"I'm a lot of things tonight," I said. I walked over to my carry-on and peered inside. Yup. The vibrator was still there. I knew Perry was fairly inexperienced with sex so there was a good chance she'd never used one with anyone other than herself, and even on her own I couldn't be sure.

She walked over to me and I told her to take it all off.

"Slowly," I added.

"Are you sure you don't want to sit down? We could re-enact the scene from *True Lies*."

"Oh, baby, what we're about to do will never be in any James Cameron film."

She looked a bit nervous at that, so I walked toward her and helped pull her shirt over her head. "Do you want me to help you?"

"I think I got it," she said. I stepped back a foot, her breasts still in groping distance, and watched as she shimmied out of her jeans.

"Don't you think we should turn off the lights?" she asked, that strain of insecurity breaking across her brow.

I steadied my gaze at her, making sure she felt the heat coming off of it. "I want to see every single part of you. I wouldn't have it any other way. Show me."

She reached behind and undid her bra, and my erection twitched. I'd never felt so thick and so hard before. Even she was impressed, and I'd been impressing her a lot lately.

She slipped off her underwear next and tossed it across the room with a flick of her foot.

I grinned. "Perfect. Now get on the bed, all fours, facing the wall."

She hesitated but I grabbed her around the waist, pressing her full breasts against my chest, my cock a pylon of steel against her. I kissed her hard, my tongue twisting and snaking with hers, my lips engulfing her wet ones. Then I pulled back, feeling dizzy with lust, and ordered her to get on the bed again.

She did as she was told. I added in that she had to keep facing the wall, no peeking. To her credit, she complied as I fished the vibrator out of the bag. I'd bought it just the other day, figuring she might have fantasies that she'd never learned to express. Petty as I was, it was a dildo not much bigger than my own cock. I didn't want her to start comparing mine to her imaginary boyfriend's.

I stood behind her, feeling the weight of the device in my hands, wondering if she was going to love this or if she was going to freak out. Only one way to find out.

"Spread your legs," I commanded.

She did as I asked. Such a lovely view.

I lay down on my back and slid up under her, tool in hand like a vag mechanic. The tips of her breasts brushed against my face and I teased her nipples with my tongue. She moaned in response, back arching, wanting more. I was going to give her more.

I moved back down and put one arm around her waist, pushing at her lower back until her pussy was in my face. Then I angled the vibrator around, turning it on to a low buzz, and gently pressed it into her opening while I slowly teased her cleft with my tongue.

She froze. "What the hell is that?"

I removed my mouth from her sweetness. "Nothing you need to worry about. I packed a friend along on our trip."

"It's new, right?" she asked in terror.

I almost laughed. "Yes, it's new. Now unless you're going to tell me how badly you need my cock, I think you oughta keep your mouth shut. Moaning and groaning is encouraged though."

I put my lips back on her wet ones and started stroking her clit with my tongue in slow, delicious swirls. I pushed the vibrator further into her, wishing it was my own dick she was squeezing and ignoring my growing blue balls. This was about her. This was about rocking her world. This was about rubbing it in. Literally and figuratively.

It didn't take long before it sounded like Perry was trying out for *Jenna Jameson's American Idol*. I pushed her to the brink, thrusting in the vibrator while sucking her swollen clit at just the right moment. She cried out—loud as hell—

swearing, yelling my name, moaning, spasming in my mouth and shaking from head to toe. I quickly slid out from under her, using the moment as fuel, and pressed her flat to the bed. It only took a few quick jerks from my hand before I was joining her in our vocal Olympics, coming in hot spurts all over her back. Fuck yes.

I collapsed on top of her, her ass the nicest cushion, and put my lips to her ear.

"What did you think of that?"

She only whimpered in response, her face down in the bedspread.

"I suppose we were a bit too loud. Pity the walls are so thin," I remarked, oh so casually.

She finally turned her head, her cheek down and smiling. "I can't believe you did that on purpose."

"What?" I asked innocently.

"You made me come so hard I was screaming."

"Hey, pipe down, people are trying to sleep," I said, shushing her.

She tried to look annoyed but her face looked far too flushed and blissful. She felt as high as I did. "You wanted him to hear."

"Are you saying I shouldn't have gotten you off like that?" I whispered. "Because if that's the case, I'll never give you an orgasm like that again."

She grinned lazily. "Don't threaten me."

"Don't pretend you didn't want him to hear."

"How long are you guys going to be involved in this pissing contest?"

"Until I'm certain I can piss the furthest."

She eyed me. "Dex, you're unbeatable. Seriously. Let it go."

I returned her steady gaze. "Perry, I've wanted you since

the moment I saw you. I'm not going to stop showing you off or rubbing it in to everyone I know anytime soon. Especially not to him and especially after tonight. You're mine. And you're mine alone. From now until the end of time."

A softness came over her eyes, and I hoped it wasn't pity. I cleared my throat and got off of her, wanting to downplay the heaviness of my words.

"I'll get some towels to clean you," I told her quickly, ducking into the bathroom to grab some. I came back to the bed and sat beside her, gently dabbing at her lower back until she was clean. "All done."

I tossed the towels aside and she rolled over on her back, breasts splayed, her hair coiled around her like black silk. She'd never stop taking my damn breath away.

She crawled under the sheets and I joined her, flicking off the light until it was just us in the dark, the taste of her still on my lips.

8
_____

Once again we woke up hung over. Actually, I woke up before Perry, just as the sun was beginning to rise off the gingerbread roofs around us. Damn alcohol never let me sleep in.

I rolled out of bed and quickly slipped on my clothes, wanting to get out to a nearby café and bring back something greasy for the both of us. There was one across the street that did pulled pork egg benedicts, and I was just ordering two of those, plus two giant to-go cups of Bloody Marys (I loved this town), when someone tapped me on the shoulder.

"Maximus," I seethed, knowing it was him without even turning around.

"Hello, Dex," he said in a distinctly Newman-esque voice.

I folded my arms and eyed him. "Okay, how can you say you've never heard of Vegetable Lasagna but you can do an impression of Wayne Knight just fine?"

He didn't smile. "We need to talk."

I grabbed a Bloody Mary and took a long spicy sip.

Damn, that was good. "Are you breaking up with me? No wait, did we keep you up last night?"

"Dex, this has to stop."

The clerk handed me the take-out box with the Benedicts inside, a grease spot already forming. I took another sip, studying Maximus's face. Sometimes the amount a person had changed could really take you by surprise. We all get older, but it wasn't until now that I realized how different Maximus really was from the boyish imp I knew back in college. Granted, he was always built like an ox, four inches above six feet, his hair always red and his face both tanned *and* faintly freckled. But he used to have this youthful glow about him that was kind of hard to explain without sounding gay. An energy, a vibrance. His eyes used to sparkle, and yes, this was growing increasingly homo-erotic, but it was the truth.

Now though, for the first time, I felt like I was really seeing how much older he was. I was older too. I had a few grey hairs popping up along the sides of my head, I had crinkly lines around my eyes that never used to be there, and I certainly wasn't handling hangovers as well as I used to. I was fairly close to being a normal 32-year-old male, albeit one that actually wasn't very normal at all.

But Maximus looked tired. His skin was more ashy than weather-beaten, his hair had lost some of its luster (and I noticed this because he used to douse his hair in beer and lemons until it was shiny enough to see your reflection), and there was a bit of a paunch starting up where there was only brawn and muscle before.

"What are you staring at?" he said, and I became aware that he was waiting for me to respond to something. What was it? Oh yes, *Dex this has to stop.*

"I'm staring at you, ginger Elvis in the peanut butter and

banana sandwiches era. Why do we need to talk? What needs to stop?"

He looked out the window and said, "Come with me."

I rolled my eyes and asked the clerk to put the Benedicts in a bag since I was already juggling two drinks, and ran out into the street after him.

It was pleasantly warm here in March, jeans and tee-shirt weather. The tourists were around, but not in droves, and who cared anyway because I was a damn tourist myself. I followed Maximus down the street, watching the occasional car bump by, shock absorbers getting an endless workout, until he stopped at a wide open park on one side of a church. There was a statue of Andrew Jackson on a horse in the middle, and we sat down at one of the many benches that were in a circle around it. Some were filled with people sipping morning coffees, others were filled with sleeping homeless people, but for the most part the park was dead quiet.

"All right, so what do you want to talk about?" I asked him. I was almost finished with my Bloody Mary and the longer I'd have to sit here talking with Maximus, the more I'd want to finish Perry's. "Is it the zombies? Is that what needs to stop, because while I agree that zombies have to be stopped on principle, I just don't think you and I are the ones to do it."

"Please, I'm being serious." And he was.

Still. "About the zombies?"

"You and Perry. It has to stop."

"Dude, don't take this the wrong way, but I'm not sure how many times I need to tell you to fuck off before you get it. I'm sorry Perry isn't around to kick you in the shin, but I'll be more than happy to provide an acceptable substitute. My knee, your balls. My fist, your nose. Take your pick."

"Can you just for one minute get your head out of your ass and listen to me."

The tone he was using made prickles of unease creep along my neck. Delusional or not, he meant every word. The smile disappeared from my face.

"What then?"

He wiggled his jaw back and forth and then pressed at it with his fingers. A few moments passed. In the distance, I saw mule-pulled carriages line up near the river. He exhaled slowly.

"This is going to sound strange, so just hear me out. You can swear and posture and do whatever it is you do when you hear something you don't want to hear. But for now...let me speak."

"Okaaaaaay."

"You and Perry are not meant to be."

"Uh..."

He raised his meaty hand. "Not finished. I can't really go into the details at the moment because you wouldn't believe me anyway, but I just wanted to put this idea in your head. You and Perry are not meant to be. I'm not saying this out of jealousy or hatred or spite or anything. Believe it or not, I am saying this, telling you this, because I care about you. I care about both of you. You love Perry, I know that, but not all love leads to good things. Take it from me, sometimes we want to do everything and risk everything for love and it doesn't mean shit. It all falls through. Being in love, having love in your hands, doesn't mean that you'll always have it. And in your case, it doesn't mean that good will come out of it. Wars are started over love, people are killed over love, lives are ruined over love. If you and Perry ever become something more than you are now, if you ever impregnate her, if you want a baby, she—"

And that hit me like a ton of bricks.

"I'm done listening," I interjected, and leaped to my feet as if I'd been stung with a cattle prod. I'd been listening in a state of disbelief, in a state of good humor, in a state of reluctance, not really understanding a single word this crazy man was saying, but bringing Perry into it, bringing a pregnancy into it, that was too much. I had my limit and that was it.

I stood over him, feeling red hot rage flow through every part of my body, daring me to let loose on him. "Don't you ever talk to me about this again, you understand? Don't you fucking dare. I can't say what I'll do to you if you do, but I can say it won't be pretty. And I mean it. You're a sick, jealous son-of-a-bitch. You know that Perry had a miscarriage, with my baby, you know that, and you have the fucking nerve to drag me out here and tell me this shit? You have another thing coming, and I don't know what it is, but you're not going to like it. Now you're going to shut your fat mouth and never bring this up with me—or her—again or so help me god, I'll be straining your dick through your teeth."

I tossed my empty Bloody Mary at him, the ice rattling out of the cup and raining down on him before he had a chance to duck. Then I stormed back into the Quarter, trying to swallow down the parasitic anger. I couldn't even begin to fathom what he was trying to do, but all I could figure was that I had majorly underestimated him. He was either more jealous of me or more in love with Perry than I had thought. No wonder he was looking so ugly if this was what was eating him up inside.

By the time I got back to the bed and breakfast, I was a lot calmer. I'd also finished Perry's drink which helped. I got her a new one but the Benedicts were cold. She didn't care though. She'd been worried when she woke up and couldn't find me around. To see her worry like that about me pretty much melted my heart.

I decided to keep what Maximus said to me a secret. It wouldn't do Perry any good to know how obsessed with us he was, and it would only freak her out. I just wanted to get through the next week or so without being arrested for manslaughter. As much as the idea of zombies interested me, I was all for shooting at the haunted house, seeing the usual funny lights and maybe something chilling on the EVP recorder, and getting the hell out of Louisiana. I wanted to go back to my normal life, with Perry in my bed and Fat Rabbit on the couch, and unspoken dreams of her and I together.

Unfortunately, just because I felt that way didn't mean Perry did. She was excited about the potential zombie situation and was looking forward to meeting Rose at noon. She'd told me that Rose had interested her since there weren't many people out there who could see ghosts, at least none that we knew. She wanted to see if Rose ever had a Pippa in her life and wanted to know what other abilities she had. From what I saw last night, she at least seemed to have the ability to make other people zone out. She'd be an excellent spy, though I guess it helped with bartending as well.

We met Maximus down in the lobby at twenty minutes to twelve. He was chatting to the plucky receptionist, who was batting her grey hair down nervously, obviously charmed by the fuckhead.

"Vegetable Lasagna," I called out. "Let's go."

He turned to face me and I had to immediately forget the terrible things he'd said to me earlier, otherwise I'd never even make it through the day.

I forced a smile and jerked my head toward the door.

Then I grabbed Perry's hand and pulled her outside. She was wearing leggings and boots again, with a skull-embossed sleeveless dress on top. It was so nice to see her showing more skin, although I'd probably find it a lot more distracting as the months got warmer.

It wasn't long before we were outside of Nameless. The bar looked different in the daytime, both sweeter and older, like so many of the buildings in the Quarter. Strands of Mardi Gras beads hung from the sign and awning, tossed there only weeks ago.

Now that I was really getting a feel for the place, I could sense this vibe of resilience underneath the rough city streets, this pride and strength to keep going, to rebuild, to forge on. But even with that spirit everywhere, I could sense spirits of another kind. Sprits of history, spirits of loss, spirits of revenge. This didn't happen often to me, only a few times when I used to live in New York, but now that I was sober I could feel a layer of supernatural chaos underneath everything. I wondered what looking though the Veil here would look like.

As we waited for Rose to show up—the bar had already been open for several hours—I studied Perry. She seemed to be okay at the moment, not edgy or nervous like she could be if she was experiencing the same feelings that I was. The minute she looked even the slightest bit uneasy, I'd be there telling her she wasn't alone in this. Until then, it was another thing I was keeping to myself.

Finally Rose poked her head out of the bar. She was wearing worn jeans that fit her like a glove and a dark grey tank top that showed the slightest sliver of her flat belly. She was in good shape, looking as if she ran several miles before breakfast. I wondered if the Rose that Maximus had known was softer in body too.

"Y'all ready to meet the Mambo?"

"I can *do* the mambo," I said. "Mambo Number Five."

Perry let out a derisive laugh. "Thanks, I *just* got that song out of my head."

I shrugged. "Well, it was my song back in the day, but I never got to sing about Perry."

"You guys can be cute later," Rose said. "In private. Without me there. Let's go."

"There is no private for these two," Maximus muttered as he brushed past me, following Rose. I was almost fooled for a second into thinking this morning had never happened. There was no delight in our loud antics anymore. Well, no petty delight anyway. That *was* some top-notch sex.

Rose took us around the corner to a half-empty parking lot near a venue called One-Eyed Jacks. which she assured us was the best place to see live music. She said she saw Queens of the Stone Age play there to only 900 people. I decided I hated Rose after that.

She drove an old crew cab truck that was cherry red and rusted in parts. It groaned and creaked as she eased it out of the Quarter and around numerous detours from endless construction work, but assured us that the old beast would probably outlive her. It was funny hearing her speak. At times Rose looked and acted like she was our age, but at others she came across as a toughened old lady. Maybe that's what Maximus had meant by her becoming harder. Maybe whatever life threw at her, whether it was Maximus or owning a bar, or seeing the supernatural, just made her wiser. I didn't think it was possible to be both soft and experienced—your battles caused the scar tissue. I knew I definitely had mine.

"Where does Mambo Maryse live?" Perry asked as Rose pulled the noisy car onto the I-10. We were sitting in the crew cab together and I was having a flashback to the days when we were first getting to know each other and we had to share the back of her cousin's truck with a crab trap. Had never been so thankful for a crab trap in my life.

"She had a nice place on the outskirts of town, used to do readings there back in the day. But after Katrina, her place was damaged. She moved further West, a house on the bayou."

"By herself?" Maximus asked. "Isn't she ancient? When I last saw her she looked like she was going to keel over."

Rose shot him a dry look. "She's stronger than she looks. She has her apprentice taking care of her now. She lives in a cabin further out in the swamp water, the kind you have to take an air boat to get to. Anyway, she's living with Maryse now, well most of the time."

"So how did you get to know this Mambo?" I asked, watching as the industrial buildings melted away into endless stretches of swamp water, duck blinds, and billboards.

Rose eyed me in the rear view mirror, her eyes mirroring the grey water around us. "My family was very much into the occult. Well, my ma was. Dad was a cattle farmer and just turned a blind eye. She never practiced Voodoo but it fascinated her. She got to know Mambo Maryse in the eighties, stayed friends with her until she died. Then I stayed friends with her. My ma was an immigrant so she didn't have any family on this side. I looked to Maryse as a viper-tongued maw-maw, a grandmother, especially after my dad died too."

"Sounds like my kind of woman," I told her. "But you said she's sick now?"

"They say old age, and I reckon that makes sense, but..."

"You don't believe it," Perry filled in.

Rose brushed her hair back but it wouldn't respond, her frizziness mocking her. "It just doesn't feel right. I've tried talking to Maryse about the illness, about what's ailing her, but even last week she said it was just her time. She said... the stress was too much."

"Mambos have stress?" I asked.

"Ones that are being shunned by the community? Yeah, they have stress, sugar."

Maximus looked at her askance. "Shunned?"

Rose exhaled slowly. "The last two years or so, the other Mambos have been accusing her of being a Bokor, like the person who's raising the dead and creating the zombies. I don't really know why. Maryse hasn't done anything then and she certainly isn't doing anything now."

Huh. Well that was at least a little suspicious. The Voodoo community shuns this Mambo a few years ago for going to the "dark side," now she's ill and zombies are tearing up the ghetto.

I glanced at Perry, wondering if she was thinking the same thing. Her brow was furrowed, the wheels spinning; it was safe to say we were on the same page.

We lapsed into silence after that, Rose glancing at us on occasion, as if she could see the suspicion on our faces. After a while, the tension was too much for the giant jackass ginger and he started asking Rose about the people who used to work at the bar, harmless small talk, although I could sense rehashing the past was a bit leaden for both of them.

Fortunately, the Mambo's house wasn't too far outside the city limits. It was amazing how quickly the landscape changed, how the dark, murky waters, flocks of birds, and weeping trees took over civilization in an instant. Rose turned the truck onto a dirt road and we bounced down it, my eyes torn between the beauty of the dark swamp around us and the beauty of Perry's bouncing breasts.

The further we went, the more it looked like we'd never see a human soul again, until finally, rising up like a beacon, was a small, one-level house, bright white with green trim and a screened-in porch. The swamp water lapped a few feet away, and I noticed a low makeshift wall of sandbags sat between it and the house. There was also a small dock with a metal air boat on one side and a rowboat with peeling paint on the other. The inlet was flanked by drooping trees rising right out of the water, white egrets flapping noisily to and fro. Crickets and unknown insects chirped loudly, despite it being afternoon.

We parked the car beside two others, a small rusted Toyota and a brand new Range Rover.

"Does she have company over?" I asked.

She shook her head as she jumped out of the truck. "As I said, she's shunned. Ambrosia keeps her Rover here since you can't drive to her cabin anyway."

"Ambrosia?"

She tried to a hide a smile. "Ambrosia Paris. It's the name of her apprentice."

That figured. I got out and was immediately met with the musty stench of the water, which was enjoyable in a weird way. I was also met with the sudden whine and pinch of mosquitoes.

I slapped my arm in several places, swearing. Mosquitoes were my nemesis these days. Back when I was on my medication, they never even bothered me, yet lately it was like my pure blood had been attracting them like crazy and now I was in Malaria City.

Rose leaned into the truck and pulled something out of

the glove compartment. She tossed it at me and I caught it. Good ol' fashioned Off!

"I don't even get bitten anymore," she said, "but you three won't be so lucky. Spray yourself up."

I clouded myself in a toxic mist and did the same to Perry before reluctantly giving the spray to Maximus. I guess it was more like I threw the spray at him, aiming it at his head. Big dumb oaf had quicker reflexes than I gave him credit for.

We waited for him to finish, then walked up to the house, following a stone path lined with translucent, reddish flowers that were shaped like bells. Butt ugly landscaping, if you asked me.

"Carnivorous plants," Rose said, nodding at them with a grin. I was starting to get a distinct *Little Shop of Horrors* vibe from the place and the feeling doubled once we climbed up the steps and opened the rickety screen door to the porch.

The porch was lined with plant after plant after plant, some hanging from the roof, others seeming to grow straight up from the ground, breaking through the slats on the porch floor. There was also a mess of dried herbs, a bunch of jars filled with thick goo and what looked like embalmed reptiles, and a small fridge that hummed in the corner. I didn't want to know what was in there.

Rose rapped on the glass door while my eyes were still searching the porch for more weirdness. I found it when I recognized a few beehives stacked in beneath a large Venus fly trap.

"Those don't have bees, do they?" I asked. "Because I'm allergic. Seriously allergic." And though I'd packed the Epi-Pen in my luggage, I hadn't been smart enough to bring it with me. Then again, I didn't know we'd been venturing out into an honest to God Voodoo hut on a bayou.

Rose shook her head. "They've been empty for a long time. Maryse used to use the beeswax for a lot of things."

I swallowed hard, trying to slow my heart. That whole thing put me on edge and I had to remind myself that Maryse probably wasn't much different from our old Medicine Man friend, Bird.

The door opened and I was expecting to see some horrible haggard old witch. Instead it was a smiling young woman. I was actually a bit taken aback. This woman was smoking hot.

"Hello, Rose," she said in a very light Creole accent. She smiled brighter at the rest of us. "You must be the ghost hunters. I'm Ambrosia. Won't you come in?"

Hell yes, we'd come in if she was showing us the way. She was a very light-skinned African American with pale green eyes, tall in stature. Her hair was shiny and wavy, rich like dark chocolate, going all the way to her ass. And what an ass. It was one of those shelf ones you were tempted to place something on, just to see if it would stay. I could bounce fucking nickels off that thing, if not smack it a few times with my dick.

I felt coldness from beside me and looked down at Perry, who was looking straight at Ambrosia with a worried look in her eyes, her lips pressed into a thin line. Ah shit, I'd been ogling the woman, hadn't I? Jenn had never cared who I ogled, but Perry wasn't built like that. I had to keep my old habits in check when I was around her and remember that she was a lot more insecure than she looked.

I put my arm around her and gave her a squeeze while I introduced us to Ambrosia.

"I'm Dex, this is my girlfriend Perry." I looked over at Maximus. "That's Maximus Douchekabob. It's a foreign-sounding last name, but he's actually from here."

Maximus glared at me before offering Ambrosia his hand and a shy smile. Well, wouldn't you believe it, Maximus was smitten with her as well. I guess he wasn't the racist redneck I'd pegged him out to be.

We followed Ambrosia inside and I did my best to keep my eyes off her jean-clad ass. I kept them on Perry's breasts instead and it worked out even better.

Maryse's place was fairly large for being one-level, though it suffered from the same amount of controlled chaos and clutter as the porch did. Thankfully there was nothing of the heebie jeebie variety inside, just stacks and stacks of books and magazines, floral upholstery, watercolor landscapes, doilies, lace, dolls, and dust.

"Why don't you take a seat," Ambrosia gestured to the couch, the gold bracelets around her slender wrists jangling. "I'll go see if Maryse would like to see you."

She disappeared down a dark hall, and Rose, Perry, and I took a seat on the flowery couch while Maximus tried to fit his frame into a wicker rocking chair. We waited for a few tense minutes, all of us taking in the sights of the house, except for Rose of course, who was texting someone on her phone.

When I got bored trying to figure out what kind of reading material a Voodoo priestess tried to keep herself busy with (books on chicken sacrifice, and romance novels, probably), my mind drifted over to Maximus. He was sitting there in the rocker, awkwardly I might add, and avoiding my eyes. Which was just as well, I'd been avoiding his eyes too. But the words from the morning kept filtering into my head like tiny drops of acid, making me pay attention to them. Even though I couldn't figure out the why aspect of what Maximus had told me, other than he was an obsessed psycho, it was the way he said it that was getting to me. He had been sincere, and when he said he was worried about us, he meant it. And that was the scariest thing of all.

"She'll see you now," Ambrosia said, coming back into the room. "She's awake. I'm just going to bring her tea, but you guys can go right ahead. She's a bit tired and you might not get much from her, but I'm sure she'll be happy to see you, Rose."

The way that Ambrosia said Rose threw me off a bit. Now I had to wonder if there was bad blood between these two. Perhaps the young Voodoo apprentice was worried about Rose stepping on her toes. Or vice versa.

I kept my observations to myself as we walked down the darkened hall, the matte lamps that hung overhead in shapes of flowers flickering as we went under them.

Rose knocked on the door at the end and slowly opened it when she didn't hear a response.

Here the room was dark, all the blinds drawn shut, the air cool and damp. There was a large white, four-poster bed at the end with mosquito netting draped all around it, a ghostly look. I could see the shape of a small woman sitting up in the bed, just her hazy, dark outline through the netting. It gave me the fucking creeps.

"Mambo Maryse?" Rose asked gently as she slowly approached the bed. The three of us hung by the door, watching her, unsure of what to do. I grabbed Perry's hand. To reassure her, of course.

Rose drew back the netting and we all tensed up. She was going to be dead, with spiders coming out her eyes and a snake for a tongue, I just knew it. But all we saw was a skinny little white lady with long grey hair, nestled into a mound of fluffy pillows. It was too dark in the room though to figure out where she was looking, even though enough light had come in through the curtain to be reflected in her eyes.

"Can you hear me?" Rose asked, standing at the foot of the bed. "Ambrosia said it was okay to talk to you. I have some friends here you'll want to meet."

Maryse didn't move or make a sound. Rose went for the curtains. "Here, I'll let more light in."

"No!" Maryse suddenly screeched, her voice hoarse and louder than I expected. "The light, it burns."

Christ, what was she, a vampire?

Rose spun around and nodded frantically. "Okay, okay, don't worry. We'll leave it dark. I didn't know."

"Of course you didn't know, you're barely around," the Mambo sniveled, settling back into her pillows. "Everyone is shunning me, including you."

Rose sighed and looked over at us, as if we were supposed to say something. The thing is, I didn't know what. The whole Voodoo zombie angle was Rose's idea, not mine. I wanted that haunted house and I had a feeling an ailing Voodoo priestess would be no help with that.

"Maryse, I have some people here I'd like you to meet. Ambrosia told you about them, didn't she?"

"Ambrosia tells me a lot of things. I never listen."

Wow, being Maryse's apprentice was starting to sound like a pretty shitty job. I started to wonder what Ambrosia's deal was when I felt my gaze being drawn to the bed. Maryse was staring right at me, I could feel it.

"Who is that young man?" Maryse asked in weird disbelief, a crooked finger extended in my direction.

I pointed at myself. "Me?"

"You seem familiar."

Well, that certainly wasn't possible. I looked up at Maximus hulking over me and elbowed him. "This guy, I've heard you met him before." I shot him a look to step forward. Apparently he was feeling nervy too.

He cleared his throat and came toward her, one slow step at a time. "Mambo Maryse. Do you remember me? It's Maximus."

She fell silent. The whole room did. Outside, you could hear the crickets and cicadas, the drone of dragonflies. Finally she said, "I don't think I know you. Who is this man, Rose?"

Rose tilted her head at him apologetically before answering her. "He was my...we worked at the bar together. I know you can't really see him now, but he was tall, handsome, with red hair. We were...together. A lot. You *know* him, Maryse."

More silence. I was about to say "Ouch" on his behalf, since he failed to make an impression on her over the years, but suddenly Maryse sat up straighter, her posture rigid in the dim light.

"Jacobs," she whispered.

The way she said his last name made chills run down my back, stopping at my balls, and continuing to my toes. Perry applied pressure to my hand, perhaps feeling the same way. Except for the balls part.

"That's right," Maximus said, his voice shaking a little. "Maximus Jacobs. I used to be in love with your Rose here."

"But..." Maryse trailed off, shaking her head. "You're mortal."

Rose and Maximus's eyes flew to each other, both of them wide and shining with horror.

"Of course he's mortal," Rose said quickly, trying to laugh it off. "He—"

"No," she interrupted Rose, her focus back on him. "No, you changed. You've gone rogue. I remember now."

I raised my hand even though she probably couldn't see me. "Uh, miss Voodoo lady? I hate to break it to you but this dude's been mortal for a long time. He was my college roommate and I drank him under the table time and time again."

"You," she seethed, her finger pointing at me again. I cringed a bit, feeling like she was poking into my soul. "You. I know you, I know about you! You're the *exception*."

I raised my brows and looked down at Perry. She was shaking her head in confusion. "Exception to what?"

"Get out," she suddenly yelled, her glinting eyes on Perry now. "Get out, all of you, you too, Rose! I'm tired of people just showing up in my life and wanting things from me, disturbing everything. You're all a bunch of idiots, dabbling in things you don't understand, bending the laws with no regard for this world or the one next to us, or the one above us or the one under us. I'm too old to deal with this baloney anymore."

And with that she flopped back on the bed and pointed at the netting. "Now close the netting and leave."

Rose quickly did as she asked, looking flustered, and we all got out of that room as quickly as we could. Rose closed the door behind her and we scrambled out into the kitchen just as Ambrosia was coming toward us with a pot of tea.

She gave us a waning smile. "I suppose I should have warned you that she's got a bit of dementia and has been talking gibberish for the last few days now."

"Yeah," I said carefully, "a little warning would have been nice."

She beamed at me, her teeth so white, lips so full. I felt kind of dazzled. "I'll go bring her the tea, but I'd love to talk to you guys more about all of this, even if she doesn't want to. I have a friend whose blues band is playing in the city at

Deep N' Easy. Why don't we all meet there tonight? I'll even put you on the guest list."

I looked to the others for their opinion. The women looked less enthused than the men, but Rose still nodded brusquely and said, "Sounds good, see you there."

We left Maryse's swamp house in a hurry, and all I could think about as we got back in the truck was how that frail old witch said she knew me. She obviously did have dementia, I mean she was surprised that Maximus wasn't immortal anymore and probably saw a bunch of pixies dancing around her head, but it was the conviction in her words that was doing me in.

I had too many strange messages for one day. The Big Easy was turning out to be harder than I thought.

9

"Well, what did you think about that?" Perry asked as we closed the bedroom door behind us. It was the first time we'd been alone since the morning, and the whole drive back into NOLA was filled with shitty radio, none of us even daring to talk about what had just happened. Well, I wanted to talk about it, but both Rose and Maximus were so uncomfortably tight-lipped that I wouldn't even get any joy out of ribbing him.

I walked straight over to the bed and flopped face-down on it. I felt utterly and completely drained. I turned my face to look at her. "Come lie with me," I mumbled against the sheets.

She lay down beside me, on her back, her eyes on the ceiling. "That was weird."

"What isn't weird anymore?" I pointed out.

"True," she said, folding her hands across her stomach. She turned to look at me, her expression earnest. "Have you seen that woman before?"

"The crazy Mambo?" I shook my head. "No, never.

Granted, I couldn't really see her since she's apparently a vampire as well. But no. You believe me, right?"

"Of course I do. I just think it's weird."

"As weird as her saying Maximus is immortal?"

"If not weirder. Obviously she is just a crazy old kook." Crazy, and yet part of me wanted to believe her.

"She's white, too," she said. "I expected her to be Haitian or something."

"Well, Ambrosia's of mixed descent."

At the mention of Ambrosia's name, Perry stiffened. Interesting. It really did seem like my woman was jealous and I was finding it immensely flattering. I spent so much time wondering about Perry's true feelings for me, if they were more than a sexual fixation, so it was really nice to see she cared about me at least that much. I really hoped I wouldn't use it to my advantage, because that was definitely something the old Dex would do—make them jealous to see if they cared.

Nope, I told myself, *you have to be more mature than that*. I reached over and tugged at the band of her leggings, trying to get her attention.

"Hey, kiddo."

She relaxed and smiled at me. "Hey. Sorry, I guess I'm just tired too. Jet lag finally catching up to me."

"We could nap until we went to the bar."

"Right. Like we would ever just nap."

I frowned in mock disgust. "Hey, you don't see me pawing you right now, do you?"

I turned over on to my side and pulled her to me, wrapping my arm around her waist until she was pressed up against me. "Let's just sleep," I whispered in her hair. "We've earned it."

We were out in seconds flat.

≈

DEEP N' EASY was located on Frenchman street, just out of the Quarter. Perry and I trailed behind Rose and Maximus as we walked down the rough sidewalk, peering at the never ending vibrancy around us, from the open-air bars spilling out onto the street, to the endless music coming out from all directions, to the various tattoo shops.

I pointed to one of them. "Ever think of getting a tattoo?"

She shrugged and bit her lip. "I have some ideas…"

"Tell me," I said. I never pegged Perry to be one of those types; she seemed too indecisive for that.

She shook her head, suddenly coy. "No, it would be a surprise."

"A surprise?" I both loved and hated surprises. "Is it a picture of my cock? Did my letterman jacket give you the idea?"

She rolled her eyes. "I'm not telling you." She kept walking, trying to catch up with Maximus and Rose. I waited a few beats, concentrating on her, hoping I could get a thought out of her and find out what the surprise was. All I got was the sharp stab of a headache instead.

I hurried after her and she tossed me a smug look over her shoulder. She was enjoying her tattoo secret too much. I supposed I hadn't been too forthcoming with my "Within your Light I Lose the Madness" on my back either.

"Is it a fleur-de-lis?" I asked, rolling up my t-shirt sleeve to show her the one on my insanely buff arm. "Considering there are fleur-de-lis all over the place here, you'd fit right in. And we'd match."

Her eyes paused on my muscles briefly before her blasé look returned. "That's pretty lame, Dex, even for you."

"More or less lame than the cock?"

"Would y'all hurry up?" Rose yelled. They had stopped outside a bar, the slow thumping of bass pounding through the brick walls. The light inside was bathing everyone in red.

"Deep N' Easy," I remarked, reading the faded sign. "Just the way I like it."

Rose shook her head, unimpressed, and we followed her inside where we lined up in front of the bouncer. I leaned into her. "You never smile, do you, Rose?"

She rolled her eyes and told the bouncer our names. He checked us off the list and told us to go inside.

Ambrosia spotted us first, waving casually from a table near the stage where the band slowly rumbled on. Like last night, it was a three piece set-up, but with a somber, coal-colored singer on acoustic guitar. His soul was bleeding out through the strings and I was excruciatingly jealous.

We sat down and Perry immediately got up and told us all she was getting the first round of drinks.

"Tell them you're with locals!" Rose yelled after her. "Don't let them give you the tourist price."

Ambrosia smiled at Maximus and I and I felt strangely giddy inside. It didn't make any sense and I had to shake my head to get rid of it. Fortunately, no one else had noticed. They were all staring at the band while Ambrosia explained who they were.

"Dead Frog's Blood," she explained.

"Poetic," I said. "I guess they aren't known for being upbeat."

She leaned toward me, her eyes sparkling. "Oh, Mr. Foray, something tells me you know a lot about the blues. Even the blues can have a happy tale to tell."

"Mr. Foray?" I repeated. "You make me sound so old."

"Well, you can't be more than twenty-five," she said sincerely.

"Is it because I'm immature?"

"That." She winked at me and then tossed her hair over her shoulder. "And your girlfriend can't be much more than twenty-one."

"She's twenty-three," I explained.

"And how old are you?"

I swallowed. "Thirty-two."

"That's quite the age difference. I'm impressed."

I shrugged. "You gotta get them while they're young before they know what they're getting into." I played it off like the age difference between us didn't plague me from time to time. That little niggling fear that I wanted what I wanted from her because I was older and ready for more in life, while she was still young and almost virginal (well, a little more experienced after last night), and probably had fields of wild oats in her left to sow. I didn't want to think about that.

Perry came back with the drinks: a pitcher of local brew for everyone else, a mint julep for herself, and a Jack Daniels and lemonade mix for me. It wasn't exactly what I wanted but it would do the job.

We all clinked glasses across the table and got down to business. Maximus explained to Ambrosia about the haunted house we wanted to film, while Rose told her that perhaps we were better off looking into the whole zombie epidemic. Ambrosia wasn't as thrilled with that idea.

"Rose," she said with a smirk, "sending tourists off into the inner city isn't the smartest thing you could do."

"We'd be with them," Rose said, pointing at Maximus. "We're not tourists."

"Right, as if that makes a difference," she said. "I'm half

black and I'd still get held up in seconds, *if* I was lucky. Trust me, I want to figure out what's going on as much as you do, but I don't think they came here to dig up Voodoo. Just ghosts."

"Well," Perry spoke up, a strange fire burning in her eyes as she looked at Ambrosia, "personally, I think investigating this whole zombie thing is a lot more interesting than the whole haunted house deal. I mean, I hate to sound condescending about the afterlife, but this is something new to us."

If Ambrosia was put off by Perry's argument, she didn't show it. She smiled gently at her and said, "You'd be right about that. For as long as I've been studying Voodoo, I've never seen a single case of this happening."

I laughed. "Sure, but you can't be much older than... what, twenty-eight?"

"I'll pretend that was a compliment. I'm twenty-six. But I'm a descendent of the great Marie Laveau. Perhaps you've heard of her?"

I sipped my drink. "I don't know, I hear a lot of things. Who is that?"

Rose spoke up. "Ambrosia's mother claimed to be the daughter of Marie's son."

"Not claimed," Ambrosia said, glaring at her. "Proven. I have the DNA."

"Even though Marie's children by Paris both died at a young age of yellow fever," she countered.

Ambrosia ignored her and turned her million dollar smile on us. "To get back to the story, it is fascinating, Perry, you're right. I just don't think it's safe. Zombies are one thing, but those neighborhoods, the real people, they're a much bigger threat to your safety. Maybe after you get some haunted house footage, we can look into it more."

"That's just what I was going to suggest," Maximus said, directing his goofy smitten gaze at her.

Right. Suggest. Like Maximus wasn't all about telling us what we could and couldn't do.

"So where is the haunted house?" I asked.

"Yes, and is it anything like the haunted mansion in Disneyland?" Perry added.

With a defeated sigh, Rose told us about the house, pretty much repeating what Maximus had told us: paranormal activity had doubled, as it had in many parts of the city post-Katrina, and a lot of researchers had been in there without picking up on anything too wild. Aside from the spike in the supernatural, there wasn't anything too unusual about the house. It was built at the turn of the century and was used as a boarding house for many years before becoming a squatter's paradise. Then the storm surge caused the breeches in the Industrial Canal and flooded the place. It was hard to tell if anyone had died inside.

"Tomorrow night we'll go and shoot it," Maximus said.

"Don't we need special permission from the city?" Perry asked.

"You don't need permission to do anything here," Rose said dryly. "The Wild West, remember? The City that Forgot to Care."

To accent that last bit, the band ended with a sad crash of the symbol and Dead Frog's Blood exited the stage and Ambrosia got up, going around to each table and collecting tips for them.

When she came back, the music had turned to CCR over the speakers and she held out her hand toward me.

"Pardon me, Perry," she asked, though she was gazing straight at me, "but do you mind if I dance with your man?"

I could hear Rose suck in her breath across the table and

was so certain that Perry was going to tell her to fuck right off, but instead she threw her head back and smiled at Ambrosia, "I don't mind if he doesn't mind."

The thing was, I didn't mind dancing with Ambrosia. I was tempted to touch her skin to feel how smooth it was. These were bad, bad urges and I didn't really know why I was feeling them. Obviously I had a libido that just wouldn't quit and I knew I was a pervert deep down at heart. But I shouldn't have been thinking those thoughts with a gorgeous woman right beside me, the one that was mine, the one I loved, but I was. I didn't understand.

Realizing that I hadn't given her an answer and was leaving her standing there, that everyone was waiting for me to say something, I opened my mouth to say, "Actually I'd rather give the first dance to Perry here." But I didn't say that, because Perry looked at Maximus and said, "And while you guys dance, I'll dance with Maximus here."

I choked on my words before they could come out, feeling like I was kicked by a sharp-toed boot. Maximus looked just as surprised as I did, but he said, "I'd be honored, little lady," and got out of his chair, as if he were a chivalrous gentleman doing her a favor.

Perry got out of hers, not even meeting my eyes, and together they went off to the dance floor. It took a few seconds for me to recover, so I shot Ambrosia my most becoming grin and leaped to my feet.

"You better be careful," Rose said under her breath. I gave her a funny look, but she busied herself with her beer, like she'd never said anything.

I tried not to look at Perry and Maximus dancing together, having horrifying flashbacks to Rudy's Bar in Red Fox, New Mexico, and once my arms were around Ambrosia and I was feeling the softness of her skin, I couldn't even care less what Perry and Maximus were doing. All I could think about was this exotic woman in my arms, the elegance of her dance moves. Sure, we were dancing to "Bad Moon Rising," but we managed to make it work.

"You're an interesting man," she said slyly, pressing herself to me. "All of you are. Your girlfriend. Rose's ex-lover. You're all very unique. But you're the most unique of all."

I raised a brow at her and grinned cockily. "Oh yeah? How so?"

She pondered the question for a moment. "You have a very large aura."

I grinned even wider. "That I do."

"It's very powerful. You're a lot stronger than you look. You've got a lot of willpower."

"I do?" At the moment, I was afraid I didn't have any. Suddenly thoughts of Perry entered my mind and my heart directed my attention across the dance floor. Perry and Maximus were dancing together. Jealousy kicked me in the gut, making me bleed, but the longer I stared at them, the more I realized how awkward they looked. Perry looked like she'd rather be getting a root canal, and Maximus was staring at Rose. Silly girl was trying to make me jealous now. God, I wished I could have been annoyed about that but I wasn't.

I looked down at the cocoa-skinned temptress in my arms, and suddenly I had a feeling I knew what she was doing. She was a Voodoo priestess in training and one hell of a hardcore flirt.

"Thank you for the lovely dance," I told her, my feet coming to a stop before the song was over. "But I'm afraid I've got a thirst that just won't quit." I nodded at the bar.

She smiled slyly, satisfied. "I knew it. More strength than most people, and more willpower than you think."

I threw up my arms. "Too bad you ain't a drink, baby," I said lightly, and made my way over the bar. I heard her giggle behind me.

The second I was away from her and the bartender was handing me a Jack and Coke, local priced, I felt like a huge weight was lifted off my shoulders, a layer of gauze peeled away from my eyes. I leaned back against the bar and watched as the song ended and Perry and Maximus went back to the table. She didn't look for me. I knew she was smarting over the whole Ambrosia thing, and even though I planned to turn her down, Perry's insecurity wasn't going to believe that. Besides, I probably had been staring at Ambrosia like a fool, just like Maximus was staring at her right now. I guess I wasn't exactly the man to instill a sense of faith in people.

After I downed my drink and ordered another one, plus another Mint Julep for Perry, I went back to the table. Everyone was talking about ghosts, some of the worst they'd seen, and Rose was doing most of the gabbing.

I passed Perry her drink, to which she politely, albeit stiffly, thanked me. She turned to Rose. "So tell me, do you just see ghosts or is there more?"

She cracked a rare smile. "There's more. If I concentrate hard enough, I can put people in a trance."

"Like the Beard Man at your bar," I said.

"Beard Man? Oh, Daryl. Yes. Like that. He never heard a word we were talking about. In fact, he wouldn't have heard anyone. It's almost like an invisibility cloak of sorts, comes in handy on occasion. I reckon it would come more in handy if I used my ability for bad, not good, but that's only 'cause being bad comes up more often."

"Is that it?" Perry asked.

"That's not enough?"

"How long have you had the whole trance hypnotist ability? Do you know where you got it from?"

She wiggled her lips and then said, "No idea. Just sort of discovered it one day."

I called bullshit on that. But perhaps she didn't want to talk about it. Maybe not in front of Maximus or Ambrosia. Maybe not in front of me.

Soon, while Perry got to discussing our time with Sassy(quatch), the band began to file back on stage. I felt like I was about to waste an opportunity if I didn't act now.

I got out of my chair and stepped onto the low stage. The guitarist looked up at me in surprise. "Where y'at, son?"

"There's a woman I'd like to impress," I told him. "And she does love the sound of my voice. Do you think I could sing the first song? There's a round of drinks for you fellas in it."

That was all it took to seal the deal. I told them the song, knowing they'd be able to swing it, then grabbed the mic and brought it up to my mouth.

"Good evening, ladies and gentleman," I said, my voice booming across the bar. Perry, Rose, Maximus, and Ambrosia all swiveled their heads in my direction while most of the patrons looked up in passing interest. "I know I'm not who you expected to see tonight, but the fellas here were gracious enough to grant me this song, this song I dedicate to the beautiful, the sexy, the crazy, Perry Palomino."

I gestured to her dramatically with the swing of my hand, and even though we were already in a red light's glow, I knew her face was turning redder.

I looked at the guitarist and said, "Hit it, boys."

They sprang into a sparse but soulful rendition of Otis Redding's "That's How Strong My Love Is."

A few people in the bar clapped at the old favorite, including Rose and Ambrosia, who were looking impressed when I hit those first notes with smoothness to spare. Maximus, however, was looking at me like he wanted to light me on fire. It didn't matter what he thought. This song was for Perry.

"I'll be the moon when the sun goes down," I sang to her and only her, "just to let you know that I'll be around."

I had sung a similar song to her in Seattle, back at the Shownet Christmas party, the start of that beautiful, devastating night. At the time, I sung "This Guy's In Love with You," and I sung it with as much feeling as I could muster, because I was in love with her, I was in love with her deeply, and that song was the only way I knew how to express myself. She had no idea how I felt, even though I felt like half the Shownet staff must have had some inkling after that.

Now I had told her how I felt, she knew I loved her, and yet this Otis Redding song held as much passion and conviction as the one before. Because I still felt like what I had in my hands could slip through my fingers at any moment, and what I thought I might have in the end could turn out to be nothing at all.

When I was done, a layer of sweat on my brow, my hands shaking from adrenaline, the smoke in the bar was thick and I could barely see our table. But I could feel Perry watching me. I hoped she realized every word I sung was true.

"How about that from a white boy," the guitarist said lazily into the mic. "Everyone give him another hand, his Redding almost puts mine to shame."

I knew that wasn't true, but I took the compliment

anyway and went to the bar, ordering the band a round of drinks.

Perry appeared at my side, looking shy and embarrassed.

I smiled softly at her. "Hey, kiddo."

She swallowed, licking her lips. "Thank you."

"For what?"

"For that...for...trying to make me feel better."

"Perry..."

She shook her head quickly. "I'm sorry. I'm being a jerk, I know. I just...I see the way that girl looks at you, how beautiful and thin she is, how you guys looked so good together, and I... I panicked. Dex, I'm not used to being with anyone, let alone someone like you. You have no idea how fucking hot you are."

"And you have no idea how goddamn sexy, beautiful, and amazing you are," I answered back.

"You forgot crazy."

I put my hands around her waist and pulled her to me. "Baby, we are *both* crazy. That's why we're made for each other."

Then I kissed her hard, not caring who saw. And there were quite a few people that did. They applauded again and we both grinned against each other's lips.

Now that we got some of those misunderstandings out of the way, the rest of the night went smoothly. I pulled Perry onto my lap, so Ambrosia turned her charms to Maximus for a while, then decided to make her rounds of the bar, seeing a bunch of people she knew. Rose proceeded to get a little drunk, which you'd think would make her looser and more carefree, but it didn't. If anything, she got more uptight, more worried, her eyes scanning the bar.

Pretty soon things were getting loud and rowdy and

people were dancing. Ambrosia was dancing from man to man, all of them fawning over her, while I kept Perry close to me, trying to keep my eyes on her, even though sometimes I felt compelled to look in Ambrosia's direction. When we worked up a sweat, Perry excused herself to go to the bar and get us some water, sensible girl that she was. I sat back down at our table and watched her go, enjoying the view of her ass, the swing of her hips, the shake of her hair. She seemed a little more confident than she was earlier, and while I hoped it would stick around for a while, I knew it wasn't going to be an overnight thing with her. It didn't matter though, she was worth all the effort and then some.

Perry was being chatted up by a huge black dude who had eyes for only her cleavage. I would have stepped in, especially since he looked like he was saying some pretty cheesy shit, but Perry was giving him her patented "Piss off" look and blatantly ignoring him.

The man kept on leering at her though, and I continued to put faith in Perry's handling of the situation when the unthinkable happened.

In mid-sentence, whatever gross pick-up line he was trying, the man stopped talking. He reached up to his throat and held it, eyes bulging, skin growing slick with sweat that glistened under the red lights. Perry looked at him in concern at first, followed by shock. The man keeled over onto the floor, hitting it with a thud that shook the bar.

Someone screamed, then everyone screamed. People ran. Perry stumbled backward, looking horrified, more at herself as if she did something to him, but I knew she hadn't. Someone bent over the man and felt for his pulse. I read his lips. "Dead."

I got up and pushed my way through the frightened

people, making my way over to Perry and taking her into my arms.

"Dex," she whimpered into my chest as I stroked the back of her head. "He just fell."

"I know," I told her, watching as someone else listened for his heartbeat and verified what the other man had said. He was dead. Heart attack, who knew.

The ambulance pulled up just as we were leaving. I wanted to get out of there before the police started pulling people aside for eye-witness reports. We were done dealing with the police after what happened in Snowcrest, and Rose was quick to tell us we did the right thing, especially considering the way the cops were in NOLA. They could help you or royally screw you.

The five of us went around the corner, nervously peeking around at the flashing lights. We saw the man's body get pushed out in a body bag and placed into the ambulance.

Ambrosia lit up a cigarette—I'd seen her smoking socially in the bar—and Perry stuck her hand out.

"I'd like one please," she demanded, her voice shaking.

I would have said something about that, but she'd just seen a man die right beside her. She could have the whole pack if she wanted it.

While Perry smoked, Ambrosia told us about the man. She'd danced with him earlier. His name was Tuffy G (because of course it was), and he was an okay guy, he just got a bit pervy when he got drunk. As far as she knew, he was a bit overweight but there was nothing wrong with him. He was in his early thirties and lived somewhat close to the haunted house we were investigating. He tiled bathrooms for a living.

"Well, I guess sometimes people just die," I said.

Ambrosia shot me a dirty look that still managed to look sexual. She flicked away her cigarette butt. "You know, for someone who sees ghosts, you don't seem to have a lot of respect for the dead."

"Dex doesn't have a lot of respect for the living either," Maximus put in.

"Shut it, ginger balls."

"We should get going," Rose interrupted us before we could get into another sniping war. "I have to open tomorrow."

"I'm sorry that ended in a bit of a bust," Ambrosia said apologetically. "Still hope you had a nice time. And I wish you the best of luck with the house. If you need anything before you go, here's my card." She handed it to me and I slipped it in my pocket. She looked us all in the eye. "Seriously, if you need anything at all, I'm happy to help. I don't care how ludicrous it sounds. I like you guys."

Rose grumbled something and then started walking down the street toward her truck. We said goodbye to Ambrosia and hurried after her.

Back at the bed and breakfast, Perry was still in a state of shell-shock. I ran her a bath, making it overflow with sweet-smelling bubbles, and led her over to it. I bathed her while she sat there, and I made her drink a glass of bourbon that I'd bought earlier in the day.

"Do you want to talk about it?" I asked her as I ran a washcloth down her milky white back.

She shook her head. "I'll be okay." She looked up at me. "Dex, make love to me."

I cocked my head, not hearing her right. "What? Now?"

"I need to feel you," she said, her voice barely above a whimper.

"Okay, baby," I told her. I brought her out of the bath,

quickly dried her off, and then carried her over to the bed. I lay her down on it, then slowly, gently, covered her silken body with kisses, from the curve of her shoulder to her delicate ankle bones.

While I was inside, staring deep into her eyes, pushing slow, pushing soft while I was so hard, I felt a tingle at the back of my neck, a wash of heat covering my head.

I love making love to you, Perry's thoughts crept into my brain. *I need you, I need you.*

I couldn't help but smile and took us both over the edge. It wasn't quite I love you. But it was a start.

10

"Dex, wake up." Perry was whispering harshly, trying to shake me awake.

I slowly opened my eyes, the room dark except for the streetlights that were being filtered in through the gauzy curtains.

"What is it?" Where was I? I sat up and looked around. Perry was beside me in bed, topless, her breasts glowing in the dim light. We were in New Orleans. The bed and breakfast.

"There's someone on our balcony, she says she wants to speak with you."

I shook my head, blinking fast, swallowing the terror. "What?"

I looked over to the French doors. There was a silhouette of a woman standing on the other side of them. The curtains billowed, a ghost dance.

Perry whispered in my ear. "She says she's going to take me with her, all the way to hell."

I spun around to see what Perry meant by that but

suddenly she was gone. I was alone in the bed. The woman wasn't on the balcony.

My teeth began chattering, my limbs turning to blocks of ice, holding me to the bed. The fear came so suddenly, so strongly, that I couldn't breathe, couldn't think, couldn't do anything.

I just knew that someone was in the room with me. It wasn't outside anymore.

It was in.

"Dex," Perry's small voice called out from the bathroom. "Dex, she's in the mirror."

I tried to call out to her, but my teeth were chattering too much.

"She says she'll give me the baby if I step through the mirror."

No! I tried to scream, but now my jaw was glued shut and my lungs were filling up with internal screams and fluid as cold as dead bones. Dirt began to fill the room, raining down from the ceiling.

"I have to go," Perry said, her voice just an echo. "I'm sorry, baby."

I blinked in my rage, and my mother stood at the edge of the bed, waist deep in the dirt that was rising around the bed like floodwaters. She picked some up in her hands. "I'm coming back for all of you, Declan."

Then she threw the dirt on my head, again and again and again, until it filled my mouth, my nose, my ears, and finally my eyes.

It was all over.

I was dead and buried.

~

"ARE YOU SURE YOU'RE OKAY?" Perry asked during breakfast, gently pushing my hair off my face.

"Are you sure *you're* okay?" I said right back to her, returning her suspicious look. "You're the one who had someone die right beside them last night."

"And you're the one who woke me up in the middle of the night, acting like *you* were dying. So that's two scares for me."

I looked around the breakfast dining room of the B&B. We were alone, drinking cup after cup of dark coffee and pulling apart flaky beignets, having gotten to breakfast just at the cut-off point. We were probably pushing our luck, but the breakfast server was sitting outside on the veranda and smoking away, not really caring.

"Well I'm fine, I just had a nightmare."

"How often do you dream about your mother?" she asked. I had to tell her what happened, everything except the baby part. But anyway, it was just a dream; it wasn't real. When things got real, then that's when they became something. This was just my overactive imagination coupled with my raging hormones. Weird shit like this happened all the time.

"Not very often," I said truthfully.

"More after you saw her in the motel in Canada?"

I shrugged, hoping she'd drop it. "Doesn't seem like it. Hey, are you sure you're up for shooting tonight? I mean, after last night, I wouldn't be surprised if you wanted to back out of the whole thing."

She shook her head determinedly. "No, I'm good. I mean, I feel kind of icky, like...dirty. I don't know, I can't really explain it. I feel...tainted. Like that's going to stick in my head for a long time. But I feel okay otherwise. I'm not scared, if that's what you're worried about."

"I'm just worried about *you*, kiddo. And frankly, we want you to be a little bit scared. Haunted house TV show, remember?"

She glared at me mockingly. "Still the sadist, aren't you? Like the time you made me climb the stairs in the lighthouse."

"I was just trying to look at your ass," I admitted, stuffing the pastry in my mouth.

Maximus had left the B&B early, perhaps to visit Rose or stock up on more flannel shirts and pomade. He left a note but all it said was to meet him in the lobby at 7PM, so Perry and I decided to have a nice touristy day in the Big Easy together. Fluffy, sexy fun between the bookends of death.

At least that was the plan. And we did follow through with it, for the most part. We took a ride in one of the red velvet lined, mule-drawn carriages. We had crawfish and Bloody Mary's down by the river. We watched a few buskers in Pirates Alley and peered in people's yards in the Garden District. We took the streetcar (wasn't called Desire, but it did set Perry off on an endless—and terrible—Blanche DuBois impression). We got a bit sunburned and humored a couple of crazy drunks.

But then I got restless and curious. I wanted to find an authentic Voodoo shop and do a little research of my own.

"So much for a happy fun date," Perry said as we peered into an in-your-face store, Reverend Zombie's Voodoo Shop on St. Peter Street.

"Well if this place can't tell us about zombies, I don't know what will," I noted, as I spied a sign in the display window among the figurines and potions that said, *Come on in and shop for a spell.*

We entered the store, surprised again, this time to see it quite busy and not with just tourists. It wasn't hard to see why: there were tons of statues among all the occult books and unnerving masks. It was a bit creepy having so many eyes on you, whether they were inanimate or not. I felt like nothing was inanimate in Voodoo culture.

There was an adjoining tobacco shop that was capturing Perry's interest, so I decided to nip it in the bud right there.

"Hey, I saw you have that cigarette last night," I warned her.

She shot me an annoyed look. "What are you, my dad?"

"No, I'm your concerned boyfriend who doesn't want you hooked on the stuff."

She looked up in exasperation. "Right, Dex."

"Hey, for every cigarette you smoke, I'm going to smoke one too."

"Now that's mature."

"Can I help you?" A mustached, bow-tie wearing, white guy with knee-high Doc Martens stopped right in front of us. He kinda looked like he was heading to a Marilyn Manson concert—in the 1920s—and got lost along the way.

"Can we help *you*?" I asked.

He smiled. "I work here. My name's Ezekiel. Let me know if you need any help with anything."

He turned, ready to go greet the next customers but I reached out and touched his arm lightly.

"Hey, uh, Ezekiel?"

He stopped and smiled pleasantly. I noticed he had weird markings tattooed up and down his neck. "Yes?"

"Hi." I nodded at Perry. "We're not from here."

"I figured."

"We're actually visiting friends...and she said she'd heard some rumors about some bad juju going on in the city."

"Bad juju?" he repeated. I had a feeling I was insulting him.

"Sorry," I quickly said, flashing him a smile. "I meant, bad...stuff. Regarding local Mambos. Some of them are raising zombies in the ghetto."

He raised his brows as far as they could go. "Mmmhmm?"

Perry spoke up. "We were wondering if you knew anything about that. We don't know much about your culture, so whatever you could tell us about what's real and what's not would be really, really helpful. We don't want to go around perpetuating a stereotype."

"Oh, thank god," Ezekiel said dryly. He sighed and gently fingered his mustache. "Look here, I've heard these rumors too, but they must be just that. There have always been priestesses who try and use the spirits for destruction instead of healing, pain instead of love. They're in every religion. But even though there are a few of them in the state at the moment, it doesn't mean they'd bother with zombie rituals. That's outdated, back to the old days when people owned slaves. That just doesn't exist anymore. Curses, hexes, those are way more plausible. The zombie rumors are probably just kids on bath salts, that's all. Everyone points the finger at Voodoo when the first weird thing happens in this town."

"You say there are a few of them at the moment, a few of the Bokors," I said. "Could you tell me their names?"

He looked shocked that I asked. "Of course I won't. I'm not a snitch. Voodoo has a karma aspect to it, you know. Now, if I can interest you in some books on Voodoo, you'll probably find them a lot more helpful."

"Is one of them Mambo Maryse?" Perry asked quickly.

We both watched as Ezekiel's eyes narrowed slightly. Then he smiled. "I have no comment on that."

He looked over my shoulder, making eye contact with a couple who had just entered the shop, and muttered, "Excuse me" while he went after them.

"Well, at least we know that's the truth; Mambo Maryse really isn't the most popular Mambo in town. Do you know what *is* the most popular Mambo?"

She nodded then shot me a sly grin. "You're two seconds from getting that song in my head again, aren't you?"

"A little bit of Perry in my life," I sang into her ear. "A little bit of Perry by my side."

I grabbed her hands and spun her around the aisle, narrowly missing knocking over a few Voodoo statues. Now *that* would have been bad juju.

After we left the Voodoo store, feeling no better or worse about the whole zombie situation, we headed back to the B&B, grabbing a quick bite of dinner at a nearby café. I voiced my suspicions to Perry about Maryse being behind the walking dead.

"Well, that's pretty obvious," she noted over her piping hot jambalaya that I kept stealing bites from. "She's shunned from the community, apparently for becoming a bad apple. But that Ezekiel dude did say that there were others."

"Since we have Maryse in front of us though, shouldn't we start with that?"

Her forehead scrunched. "I thought you just wanted to film the haunted house and get out of here."

"I do," I told her quickly, feeling like we were one bad joke away from turning into *Scooby Doo*. "Really. It's just bugging me."

"It's bugging me too," she said. "I'd like to poke around a

bit more, though obviously Maryse doesn't want anything to do with us."

"Ambrosia could probably help," I said, and got glared at. "What? She did say she'd help us with anything."

Perry's eyes narrowed even more. "What if Ambrosia's the one behind all of this?"

I scoffed at her. "She's an apprentice; she's not even a priestess Mambo person. And does she look like she'd try and raise the dead?"

"Yes. She does."

You're just jealous, I thought, but I kept my mouth shut. I didn't want to start a fight, though I knew that's why Perry was saying that stuff.

"Even if it were her," I said, trying to placate Perry, "the question would be why?"

"To prove herself."

"But why?"

"To show how powerful she is."

"Kiddo," I said deliberately, "I think you're grasping at straws here."

"Straws are all we ever have." She shoved a forkful of chorizo in her mouth.

I reached over and put my hand on hers. "Not true. We've got this haunted house tonight. We'll go there and film the shit out of it. Scare ourselves silly. Leave with a pretty fuckawesome show. Sound good?"

She exhaled sharply through her nose, then nodded and continued eating.

∾

"Take a left down here," Perry said to Maximus as she squinted at the Google Map on her phone.

He was behind the wheel, me in shotgun, Perry in the back. We were allowed to borrow Rose's truck for the expedition, which was a lot cheaper than a rental car, while Rose had to work at her bar. I wished Rose were with us—not only did she know her way around the city better than Maximus, but she would have diffused the awkward tension between the three of us. Thank god Perry still had no idea what Maximus had warned me about, otherwise the whole thing would have probably been called off. I didn't even know how *I* was managing with everything. The only thing that kept me from wanting to kill him was trying to remind myself that he was crazy jealous of us, and I had to just pity him instead.

The neighborhood we were driving in was creepy as fuck. Half the people looked like zombies already, just sitting on their porches in the dark, watching our truck rumble past. Every second house looked abandoned, with giant red X's spray painted on them, a haunting reminder of the damage that Katrina had caused. Curiously, some of those houses had people in them, too scared or too stubborn to paint over the markings.

Just as I was about to suggest we head back to the safety of the touristy areas, Perry pointed up ahead at a large, looming house. "There," she said, "that should be it."

We pulled up in front of it and got out of the truck. Yeah. This place was definitely haunted.

I'd never been to Disneyland, but from the way Perry was eyeing it, mouth slightly agape, I had to assume it looked like it belonged there. It was too perfect. It was three-stories high with an attic on top, all grey with peeling layers of faded paint, maybe once yellow or cream. The porch wrapped around it completely, and cracked white pillars stood on either side of the wide stairs, supporting the iron-trimmed overhang. On the first floor, all the windows were boarded up while the ones on the rest of the floors were either cracked or broken. The house was completely dark, except for the attic window. I couldn't tell if there was a little bit of light coming from there or the glass was reflecting the streetlights below.

I nodded up at it. "Do you see that?"

"Yeah," said Perry, her voice quivering a bit. I guess this was already turning out to be more intense than we planned. "Maybe there are some squatters still inside. Are you sure this is safe?"

I shrugged my shoulders. "I couldn't tell you." I looked to Maximus. "So what's the plan, *boss*?" I asked derisively. The wind began to pick up, a hot breeze that rustled the live oak and weeping willows that lined the house's yard, obscuring most of the place from the road. Shadowy shapes danced before us.

"The plan is we get set up right here," he said, gesturing to the overgrown yard. Might be safer than doing it on the street or inside."

I looked behind us. The street was totally empty, only a lone car parked further down it, by the only dwelling that looked inhabited. Still, considering we weren't in a good neighborhood to begin with, it made sense to keep ourselves and our equipment away from roving eyes.

"This place is just..." Perry said absently while I fished my camera gear out of the back of the truck.

"Creepy?" I supplied.

"More than creepy," she said with her eyes riveted to the attic window. "It feels both dead and alive. Not just this house, but this whole street, this whole area. How many people must have died here thinking they were going to survive? How many people must have clung to the hope before they realized that help was never coming? All the regret and death...it's everywhere."

"Easy now, kiddo, we're just here to film this, not make a tribute to the tragedy."

She looked at me with annoyance. "But people can't just forget. No one really knows unless they've been here and looked around them and felt it. No one understands what was really lost."

"Except New Orleanians," Maximus spoke up gruffly. "They all know, every single one of them. And Dex is right. Let's not make this more than it is. I know you're feeling things right now, and hell, I am too. Everywhere I turn in this city, I feel like I'm picking up on one more lost soul..."

I turned to him. "You are? I'm not feeling anything."

Okay, that wasn't true. I did feel the supernatural layers were thinner in New Orleans, that there was this sick electricity in the air, that I could spot the dead around me if I really wanted to. But I didn't want to. Because to spot them was to let them all in, especially the ones I wanted to keep out. *Her*.

"You need to keep your eyes open," Maximus said after studying me for a few moments. "Retrain yourself. Then you'll see. You can start with tonight." He nodded at my camera. "Let's get this going. I'd rather not be here very long."

And, as if he'd been waiting such a long time to do this, Maximus launched into our plan of attack. I had to admit he was a lot more thorough than I usually was, and that only made me hate his plan even more. But, as Jimmy had said, he was the boss tonight and I had to bite my tongue until I made it bleed.

There would be no exploring first and filming later. We had only one chance and it had to be our first one. Spirits didn't reappear twice for the sake of cameras. And there would be more than one camera as well, Maximus was manning the other. Perry would stay with either of us, and she would be silent for most of the filming. We could do a voiceover with her later, but Maximus didn't want her talking for the sake of talking. He said it ruined the atmosphere for us and the ghosts. Instead, she would just react and use the new infrared device that Maximus had brought, one that not only showed the warmth of objects around us but the magnetic fields as well.

I was given an EVP, to keep it attached to my belt and running the whole time. I knew the shit worked and I even had one of my own that we recorded Pippa's voice on, but Maximus said our own equipment was probably inferior and possibly warped due to all the data we'd captured on it. Whatever.

"Now are we ready to go hunt some ghosts?" he asked us like the douchiest substitute teacher, trying to sound commanding and relatable at the same time.

"Fuck you," I said, while Perry sighed.

She reluctantly led the way up the weed-strewn path to the house, my camera on her, Maximus and his camera behind us. The tall grass waved in the wind and tickled my legs, scaring the crap out of me already. The porch swing swung back and forth, as did two rocking chairs. Surely the wind wasn't strong enough to make those move on their own...

"Are you filming that?" Maximus said from behind me, once again nearly making me shit my pants.

"Yes, jackass," I sneered. Man, listening to the playback of this was going to be fun.

We climbed up the steps and stopped. The two rockers chairs slowed, then stopped moving entirely.

"Are you getting anything on the reader, Perry?" Maximus roared over my shoulder.

"Jesus, man," I said, glaring at him. "Do you have to be so loud?"

He gave me a half-smile. "Sorry, I'm excited."

"Well go be excited somewhere else, and preferably not behind me where I can't see what you're doing."

"I can see two cold spots on the reader," Perry said, squinting at it, perplexed.

"Really?" Maximus yelped and basically pushed me aside to get to her. He looked down at it and grinned. "Well, I'll be damned. It's one thing to know there are two men sitting right there, it's another to see it."

"Wait...wait...wait," I said, throwing my arms in the air. "What?"

"Yeah, what?" Perry asked. "You can see them?"

He nodded. "It's a gift."

"We have gifts too," Perry said defensively. I think it's the first time I ever heard her get defensive over it, like she was almost proud.

"Well, what are they doing?" I asked. To say it was unnerving that they were there and neither Perry nor I could see them was an understatement. Maybe Maximus was pulling our leg.

"They're looking at us and shaking their heads," he said. "They look old...overalls...grey hair."

"Black or white?" Perry asked.

"Black. Probably from the 1940s. Must have lived here back then."

"You are full of shit," I said to him.

His smile dropped and he looked at me. "I can assure you, I am not. I can see things you guys obviously can't."

"Why are they shaking their heads?" Perry asked. "Are they warning us?"

"Could be," he mused, studying them...or absolutely nothing. Or splintered old rocking chairs. "They don't mean us any harm. If anything they're trying to tell us something."

I folded my arms but kept the camera rolling. "Hey, you're the ghost whisperer, you fill us in."

He frowned then jerked back. "They're gone."

Perry sucked in her breath. "He's right. Look." She showed me the gadget. The blue shapes were gone.

"Guess the dead don't want to talk to you either," I told him, slapping him hard on the shoulder.

He glared at me and then motioned for Perry to continue inside. The door to the house was boarded up with rotten wood in an X across the window, but the knob was still there. Perry tried to put her hand on it then snapped it away, shaking out her fingers.

"Is it cold?" Maximus asked.

She shook her head and shot us an embarrassed look. "Spider webs. Ugh."

I didn't know if she ever saw the day coming where she reacted more strongly to a spider web than she did to some old dead guys, but here it was.

I leaned over and turned the knob, tempted to sneak a kiss on her neck. Then I remembered Maximus was filming us for the show. Then I remembered I didn't care and kissed her anyway.

She smiled, her eyes twinkling as she gazed up at me, and Maximus was clearing his throat in no time.

"Come on, let's act professional here," he drawled.

Yes, because the three of us were such old pros. The only reason we couldn't compete in the ghost hunter Olympics.

I smiled to myself at my own little joke, but it didn't take long before my smile faded. The moment we stepped into that house, everything changed. Whatever was on the porch, the old men, whether they did or didn't exist, that was harmless. That was benevolent energy. Inside, in the dark, coffin-like air, the absence of sound, the house felt like it was holding a hundred ugly secrets, and the moment we walked through the door, through that threshold, it had already begun conspiring to hold us a secret as well.

"Uh, guys," I said, looking around me, trying to take the house all in. "Are you feeling this?"

Perry's dark head bobbed up and down in front of me. Maximus fiddled with his camera. "I'm putting this on night vision, can't see a thing in here like this."

That didn't really help me. There was little light coming in off the streets since the windows were all boarded up, and I couldn't find the flashlight I'd packed. The one on my camera was piss-poor but it would do. I could see a white glow in front of me though as Perry brought out her iPhone and put it to the flashlight application—just like old times. I did the same, and though the room wasn't illuminated, with both our lights going we could at least see what was in front of us.

First of all, it was apparent that no one had been inside for a very, very long time. The creaking floorboards were covered in a thick layer of dust that only our footprints seemed to have disturbed. There was some furniture scattered about, stained, old, and with holes in it, although not as dusty as the floor. Beside the furniture were the plastic covers, discarded once squatters found their way into the old house and decided to make it their home.

I could see from the way her phone's light jerked that Perry was scared. I'd learned to recognize those subtle movements, episode after episode. She was always so afraid to let me know how she was really feeling, how vulnerable she really felt. Here, I couldn't help but feel the same way. It wasn't that there was anything menacing in the corners, or that we were being watched by unseen forces (although, if I really let myself think about it, I would have felt that too), but that we were somewhere we really weren't supposed to be, yet somewhere that...knew we were coming. The house felt like it was expecting us. I was seconds away from saying that, but didn't want to make myself look like a chump in front of Maximus.

We continued to walk into the inky abyss, across the ragged old rug that went across the living room floor to the stately stained glass windows that must have looked out to the backyard, except those windows too were boarded up. I felt like we were in a house-sized coffin and every step we took forward was a step into the ground.

Maximus was now in front of us, relying on his night vision through the camera. I could see the faint shapes of things over his shoulder and knew we were about to walk into the kitchen and pantry. For a split-second I thought I saw someone standing over a cutting board, giant knife in hand, slicing something gruesome. But once I shone my phone in that direction, I saw it was just the refrigerator, its chrome trim gleaming against the blackness.

"Are you guys picking up on anything?" I asked. The EVP recorder wouldn't tell me any of its secrets until we were done and had uploaded it to the computer.

"It's cold in here," Perry said softly. "Everything is cold. But nothing like it was with the two men outside."

"I'm getting nothing," Maximus said. "Are you getting the magnetic readings too?"

"I don't think so," Perry said.

"Why don't you aim it at the ceiling," I told her. I could barely see her turn around in the dark to give me a look but she did as I suggested.

"There's..." she trailed off. "There's heat upstairs. I can't tell what though. And the magnetic fields look a bit warped. What does purple mean?"

Maximus made a noise of agreement and cleared his throat. "Purple means something. Next stop, second floor?"

I knew we'd all be going up there even if we said no. Part of me wanted to play chicken—be a chicken—and hightail it the fuck out of there. We'd been in haunted lighthouses, hotels, islands, and mental asylums before. All of those places had given me the same heebie jeebies as I was feeling now. But this place felt different. This house felt like it was a mixture of dead and alive, old and new, bad and...worse. There was something more than the dead at play here, but the feelings, the vibes, they were so abstract that I couldn't put my finger on it. I felt like I was in one of my nightmares, unsure if it was real or not, but certain that it meant something for somebody somewhere.

"Dex," I heard Maximus say, and I turned my head to follow his voice. He and Perry were lit by the glow of her phone, standing underneath the doorway out of the kitchen. Somehow they had gone past me, back the way we all came, and I hadn't even noticed.

"I'm here," I told them, feeling shaky. I wondered how long I had been in my head like that. I followed them out of the kitchen and back into the main room. There was a grand staircase that led up to the second floor and together we climbed it. Maximus was leading the way now, Perry behind him, and me at the end. I guess the laws of our show dynamics were changing now that we were inside. I hoped Perry felt at least a little bit comforted about being between the two of us, because I was freaking out by being at the end, feeling like something dark and heavy and horrible was following up the stairs behind me as we went, nipping at my heels.

My mind wanted to imagine my mother, her lithe, snake-like form, her torment, her terrible words. I could almost feel her, her wide black mouth and sharp teeth, her sharper tongue, her blacker heart, wanting me to suffer.

But I couldn't let my mind go that way. I couldn't let my own demons get in the way of everyone else's.

The second floor was a little bit easier than the first. For one, half the floor was divided into rooms with closed doors while the other half, the half facing the street, held a couple of chairs that must have had quite the view over the streets and gardens. The windows weren't boarded up here. They were open and broken, with the hot breeze flowing through the jagged holes, stirring up little clouds of dust that rose from the various chairs and coffee tables. If this was a boarding house once, this must have been the breakfast area or a lounge, a place for people to relax and get some sunshine. Now the only light was the one coming off the street, and though it was eerie in its own way, it still let us see what we needed to.

"Should we go into each room?" Perry asked, and I was surprised by her tenacity. And a little impressed. I had assumed everyone was as scared and eager to run away from this place as I was, but that didn't seem to be the case now. Maybe it really was in my head, feeling that the whole house was against us, that living and dead forces were at work. The thoughts about my mother should have been the first sign that I was alone in feeling this way.

Take it easy, I told myself, inhaling deeply through my nose. *So you've had a few bad dreams, you're doing okay.* You're doing okay.

"Yeah, why don't you try the first door?" Maximus said, and it struck me how much he sounded like me when Perry and I were doing the show together. There was a brief time when Perry and I had stopped doing the show and Maximus had gone to Portland—with Jimmy's blessing I might add—with hopes that he'd be able to convince Perry to do the show with him as the cameraman. It hadn't worked out, because my poor woman got fucking possessed and Maximus plead allegiance to the nation that is Palomino. But I had to wonder how long he'd been waiting to take over this role.

"Okay," Perry said uneasily, stepping toward the first door. Now that I wasn't the one ordering her around, now that I wasn't the one who was in charge and worried as shit as to whether or not we were going to get a show worth showing, I could see how demanding the job was. I had a glimpse of it when we switched roles up in Canada, but Sasquatch was an entirely different ballgame and now I was even further removed.

Perry placed her hand on the knob and the door swung open, creaking loudly. The room was entirely empty, except for an open window and a woman who stood beside it.

"Shit!" I exclaimed, my heart attempting to leapfrog out of my throat.

"What?" Perry asked, swinging her head toward me. Her eyes were wide and white in the light of my phone and I adjusted my camera so it would pick it up.

"Didn't you see that?" I said, trying to tame the panic in my voice. "The...the woman?"

Maximus and Perry exchanged a look—fuck I hated that —and then looked back at the room and at their gadgets.

"The temperature didn't change," she said, peering at the device. "But I thought I saw that purple glow, just for a bit."

I didn't know if she was trying to make me feel better or not. I appreciated it, but it didn't work. I just nodded and said, "Never mind."

We went to the next room and the next room and the next, Perry opening them all as if they held some hidden prize we'd won on the spinning wheel. But there was nothing inside, nothing that they saw or that I saw.

"Next floor," Maximus said in a deadpan voice, as if he was that droopy-faced dog in that cartoon that always said "going down." I could have smirked over that at any other time, but both Perry and I just nodded, tensing up and preparing for the next level.

Together we walked around the corner and made our way up the next set of stairs. Dust and cobwebs covered the railing, and we all tried not to touch it as we walked up the stairs, each one groaning as we went.

We were halfway up when one of the groans turned into a crack. Perry cried out, her legs falling through the stair, the wood splintering around her. I yelled and made a move to grab her, getting her arm hooked underneath mine as the entire stair disintegrated beneath her feet, sucking her body under until her lower half was dangling into the unknown.

"My Lord," said Maximus, turning around at the top of the staircase and coming back down toward us to help. He was only two steps away when the stair beneath him broke as well, splitting under his weight. He yelped and fell, holding his camera high in the air. Luckily his chest and arms were too big to slip through, though I was starting to think the whole staircase might collapse beneath us at any minute.

"Fuck shit fuck," I swore, trying to figure out what to do. Obviously Perry was first, but as much as I hated Maximus, I couldn't have him get hurt either. I placed one foot on the wainscoted wall and the other on the railing, and pulled Perry straight out of the hole. Once she was able to get her footing on the step I was standing on, I crab crawled up the railing and wall to Maximus.

I looked down at his pale, sweating face and offered my hand.

"Come on, Dickweed. Your day's not done yet."

I hoisted him up, my grip wrapping hard around his elbow, my shoulder straining. I didn't know if old Dex would be able to get him out, but I was new Dex for a reason, if not for this reason. With some strain and effort, Maximus was lifted out of the hole in the stairs and climbed onto the next one which thankfully supported his weight. I then told Perry to take a flying leapfrog onto his back. It took her a few seconds to realize what I was asking, but she did it, jumping clear across the hole that nearly swallowed her and coming to a thud on him.

Before the step had a chance to break under both their weight, I got into a squat and yanked hard under Maximus's arms, pulling him and Perry forward before anything gave way beneath them. The three of us collapsed onto the floor, taking a few moments to breathe before we got to our feet.

"Thanks, man," Maximus said, avoiding my eyes and walking away. I gave him the finger behind his back while pulling Perry closer to me. I kissed the top of her head and said, "Third floor's a charm."

She couldn't even muster a smile. I couldn't blame her. I squeezed her shoulder and told her we were almost done.

The third floor was a lot like the first floor. More or less one giant room instead of a bunch of tiny little ones. There were two rooms at the end and a bathroom, something I assumed either richer boarding guests or the owners would use, but the rest of the area was one big game room with leather couches still covered in plastic, shelves of books and game boards and picture windows. Dust still covered the floor, but everything else looked somewhat fresh and new, as if some ghostly couple had pulled down a game of Monopoly and entertained each other for a few nights.

But as much as this floor held my attention, it was the attic that was calling me. A door at the end of the room must have been the way up. I looked at Perry and Maximus, who were chattering to each other about cold spots and purple waves and this and that, and felt like they were speaking in an alien language. The thing that I was after, the thing that I understood, was upstairs, and upstairs was where I had to go.

I walked to the door and opened it, not at all surprised to find a flight of stairs leading up to the next level. I looked behind me first, but the two of them were paying no attention to me, so I walked up the stairs. They were much more solid than the ones earlier; in fact they felt like pillars of strength, wrought from the earth itself.

Once I got to the top of the stairs, it took me awhile to understand what I was looking at. I mean, it really took me awhile. Instead of a boring, dark attic as I had expected, I was looking down the length of a well-lit room. There were flickering candles in the middle of the wood-slat floor, hundreds of them, some of them red but most of them black, all of them forming this giant oval. In the middle of the floor was something white and moving. It took me awhile for my eyes to focus on it, to pinpoint what it was, but when I did, a small scream got buried in my throat. It was a small white snake with yellow diamonds down its back, pinned to the floor with a knife down its middle, writhing in pain as it was forced to die an immobile death.

A strange smell of sweet baby powder and tangy copper filled my nose as a cold breeze blew past, making the flames dance. I looked up and saw row upon row of bleeding chicken feet suspended from the arched ceiling by delicate wires, the drops of blood scattering on the floor.

I didn't know what to think or say or do. I wanted to yell and scream and tell Perry and Maximus to come up here, to see what I was seeing, but I couldn't. I couldn't do a single thing because things were happening beyond my control, without pause, without consent. I was fucking losing my mind, that's exactly what was happening.

Because at the very end of the room, beyond the dying snake and where the hundreds of black, greasy candles were burning, there was a mirror. A full-length mirror. A mirror that was aimed right at me but didn't even hold my reflection. But what it did hold, what all the mirrors held lately, was my mother.

She waved at me from inside that silver, the way she looked in my dreams, the way I remembered her in life. She waved at me. She blew me a kiss. And then she disappeared.

I blinked, trying to regain control of myself, of my soul, of my goddamn bladder, when my attention was ripped from the empty mirror—the mirror that still wouldn't hold my reflection—to the space just beyond it.

A tall, hulking black man stepped out from behind the mirror. A familiar face, if not for the dead glazed eyes and drooling lips that curled up in rage as soon as he saw me. It was Tuffy G. It couldn't have been anyone else. Tuffy G, the man we all saw die in the bar, was standing in this attic with me, looking like I was next on his hit list. I didn't know what to think, but luckily my instincts were quicker than that.

I turned and ran and ran hard. I went for the stairs, feeling the floor beneath me shake and rumble as the giant undead thing came toward me. I kept running, taking the stairs two at a time until I was on the landing of the third floor. Perry was by the wall trying to get readings from her thingamabob and Maximus was filming an inanimate couch.

I screamed. I ran. I tried to warn them.

But Tuffy G already had a plan.

He lurched forward after me, and just when I felt his hand grazing the back of my shirt, I knew he went off to the side.

Toward Perry.

My Perry.

She screamed once she saw him, his arms outstretched, his mouth open, teeth bared. He grabbed her by the neck and shoulders, his fat, dead hands about to dig into her and break her to pieces. His jaw snapped violently, wanting to eat her alive.

I didn't have much time. No time to think about what was really happening, whether this was a ghost, a zombie, or a sick fucking prank. I dropped my camera to the floor, making sure the lens was pointed in the general direction and grabbed the nearest sharp blunt object, a floor lamp without the bulb. I swung it up like I was in the Little Leagues and cracked it against Tuffy G's back. When that only made him pause in mid-attack, I quickly did it again, dropping low to a crouch and swinging at the back of his knees. I swung hard enough to break any man's legs. Only

I turned my head to look at him, keeping Perry firmly in my grasp. "Yes, why?"

He was looking toward the attic door. Smoke was beginning to filter out of it.

"Shit!" I yelled. Tuffy must have knocked them over on his way after me. "What do we do?"

"We get the fuck out of here, right now," he said, picking up his camera from the ground and giving it a quick once over. He'd thrown it pretty hard, but from what I saw, only the lens looked cracked.

"Shouldn't we wait for the police or fire trucks?" Perry sniveled.

"No," Maximus and I both said in unison. She nodded, understanding, and wiped her nose. Maximus wanted the NOPD as far away from us as possible and I wasn't about to get our footage taken away from us again. Besides, between the three of us, we'd actually gotten something, I knew it.

Now the smoke was getting thicker and flames crackled at the top of the stairs, illuminating a slice of floor in the flickering light. If we stood around much longer, we'd be swallowed up fast.

"Let's go," I said, giving her shoulders a squeeze. "We have to run."

At that, there was a thump from up above us. Something or someone in the attic.

She swallowed hard, her eyes searching the ceiling. "What else did you find up there?"

"I'll tell you in the truck," I said, pulling her. I didn't see anyone else in the attic, except Tuffy. I hoped it was just the house starting to collapse on itself.

I picked up my camera, which had skittered across the ground, and we quickly hopped down the aging stairs, careful to sidestep the ones we'd broken. The fire grew louder behind us, and once we hit the main floor, I was met with the idea that the house might not let us leave at all.

I was about to warn Maximus about this, but he crossed through the front door to the porch easily and Perry and I followed. I glanced down at the door frame as I stepped over it, and noticed a thin line of salt. If I had the time to stop and investigate it, I felt like I'd discover it went all the way around the house.

Maximus was already at the truck and starting it, Perry was climbing in the front seat, her eyes begging me to run faster. I caught up and jumped in the back, looking up at the house as we pulled away in time to see flames spread along the roof.

The window in the attic shattered, the sound competing with the noisy truck as we roared off, and I wondered if it was the heat that caused it or if someone had broken the window, trying to escape. And if it were the latter, should I have felt relieved or not?

Maximus drove like a madman out of the neighborhood, all of us silent and breathing hard, pulses racing.

Perry turned around in her seat to look at me. "What happened upstairs, Dex? Where did he come from?"

"Aside from a fresh grave? I don't know." I explained to them what I saw in the attic, the circle of candles, the live snake pinned to the ground, the hanging chicken feet, then Tuffy G rising from the corner of the room, glassy-eyed and enraged. I left out the part about my mother. They would have thought I was nuts.

"I captured it all, I think. Until he started running at me and then I just ran like hell."

"Leading him to me. My god, I thought I was done for," she said with a shiver. "He was dead but he wasn't dead. I saw him on the machine for just a second before I dropped it. He was orange-red, just like the rest of us." She was still visibly upset but she was handling herself a lot better than I was. My gut was twisted up over the image of him manhandling her, over what depraved thing could have happened if Maximus and I hadn't acted fast, while my brain was warped over what I'd witnessed in the attic, the candles, the animals, my mother, the pull of the house, the salt.

"This couldn't have been an accident," I said suddenly. "Someone knew we were going there."

"No shit," Maximus said dryly.

"Well if that's what you're thinking, then why aren't we talking about it, huh?"

"I still think it's Ambrosia," Perry said stiffly.

Maximus's eyes flew to the mirror to meet mine. I knew we were thinking the same thing, that Perry didn't like Ambrosia, so of course she'd think that of her. But call it a gut feeling, I knew Ambrosia meant no harm.

"Ambrosia's not capable of that," Maximus told her. "She doesn't have the power, she's not even been initiated into the Societe La Belle Venus yet. She has years and years to go."

"Who told you that?" she asked.

"Rose did."

Perry crossed her arms in a huff. "You're both thinking with your dicks."

I nearly laughed. When didn't I think with my dick? But there were better times to make jokes and this wasn't one of them, not when a zombie nearly tried to munch on my girlfriend.

I exhaled and sat back, trying to calm myself and go over what had just happened, when I noticed we were passing the bed and breakfast.

I tapped Maximus on the shoulder. "Where are we going?"

He eyed me sternly in the mirror. "We're going to get Rose. And then we're going to see Maryse. I want some damn answers."

∾

ROSE WAS VISIBLY worried when we pulled her from her bar duties, enough that she didn't mind leaving Nameless to one of her newer employees while she got in the truck with us and headed out to the bayou.

We told her everything from start to finish, but she was particularly interested in what I saw upstairs.

"What color were the candles?" she asked.

"Black. Some were red. But most were black."

"Did they have names carved on them?"

I leaned my elbows onto my knees and eyed her as she drove, Maximus now riding shotgun. "Why yes, while this fucking snake was dying a painful death in the middle of the room, the chicken feet were swaying in the imaginary breeze, and I saw a dead man rise from behind a full-length mirror that reflected nothing back, I decided I had enough time to pick up one of the candles and get a better look at it. I wanted to know if it was scented or not." She stared at me blankly. "No, I never saw if there were names carved on them."

"Did they look oily?"

I frowned, remembering that they had. "More so than normal. I thought maybe it was the wax."

"Maybe, maybe not. It could be sacred oils. Maryse will tell us."

Maryse might be behind all this, I wanted to say. I bit my lip and sat back. Perry wrapped her arm around mine.

Soon we were coasting down the bumpy dirt road lit

only by Rose's headlights. The dark trees and swamp water flew past us, and I could only imagine what we'd see if we swung the lights that way. Probably a sea of glowing eyes, watching our every move, waiting for the next bite.

Rose parked the truck beside Maryse's house and tossed us the mosquito spray again. "Cover your mouths and noses and spray it in here. You'll get eaten alive the minute you step out of the car." While we coated ourselves with it, coughing at the toxicity, she pulled two flashlights out of the center console, keeping one for herself and giving me the other. "Don't want you taking a wrong turn and stepping into the swamp."

"Is there anything in this city that won't try and take a bite out of you?" Perry mumbled as we got out of the truck. The whine of the insects was everywhere, buzzing dangerously close to my ears. Despite how badly I stank to them, I still felt a few of them stinging at my neck and arms.

We huddled after Rose, sticking tightly to the path, and walked up to the screened porch. Before we entered, she aimed her flashlight at the water. I was right. There were eyes in the water looking at us. There was also Ambrosia's air boat. Perry made a grumbling sound at the sight and I patted her shoulder, hoping that would make her feel better somehow and fully knowing that it wouldn't.

For her sake, I decided I'd try and look at Ambrosia through her eyes and try not to discount her as easily as I wanted to. It was hard trying to think like Perry and see her in a not-so-flattering light but I did it.

We walked inside the house; Rose didn't even bother to knock.

"Hello?" she said as we stood in the foyer and I slowly shut the front door behind us. I heard things skittering about on the porch and didn't want them running inside with us, whatever they were. I wondered if there was a rodent problem in these parts and if Voodoo priestesses ever used them for whatever rituals they did.

A cat meowed from the corner of the darkened living room, scaring the shit out of me again.

"It's just Mojo," Rose explained in a hush. She aimed her flashlight over to where the cat was and we all sucked in our breath in unison.

Maryse was sitting in an armchair, upright, eyes glinting as she stared at us. A black cat was in her arms. I was starting to think this was a bad idea, no matter how badly we wanted answers. Then I remembered Tuffy G going after Perry and I swallowed down my fear and stood my ground.

"Maryse," Rose said breathlessly, "you scared us."

Suddenly the lamp beside Maryse switched on and the room was illuminated. It looked the same as before, except for Maryse's more or less lifeless body and the squinty-eyed cat on her lap. Both of them took their time to glare at every single one of us.

Maryse sucked at her dentures. "I scared you? How do you think I feel with four nitwits walking into my house at midnight? A little warning would have been nice."

"We're sorry, Mambo," Rose said, remembering the formality. "We've come here to talk to you about something very important. I know you don't want to see us again but this is a matter of life or death."

She kept watching us, me especially, and then sighed. "I guess I was a little rude last time, wasn't I? But you know how I get when I'm woken up from my nap. Now what is so urgent that this couldn't wait until morning? You're lucky I was just in a trance and not sleeping."

"Sorry," Rose apologized again, and it struck me how much she acted like a young girl when she was around the

Mambo. The hardened, tough-as-nails Rose was gone. It was almost refreshing, except Rose's strength in the situation probably would have put me more at ease.

"Where is Ambrosia?" Rose asked.

Maryse narrowed her eyes. "Why?"

"Is she here?"

"Yes. She's in her room sleeping."

"I didn't know she lived here all the time now."

Maryse waved at her dismissively. "Good care is hard to come by. I teach Ambrosia and she takes care of me. I haven't left the house in two years, you know?"

"Excuse me," Perry said politely. "I've had to pee since New Orleans. Could I use your bathroom?"

Maryse eyed her with disdain but nodded down the hall. "Second door, child."

Perry flashed her an apologetic smile and walked down the hall.

"Is there somewhere we could talk?" Rose asked.

"Is here not good enough?"

Rose shook her head but didn't elaborate.

Maryse sighed and got out of her seat, the cat leaping to the ground. You could almost hear her bones creaking. Her long, scraggly grey hair hung around her skinny face. In the lamplight you could see just how sick and old she was. Her face was drawn and ashen, her mouth lined with a million wrinkles. Only her eyes remained sharp, even though they'd clouded over slightly, like an old dog's who still knew a few tricks.

"Very well. Follow me." She gingerly made her way to the hallway, back hunched over, and turned on the flickering overhead lights just as Perry was coming out the bathroom, looking flushed and up to no good. Maryse squinted at her again and we went down the hall, Perry tagging behind me.

"What is it?" I whispered at her. "Pee smell funny?"

She looked disappointed. "I wanted to see if Ambrosia really was in her room." She nodded at the closed door beside Maryse's bedroom. "She is. Sleeping."

I felt strangely smug that Perry was wrong, because if Ambrosia was here the whole time, she probably hadn't set up the Voodoo lab in the attic, which meant that was one suspect we could cross off the list.

Maryse opened a narrow door at the very end of the hall, one I had assumed was a linen closet, but it looked cavernous until she pulled on a hanging lightbulb and began to descend down a set of stairs.

"Aren't we going underwater?" I whispered to Maximus, who was in front of me, but the stairs were only four feet deep and we found ourselves in a cellar of sorts.

A cellar of horrors.

The ground was sawdust, perhaps rock underneath, and the air was filled with a mix of competing smells—sweet and cloying, damp and musky, rich and smoky. The walls were painted red and filled with every imaginable Voodoo horror you could imagine. There were shrines in all corners of the room, statues covered in beads and jewelry, mounds of candles in every color, poppet dolls made of yarn and tribal-patterned cloths, tied together with string. There were skulls—humans and animals—hanging on the red-painted walls, along with various tribal masks. Mason jars filled with herbs, spices, and who knows what were lined up on shelves. If the veranda was the overstock room, this was where all the magic happened. Pun intended.

We were all silent, looking around us in awe, even Rose, who looked more respectful than anything else. I began to wonder how much Voodoo had rubbed off on her from being around the Mambo for so many years.

"Please take a seat," Maryse said, and sat down in a high-backed leather chair, motioning to the three wicker chairs that sat across from a round, fortune-teller style table.

"I'll stand," Maximus volunteered, as if that made him a better man or something.

Maryse gave him a look, one I couldn't read. She wasn't impressed either way, and I wondered if she was going to start pointing at him in horror again and calling him mortal.

"Now, tell me Rose, what is it that is life and death and so magnificently important." She crossed her bony white hands in front of her. Curiously, she had gold and silver rings on all of her hands with all sorts of gemstones. The weight of some of them looked like they'd break her fingers in two.

"Well," Rose began, and then looked at Maximus. He launched into what happened at the bar last night, then into his side of things at the house, and paused when it came time to tell her what I saw. Then we finished it up with the zombie of Tuffy G coming after Perry, me beating him with a floor lamp, and him running straight out the window and falling to his death number two.

"Oh," I added, "then I guess I knocked over the candles in the attic, because the attic went up in flames, and we all ran out of the house and pretty much came straight here. And to answer your question before you ask it, no I didn't see any names on the candles."

"What did the candles smell like?" she asked.

Was she kidding me?

"Like Eau du Zombie. I don't know."

She pursed her wrinkled lips until they almost disappeared into her skin. I tried not to grimace. She got up and shuffled over to a shelf of oils and pulled one off of it. She popped the top and came over to me, holding it under my nose.

"Does this smell familiar?" she asked impatiently.

I breathed in. It did. That cloyingly sweet smell, like baby powder.

"Yeah, I guess it smelled like that. A bit more coppery though."

"The blood from the poor snake," Maryse said, sitting back down. "That was the copper smell. What was rubbed on all the candles was Follow Me Boy oil. Calamus root."

"Follow Me Boy oil?" Perry asked incredulously.

"I was expecting something more sinister than that," I added.

Maryse wasn't amused. "It is called that because sex workers in the city would apply it in order to get ahead of the competition, so to speak. Every brothel had this for their ladies. It's supposed to work on sexual attraction, but the key component is dominance and control. Most likely, those candles were probably meant for the deceased man."

"Could the candles have been for any of us?" Perry asked.

She considered that. "It's possible. But considering zombies have to be controlled by someone, I would think they were there to ensure he followed through. That said, it is interesting that they were black candles. We call them black devils. Usually, if you anoint a black devil with a commanding type of oil, you're asking for revenge or retribution against someone. Or you're just being a jerk."

So either the zombie went after Perry on purpose because her name was on the candle, or the zombie's name was on the candle, the person controlling him going after their own sort of revenge. It didn't really matter since we would never find out, although Ambrosia and Tuffy did have history together. Perhaps she was after revenge.

The thought was ludicrous, the idea terribly elaborate. Still, because I knew Perry was thinking it, I decided to voice it out loud.

"Maryse, do you think it's possible that Ambrosia could be involved in any of this?"

Perry smiled while Maximus let out an audible gasp. Maryse didn't look too surprised, however.

"I can see how you'd think that, since she and I are closest to you. But in order to do what you say happened, what you're suggesting, you have to be very powerful. Ambrosia hasn't finished her training, she has years left before she's considered a Mambo. To be frank with you, I don't think she has it in her to do it, energy wise nor personality wise. She's a sweet, kind girl."

That was true all right. Very sweet, kind, beautiful. A flash of her smile, the feel of her skin.

Perry spoke up, snapping me out of it. "But what if she was working with someone else? Helping another Mambo behind your back?"

Maryse narrowed her eyes at the thought. "I hate to think that but I suppose it's possible. I'll keep an eye on her over the next while, how about that? Last thing I want is to be blindsided by my own pupil."

"And what about you?" I asked.

"What about me?"

"Obviously you have the power to do all this, to raise the dead. You know we're here and what we're up to."

"I suppose *you* would think the world revolves around you, wouldn't you?" she asked.

"Pardon?"

"These zombie rituals are nothing new in New Orleans,

and even now, this has been apparently happening for some time before you got here. To think that they are now focused on you is absurd. And no, I am not the one behind it. Contrary to what everyone thinks of me, I am not a Bokor, I do not and have never used my skills for evil. I am a dying woman, as you can see, and I barely have any energy to keep on living. Doing any of those hoodoos would kill me instantly. The most I can do for myself right now is that."

She nodded to a side table where a yarn poppet had a nail sticking out of it. An honest to God Voodoo doll.

"Who is that?" Maximus asked suspiciously.

"I don't know *who* it is," she said, folding her frail arms against herself. It was colder down in the cellar. "But it is a Nkondi. Traditionally, it is used to hunt down evil sorcerers or threats to the Voodoo community. Here I have used it to drive my illness back to the spellcaster, whoever he or she might be."

"You believe your illness is a...a curse?" Perry asked.

Maryse nodded then focused her eyes on her. "Now, if you'll excuse me, ladies, I would love to talk to the two gentleman alone here."

Maximus and I exchanged a worried look. What the hell did the Mambo want with us?

I guess Perry and Rose were thinking the same thing, because they were staring at her in confusion.

Maryse gestured to Rose. "Please, Rose, take your friend here and go upstairs and wait for us. Shut the door behind you and try not to wake Ambrosia."

Rose and Perry slowly got out their chairs, Perry's eyes wild with fear for me. I gave her a tight-lipped smile and a nod.

They reluctantly left the room. I could feel them

glancing over their shoulder as they ascended the stairs until the cellar door closed behind them.

"So," Maryse said, turning a wicked smile toward me. "Dex Foray. I suppose you'd like to find out who your friend here really is."

Maximus stiffened, his eyes downcast. I felt like I couldn't breathe. A thousand suspicions from thousands of moments clouded my head.

She continued, calmly staring at me, knowing she held all the cards. "And why of course you're the exception."

13

I chewed on my lips, wondering if I should take the bait or if this was going to end up being a colossal waste of my time. There was nothing that Maryse could know about me, certainly nothing about the two of us. "An exception to what?"

She sat back in her chair and pulled out a hand-rolled cigarette and matches from underneath the table. "Do you mind if I smoke?" she asked, even though I knew she'd do it regardless. I shrugged. She lit the match on the table and took a long hard drag. Suddenly I wanted one too, more than anything. I was sick of seeing it around me lately, tired of trying to be so good. She must have noticed my pitiful eyes because she handed me the cigarette and pulled out another one for herself. "You'll probably need that anyway."

I inhaled and was met with the comfortable arms of an old friend. My eyes closed, rolling back, and I let out a delicious exhale. It was so wrong to fall back into it after quitting, after trying to be a better man, but Dex 1.0 was somewhere still inside me.

Maryse cleared her throat and I opened my eyes, my

nerves and endorphins buzzing pleasantly. I had forgotten what was really going on. The smoke we blew out curled around our heads in silky patterns. Maximus was silent, still tense, still waiting for whatever Maryse was going to say.

"An exception to what?" I asked her again, not wanting to get too sidetracked.

She exhaled slowly. "I'm a somewhat ordinary human being. My story isn't so different from anyone else's. I was never born with the ability to see ghosts like you, Dex. It isn't in my blood. What is in my blood is this connection to the occult, to things that lie beyond what we can see. I've always been open to it, always been curious, always wanted answers. My mother was a Mambo herself and she taught me well, taught me skills that I would have never picked up on my own. I don't possess any real supernatural talent, although I can predict the future on occasion. Not because I can see it, but because I can feel others telling me. I am nobody special unfortunately, just an old woman with a lot of practice and a lot of knowledge in how to harness the magic, the energy, that's around us. That is who I am.

"Over the years, my work has brought me into many people's lives. I've met dead loved ones at séances, have done readings for rock stars that made deals with the devil. I cleanse houses of evil entities and I practice healing Reiki on poppets. I've made loves spells for couples who ended up being married until death did them apart. I've brought luck to people who have paid me for it. I've gone to Senegal to learn how to make a proper gris-gris, or mojo hand.

"Along the way I've been introduced to the lives of people who are much more...gifted...than I am. My eyes have been opened to worlds within our own, worlds I never knew existed, beings who were beyond my scope of the St.

Michael the Archangel or Yon Sue. Beings like your friend beside you, Maximus Jacobs."

I swallowed, my throat feeling thick, and eyed the familiar ginger next to me. He stared at the table, expression frozen.

She had called him a *being*.

Maryse went on matter-of-factly. "Maximus is not his real name, he chose that himself. His name is Jacob and he is a descendant of all the Jacobs. Now, what is a Jacob? Well, I didn't quite know either. The closest thing I knew to them would be the spirit guides and guardians from Haitian Voodoo. But I suppose every culture has their own version of the truth."

She looked up at Maximus. "Are you sure you don't want to explain this all yourself?"

He met her eyes, his voice hard. "Why are you doing this?"

"Because it's time, don't you think? The three of you are here and there are no coincidences. If you want to warn Dex here about what could happen, you will have to come clean as well. You can tell half the truth, even if you fear he wouldn't believe you. Even if you fear that you've been lying to him this whole time."

My mouth was so dry, but I was able to say, "Warn me about what?"

He glanced at me, shaking his head. "I already tried."

"Did you?" Maryse asked. "Then why does he look so confused?" She sighed and stubbed out her cigarette on a small green candle next to her. "Dex, I'm going to tell you a few things and I want you to follow me, to not discount it. Each thing will have its own weight to it, a blow to the reality you think you know. I'm not trying to lay out a bunch of bombs to make your head explode. But there's really no other way."

I took in one last deep drag of the cigarette for strength then steadied myself for the verbal assault.

"The first is that Maximus, as a Jacob, was immortal. It doesn't mean he's been around forever, but at least his body has been. His job, like all Jacobs, was to act either as managers, guides, or gatekeepers between this world and the ones beyond it. The Thin Veil, the World Beyond, or whatever you want to call it. Maximus was assigned to you as a guide, and you in particular. You have a gift, Dex, and those with gifts must have someone there to show them how to manage it. To contain it. Sometimes gifts, like power for a priestess, can end up in the wrong hands."

I blinked. There was nothing to say.

"Maximus was supposed to open your eyes to your abilities back then. It didn't work out so well, for several reasons. One, is that Maximus became compromised."

I looked at him.

"He lost sight of the goal and became obsessed with you and your life."

Maximus glared at her. She shrugged. "It's all in the open now, boy. You lost your way, and eventually you gave up. It happens. The job was difficult, more so because of you, Dex. You were a lot more than he had bargained for. So pushing aside his alliance to you as a friend and not his actual job, you were far too much for him to handle, for most Jacobs to handle. There's a part of you, Dex, and I'm sure if you really look inside yourself, you'll see it, that is more than normal. More than...this world."

Finally, I had to say something. Everything was going over my head, but not that last part.

"I'm not of this world?" I asked.

"You are. You were born here, I can see that. But there's more to it than that. What, I don't know. Maybe it's your lineage. But there is something in you, in your blood, that poses a challenge to someone as weak as Maximus."

He grumbled at that but didn't say anything.

"You'd pose a challenge to anyone, to be honest, even me. You aren't a Jacob, but there's a preternatural...thread... that has made you into something over the years that I can't even classify. You're very, very powerful, Dex, in more ways than one, and that's how you became the exception. The exception to the Jacobs and the exception to this one right here. After Maximus defected, you were left alone to either figure yourself out on your own, or to bury it under a mound of medication. I was told it was the latter. Meanwhile, Maximus got reassigned to guide another person with similar abilities...Rose."

"This..." I said slowly, trying to find thoughts and words from those thoughts, "is a lot to take in. Let alone believe."

"I'm not finished," she said tersely. "Maximus took care of Rose, opened her up to the world that was just out of sight. He did his duty. And when his duty was finished, he went rogue and gave up his immortality to live a human life. I suppose in his new existence, he went to find you, to maybe make right the things he wronged. Perhaps to check up on you."

Maximus looked at me for a moment before quickly looking away. "I saw you, on the internet. In the lighthouse. You were ghost hunting. I knew just from watching you that you had no idea what you had, that no other Jacob had been assigned to you. I had to get in your life somehow. When I heard about the incident in Red Fox, I knew that was the way in. I just wanted to see how you were doing."

"How very thoughtful of you," I said absently, my brain still turning over on itself.

"And then I met Perry."

And then he got my full attention.

He smiled, knowing it. "Perry was like you, just not as difficult. I'd been out of the network for some time, so I couldn't figure out at first whether she needed a Jacob as well. I had gone rogue; it was no longer my duty, but I still felt like I had to do something. Later on, I learned that Perry did have a Jacob of her own in high school. Apparently it hadn't gone very well."

"The accident," I whispered, remembering what she had told me in December while were shooting at the mental asylum.

"That's right."

"But..." I began, "say that what you two kooks are telling me is the truth, and I just don't know what to think, why would Perry's Jacob end up like that? He didn't help her. He showed her demons and made her burn down a fucking house."

"Because they're not divine and they aren't evil. They aren't good and they aren't bad," Maryse explained. "They just are. The worlds beyond here are grey, just like they are. Maximus became too involved with you and your life and your humanity. He was weak and he fell to that weakness, fell to his insecurities and his jealousies. That's neither good nor bad. It's just the nature of things."

I frowned in disbelief. "So poor fucks like myself or like Rose or like Perry, with all of these abilities and gifts and weights on our shoulders, we're assigned a guide who might be an unreliable piece of shit in the end and do the opposite of trying to help us? That's not fucking fair!"

She shrugged. "That is life. Real life is grey."

"What about Perry's grandmother? Pippa."

"She's just a woman, a woman like Perry," Maximus said to me. "She had a Jacob too. From what I understand, he helped her."

"She was put away in a mental institution," I said through grinding teeth.

"Because she still had her own free will, her own choices to make. Jacobs can only guide, we can't interfere."

"But you did," I snarled, remembering his involvement when Perry was possessed. "You did more than interfere, you stuck your dick in her!"

He flinched but calmly said, "I am not who I used to be. I have no more rules." His eyes flashed to mine. "And I was trying to save her, to save both of you."

"How is fucking the woman I love supposed to save us?"

"Because she's not supposed to be with you!" Maryse said sharply, sharp enough that my head swiveled to her, almost giving me whiplash.

"It's what I tried to tell you the other day," Maximus said under his breath.

I raised my hands, anger flowing out of me with surprising strength. "Whoa. Back up. What do you mean she is not supposed to be with me, huh? You think this is fucking funny, some idea of a joke? What, Maximus, you got her on the same prank that you tried to pull on me?"

"I wish this was a prank, Dex," she said, a hint of sadness in her eyes. "You're special. You've got parts of you that link you to both worlds, the world of the dead, of demons and unimaginable power, and the world of the living."

"How?" I exclaimed, slamming my fists on the table until it nearly broke underneath them. "How would I be linked to both worlds? I was born here, in New York, to a human mother and a human father."

"Did either of your parents ever dabble in the occult?"

I was shocked into my thoughts. No, never. My mother had been a drunk, my father had enough and left. He was a businessman. I had a brother. Both of us were as normal as can be.

And then I remembered one thing my mom said right before she died, something I thought about from time to time, when I felt like wallowing in self-loathing. *You are not my son, you are not my son, I was not me when I had you. I was not me when I had you.* Then she died, in front of my face. I had never figured out what that meant and now I was too scared to.

"Dex?" Maryse asked. She was studying me.

"What does this have to do with Perry?" My voice felt laced with acid, her name on my lips was burning me.

"Like a mortal with a Jacob," she said with deliberation, watching Maximus now, "two people with abilities shouldn't get together. The energies shared and exchanged can cause ripples, holes in the fabric of the Veil, and where there are holes, bad things can get out. And they should definitely not have children. The children would have twice the amount of power that the parents have. The world is not cut out for people like us, people on the fringe, not anymore. Science and technology and fear have replaced the open mind that's needed to embrace people like us. As you know, Dex, from what you suffered, people are far too quick to label you as mentally ill, to try and fix you with pills, when in reality there is nothing wrong with you. You can just see and do things that others can't. It can be a beautiful gift, but unfortunately the world does not see that beauty. It fears what it doesn't understand. You and Perry would produce a child that would end up going mad. And that's if you were lucky."

My heart was hammering hard in my chest, hard

enough to hurt. There was truth in her words, I could feel it in my bones, and the truth would kill me if I let it.

"What do you mean, if we're lucky?"

Her face grew very grave, very solemn. Maximus straightened up beside me, clearing his throat.

"Dex," he said carefully, licking his lips. "Because we don't know what makes you...*you*...we don't know what would happen if Perry got pregnant again. We don't know if the child would be a child at all. We already know that it would have enough power on its own to attract hosts that don't want to leave. It wasn't an accident that Perry got possessed. The pregnancy, the combination of you and her together, it was bound to happen. If there was a next time, I don't think Perry would survive it. The next entity would stay in her, forever, and take the child too. I'm sorry."

And suddenly I couldn't breathe. Suddenly I couldn't even see. The world in front of me clouded over and inside I was drowning in my sorrow and sadness. Because I believed what they were saying, even though every part of me was begging for me to ignore them, to discount them, to tell them they were liars and that they were wrong. But I knew that wasn't the case. I knew in the deep-seat of my soul that everything they had told me, from what Maximus really was, to the fact that I had a little something extra in my blood, to the fact that Perry would probably not survive another pregnancy, at least not by me, was the absolute truth. I'd never been handed so many soul-crushing, reality-bending, life-altering bombs before in all my years.

But what killed me more than anything was knowing that Perry and I could never start a family together. I could never put my seed in her and watch it grow, never be a happy, expectant couple. It wasn't like this was something I'd even discussed with her, for obvious reasons, but it was my dream that I secretly held on to and held on to tight. Now I'd have to let it go.

I'd have to let her go.

Maximus put his large freckled hand on my shoulder. "It's for the best, you know it is. It's for her best."

Maryse got out of her chair and went to rummage through a shelf, while I sat there absolutely dumbfounded.

I looked at Maximus, for once wanting his advice. "What do I do? How should I tell her?"

He shook his head and gave me a gentle smile. "You can't tell her. You know you can't. Perry is stubborn as anything and the moment you tell her something can't happen, she'll try and make it happen. To tell her this, to tell her that this part of her future is over, it would kill her. Crush her."

"But what am I supposed to do?" I repeated, feeling crushed myself, my internal organs being put through a vice.

"You'll figure it out," he said.

Maryse came back, placing a small vial of oil on the table and a Ziploc bag full of hand-rolled cigarettes. "The oil is Van Van oil—lemon verbena—it will help protect you, whether now from zombies and black magic or from dark forces in the future. The cigarettes are to get through it all. There's some special herbs in there too, ones that might help clear your mind a bit." I took the oil and the cigarettes, folding up the bag and sticking it in the pocket of my jeans.

"Thank you," I said, my voice failing me as I got out of my seat.

"You're welcome. Now I hope you take some time over the next few days and be kind to yourself, Dex. These are some large but important truths and your mind needs a way to work around them, to fit them into the life you thought you knew. Don't rush anything or make any rash decisions. Just be and feel and ask for help when you need it."

I tried to smile but failed. "It's kind of hard to take some time for myself when we're trying to film ghosts and zombies."

"Ignore the ghosts and the zombies. Just go home." She gestured to the top of the stairs. "Please show yourselves out and tell Rose and Perry that I'm sorry I couldn't be of much help."

We nodded and climbed the stairs out of her Voodoo cellar. An hour ago, zombies were the biggest concern in my life. Now my biggest concern put that one to shame.

14

Perry and Rose were understandably anxious and suspicious when Maximus and I returned from the cellar. They asked us non-stop about what happened downstairs and I kept having to lie, over and over again, with Maximus picking up the slack. We told them that she thought both of us could have information about the zombies and that she put us under hypnosis to see if there was anything we could recall at the house. We told the girls that she made them leave because they would have been too distracting for us and that Perry couldn't be hypnotized because Maryse sensed too much resistance in her. The hypnosis didn't turn up anything that we hadn't already told her. It was amazing how easy I was able to tell that lie, even right to Perry's face, and it gave me a sick sense of hope that I'd be able to keep the real truths buried.

And as for that, I didn't know what to do. All I could do was keep a little distance from her, which was actually quite easy. I had trouble even looking at her face without getting lost in the beauty, lost in the feelings, the love I had for her. I was dying slowly inside and tired as hell. The minute we got back to the B&B I went straight to sleep. I could tell Perry wanted to talk or to even get in my pants, but I couldn't do it. I mumbled something about it being the middle of the night and passed right out, swept away by blissful sleep.

The next morning, Perry was trying to rouse me awake but the minute my mind latched onto the horrible memories of last night, I wanted to stay in bed. I couldn't deal with this. I couldn't make sense of this, not with Perry there.

Thankfully, yes thankfully, Maximus knocked on our door, telling us he wanted to go through the footage from last night and see if we had enough for a show. If so, we'd stick around another day and shoot some atmosphere shots and then head home, screw the zombies.

I never thought I'd say this, but I wanted Maximus around me. He was the wedge between us, that awkward buffer, and now I wanted him back. I wanted him between me and Perry while I figured out what to do. I wanted him to keep her mind occupied so she didn't start worrying about what was wrong with me, why I was so quiet and avoiding contact with her and keeping my distance. He knew it too. When he came in the room with the equipment, he'd come in with breakfast that he pilfered from downstairs, and he didn't leave while we quickly got ready. Perry was fully-clothed in her pajamas, but looked pissed off that he was there and interrupting her morning time. I hadn't slept nude, so I just pulled on the pair of jeans by my bed, slipped on a clean t-shirt from my bag and was set.

That said, I barely paid attention to what we were looking at on the footage and kept leaving the room to go smoke Maryse's cigarettes on the balcony. They really were keeping me sane and clearing my head. I fingered the bottle of Van Van Oil in my pocket and wondered if rubbing the cigarettes with them would do anything. I didn't exactly believe in all the Voodoo hoodoo hocus pocus crap, but I'd seen more and more crazy shit over the years, fuck, more crazy shit in the last twenty-four hours alone, that told me to never discount anything.

Like the fact that your old college roommate, classmate, bandmate and overall thorn in your side hadn't even been human. He was something else entirely, an immortal being whose job in life was to act as a guide to those who could see through worlds. Only he didn't exactly like the job when it came to it and decided he'd rather forget all that and eat all my food and play all my music and be friends with all my friends. He was a fucking supernatural freeloader, and at the moment, the only person in my life whom I could be completely honest with.

"Can I have one?" Perry asked shyly, coming on the balcony to join me.

"Guys, we're not done yet," Maximus yelled from inside.

I glanced at her and sighed, deciding I might as well give her one. For all I was dealing with, now she had to deal with a distant boyfriend and the fact that part of her zombie attack was captured (albeit at a weird angle) on film.

"Here," I said, fishing it out. Our fingertips brushed against each other and I felt that deep-rooted spark, the one that always tied me to her, the one that made me want to rip her clothes off and drive myself so far into her that you couldn't tell where I ended and she began. That spark that could lead to her death, that spark that could rip apart the fabric of worlds.

This was hell. This was so much hell. All I wanted to do was take her right here, bury myself inside and never come out. Say goodbye to the worlds and the truths and the consequences. Perry was my world, and yet I was beginning to realize I had no choice but to walk away.

"How are you feeling?" I asked thickly, taking my hand away from hers. My nerves went cold at her absence.

Her brow furrowed, her features scrunched delicately. "How are you feeling, Dex? Why are you smoking now? Why won't you look at me?"

I shrugged, trying to find a way to play it off, a headache maybe, but then Maximus was there behind us.

"You kids, I think we have one hell of a show," he said. Perry told him off with her eyes, annoyed that he was interrupting us while I let out a sigh of relief.

Show...show...how could there even be a show?

"Dex," Maximus said in a warning voice, "you look a little ill. Is that headache coming back again?"

Thank you, you ginger son of a bitch, I thought. I nodded, playing it up. "Yeah, ever since that hypnosis, I just feel so off."

"You're stressed," he said, his voice dropping a register. "You're probably overthinking things. Remember what Maryse told you. To be kind to yourself and relax."

Perry's eyes were volleying between the two of us. Now I could see she was doubly suspicious, not only at the mention of hypnosis, but the fact that Maximus and I were talking pleasantly to each other.

"I get it, fuck face," I told him for effect. Then I flicked my cigarette over the railing and came back inside, leaving Perry bewildered in a cloud of smoke.

He was right though. Once I was able to push through the nagging pain in my heart, my gut that twisted from anxiety, I could see that we did have a good show. You could see Tuffy G as he came at me in the attic too, only in the darkness his features didn't come out too well. That was just as well since Maximus had to remind us that it was a crime scene now and if any of the NOPD came across the video it would look pretty suspicious if they could ID Tuffy in the shots. In fact, to play it extra safe, we decided we wouldn't show full exteriors of the house, just in case someone recognized it as the house that burned down. Inside it was too dark and old to really tell where it was.

We went through the footage a few more times. If I'd been feeling like myself, I would have been extremely pissed off that Maximus was calling all the shots, even with shit such as editing and the music, which was one hundred percent supposed to be my duty. We might have gone to the same film school, but he really didn't know shit when it came to these kinds of shows.

I was about to remind him of that when his phone went off.

"Rose?" he said, answering it. I could hear her squawking through his speaker. He nodded quickly a few times before saying, "Okay, we'll be right there" and hanging up.

"What was that?" Perry asked. She was sitting on the bed and had drawn her knees up to her chest in worry. She looked so fucking cute. I had to mentally kick myself.

"That was Rose," he said getting up, his tall, wide frame seeming to fill the whole room. "She's swinging by here to pick us up. Apparently Ambrosia was attacked by a zombie a little while ago."

"What?" Perry and I both asked in unison.

He grabbed his camera, pulling the memory card out from the computer and sticking it back in. "Let's go."

~

Rose must have been nearby because as soon as Perry was

dressed and able to smudge on only the tiniest bit of makeup, the truck was roaring up Royal Street.

Once we were in and bouncing along the rough roads of the Quarter, she told us that Ambrosia had gone to the nearest supermarket, just off the 10, for Maryse's groceries. She said she was attacked in the parking lot, the man able to take a bite out of her. She said he looked disheveled, like a homeless person, and white. Passerby restrained the man and police had him in custody. They were blaming it on bath salts.

Ambrosia didn't have the luxury of a private room, and was the only patient in there who looked to be not half-dead or dying.

Still, even in a blue hospital gown with her neck bandaged up, she looked utterly radiant. Her bed was by the window, and the sunlight filtering in made her dark hair shimmer with strands of copper and gold, her lips soft and shiny. She looked like an angel. I felt terrible for even considering that Ambrosia had been behind any of this, and even worse that I put that idea in Maryse's head.

"Hey y'all," she said to us, tilting her head, her light eyes sparkling beneath her dark lashes.

"Hey," I said, coming toward her. Her skin looked so soft and touchable. She smiled at me, and it reached so far into me it was doing something to my dick.

She smiled at Perry and Maximus as well, offering them the same warmth she was offering me. Only Rose got a colder reception, even though she was leaning over Ambrosia in honest concern.

"How are you feeling, does it hurt?" Rose asked.

Ambrosia shook her head. "No, not really. They gave me some form of morphine, so I'm feeling fine."

"I hope that doesn't scar your beautiful neck," I found

myself saying, gesturing to where the bandage was, between her ear and her shoulder.

Perry was staring at me, open-mouthed, and Rose shot me a perplexed look but I didn't care. Why were they so uptight? She had a beautiful neck, and it would be a shame to have it forever damaged by the undead.

"I hope so too, dawlin'," Ambrosia said sweetly to me. Her lids fluttered seductively and I felt warmth spreading from my heart outward. It was a feeling I wanted to hold on to, one that erased all worry and pain. I found myself gazing deep into her eyes as she said, "If I'd known you were coming, Dex, I would have made myself pretty for you."

I smiled. "You're already so beautiful."

"Dex!" Perry growled at me, kicking my leg. I barely looked at her, I couldn't. I could only see Ambrosia.

"Oh, that's right," Ambrosia said. "I'm sorry, Perry. I forgot that the two of you are together. You just don't seem like you're together. My mistake."

"Oh, fuck you," Perry snarled at her. "I've dealt with enough women like you to not believe a word you say."

Everyone jerked in shock at her words, including me. Perry turned to me and said, "And fuck you too, asshole. I should have figured you'd get bored with me so fast."

Then she spun around and marched out of the hospital room.

My eyes were wide, my heart pounding, pinching. What the fuck just happened?

Rose was staring at me in disgust. She turned to Ambrosia. "I'm going to go check on her. Why don't you tell the boys what happened."

She ran out of the room and Ambrosia shrugged. "We'll, she's a bit uptight. That's the problem with dating young girls, Dex. They don't know how to be in relationships."

What she was saying was kind of true. Her eyes were steady on mine and I felt myself nodding. But still, part of me was in agony, somewhere deep inside. I shook my head slightly and tried to focus. My hand went to the vial of oil in my pocket and I began rubbing it.

Ambrosia frowned at me but then turned her mega-watt smile to Maximus, who was gazing at her like I knew I had been. Jesus, I needed to get a hold of myself.

Ambrosia told us about what happened, and her surprise that it was a white guy. She heard through the police officer that booked the guy that he was completely deranged and had been reported missing from his family a few days ago. Although a few days ago, he was an upstanding family man with no history of mental illness. The cops were also unable to find any traces of bath salts, but they did find a low amount of Datura. The very extract that the Bokors would control their zombies with.

Soon after the nurse came in, wanting to give her another round of antibiotics to heal her wound, and Maximus and I were asked to leave.

"That was weird," he whispered to me as we walked down the hospital halls, looking for Rose and Perry.

"What was? The zombie attack in broad daylight, in a parking lot, by a white upstanding family dude?"

"That," he said slowly, "and also Perry."

"What about her?"

He swung his arms. "I don't know. It's like she totally overreacted over nothing."

Was it nothing? And wasn't this what he wanted?

"Let me deal with her," I told him.

The reception we got at the truck was Antarctic chilly. Rose was being curt with me, and Perry wouldn't even look my way. To make matters worse, Maximus was insistent that we stop at a crab shack he remembered, an authentic old thing on stilts. The view was terribly romantic as we took a seat on the patio overlooking the rippling bayou, the breeze warm and humid, the fishing boats zipping past in the distance. We ate out of perforated red plastic dishes, our crab and crayfish wrapped in greasy newspaper, drinking beer and sweet tea out of Mason jars. It was such a quintessential Louisiana moment for me, and yet I couldn't enjoy a single second of it. I fought hard to keep my mind off of Ambrosia and onto Perry, which was something I didn't want to do. Thinking about Ambrosia was easy, inviting almost, while thinking about Perry made me ache inside. It made my world spin, my hurt spasm, my lungs seize up, my guts freefall. Looking at her, thinking about her, just tore me apart. She was a dream that was seconds from becoming a nightmare, a present that was about to be taken back.

I dealt with it the only way I knew how—I drank myself into a bit of a stupor, hoping to numb the pain, the questions, the answers. When we were dropped off at the B&B, I felt like roaming the streets of the quarter, looking for my next drink, my next way out. I didn't want to go into our room, I didn't want to deal with her, with anything. But I had to.

I wasn't in the room for more than five seconds before Perry slammed it, locked it, and put her hands on my chest and shoved me backward.

"What the fuck is wrong with you?" she yelled, her eyes up in flames, her voice raw with anger.

I let her push me. I didn't fight back. I looked at the floor and gathered my strength to know what I had to do. If Perry and I could never be, if being with her would possibly one day hurt her, kill her, I couldn't do this to the both of us. I couldn't keep loving her, being with her, not like this.

I was dying inside and she had no idea. I couldn't let her see. Our world had changed on us and so damn fast.

I ignored her violence toward me and sat down on the bed, kicking off my shoes. She came right around in my face.

"Why are you ignoring me? What did I do?"

"Just chill out," I told her, giving her a dirty look. "You made a fool of yourself earlier."

She gasped. Her face flinched like I'd just slapped her. I wanted to cry.

"You asshole! You...oh, how dare you! You were flirting with her right in front of my face. How do you think that makes me feel?"

I shrugged, all forced casualness. "I don't know. You flip out and get insecure over everything. How am I supposed to know what's going to set you off?"

She shoved me again, and I reached up and grabbed her wrists, holding them between my fingers.

"Stop hitting me, you're acting like you're crazy," I told her.

And now she was crumbling. "What happened to you, Dex? Yesterday we were fine, everything was fine. What happened? What changed?"

"You changed," I said, turning it around. "You need to get over your issues."

Another invisible blow. She nearly keeled over. I knew where I was hurting her because I was hurting there too.

"Issues?"

"Kiddo, we both have them in spades."

"Don't call me that." Her voice went all steel, cold and sharp.

"What? Kiddo? Perry, I have a whole arsenal of names here I could call you, but I don't think you'd like those either."

Her eyes blazed as she leaned forward, getting in my face. "I'm not some kid, I'm your girlfriend, and I'm trying to talk to you."

"You are just a kid!" I yelled back, surprised at how caught up I was getting. I just wanted to push her away, just a bit, just to give me the space and time and distance to think things through. But now I felt like everything was coming out, all the things I kept to myself. There was no stopping it.

I pushed off the bed and began fumbling in my pockets for the cigarettes. I brought them out, the bag shaking in my hands, until Perry came over and struck them out of my grasp. They scattered on the floor.

"You think I'm just a kid?" she screeched.

"You're twenty-three."

"So what?" she spat out. "I was twenty-two when we met. You knew that about me. What changed?"

"You're not ready for this with me."

"Ready for what? For you flirting blatantly with women right in front of me? For you turning off like a light switch, ignoring me, pulling out of this relationship before it even got started?"

The madness was taking over, the rush of rage saturating my veins. I whirled around and screamed at her, "You won't even tell me you love me! Don't you dare say I'm turning off like a light switch, because I have been the only one who's been on since this thing began. You're the one who has been holding back. You're the one who lets me bleed out in front of you!"

Her lips snapped shut, her face going white. She stepped away from me, facing the wall, her head down. I was breathing hard, wishing I hadn't gotten so deep, wishing that I could take her in my arms and make all of this go away. But that wouldn't stop the hurt that would follow. The future that would crumble. We had no other choice.

"I need time," she whispered, her words breaking.

I swallowed painfully, trying to keep my own tears at bay. I took in a deep breath, shaking out my arms, hoping my feelings would go out with it.

I put on a fake smile and said, "Well, guess what, baby, now you have all the time in the world."

Her whole body shook from my words, as if they were metal knives I'd driven into her body. I realized I was holding my breath, my lungs screaming for air.

She slowly turned her head to look at me. She looked beyond devastated. Beyond hurt. Beyond everything I never dreamed of doing to her. I was so close to losing her and I was so close to keeping her.

"Fine," she said hoarsely. "I understand. I'm going to go get another room for myself here."

"Good idea," I said. The words just came. I regretted each of them.

She walked toward the door, trying to keep her head up, trying to keep from collapsing. She was trying to be strong, to be proud, to know what was going on and to know what she was going to do next.

She paused near the door, and I swore if she decided to stay, I'd tell her everything. I'd burden her with my burden if only not to do this to each other, to not make each other bleed.

You've fucked up again, Perry told herself, her thoughts coming through loud and clear. *You have the only person you ever wanted and you fucked it up again because you can never let yourself be happy. Dex will never take you back after this, and you'll never know what it's like to love him while he loves you.*

Her self-loathing for herself hurt me down to the bones.

She stared at me for a few moments, maybe hoping she could voice what she was thinking, maybe hoping that I would say something too. Two stubborn people clinging on to what they believed was right. She felt she never deserved me. I felt she didn't deserve to suffer.

I'm doing this because I love you, I thought, hoping to God that maybe she could hear me.

But she just walked out the door and closed it behind her. I collapsed to the ground, a ruin in her wake.

15

I woke up again in the middle of night, feeling like Perry was shaking me awake, whispering my name in my ear. But when I came to and sat up slowly, I realized I was alone. Perry had gotten her stuff and moved down to a room on the first floor. I didn't have her anymore. I had nobody.

I glanced at the radio alarm clock in the room. It was 3AM. I wasn't surprised at all. The room was pitch black; even the light from the street wasn't reaching through the curtains that hung there on the French doors like dead weight. All the furniture in the room sat there, hunched over like big black beasts, waiting for me to move, to say something.

The door to the bathroom slowly creaked open. I heard the shower curtain inside being moved along the bar, the metal rungs squeaking.

I sat up straighter and looked at the clock again. 3:01. Time was passing. I pinched the inside of my forearm to see if it hurt, to see if it was a dream or not. It did hurt. My heart hurt even more. The memories of the fight between Perry and I came flooding back. I did the thing I never thought I'd do—I hurt her on purpose. It didn't matter that it was for her greater good or my greater good because there just couldn't be any good in it. The pain was there, just below the threshold, threatening to bring me under. I pushed her away and I would continue to push her away until I knew she could be saved, until I knew she'd get the future she deserved, not the one that I couldn't give her.

It was because I was so lost in my misery, in my chest-stabbing despair, that I knew I wasn't dreaming. And I was so wrapped up in my own pain, my own horror, that the current one before me didn't seem to matter that much.

That was until the bathroom door swung open fully and a giant motherfucking black python came slithering out of it, heading straight for my bed.

Fuck. That was a new one.

I held my breath, wondering if I should scream, wondering how much I was seeing was real and how much was magic. How much was my mind and how much was the beyond. The gigantic inky black snake disappeared under the bed and I tensed up, waiting, knowing it wouldn't just go to sleep under there.

Fuck, fuck, fuck.

"Li Grand Zombi," a French-accented voice said from the bathroom. I looked up to see my mother climbing out of the mirror and balancing on the sink, before stepping awkwardly to the ground. She moved with unpredictable jerkiness, as if she wasn't used to the body she was in. She was no longer in the mirror. She was free.

I wished I was wearing Depends.

The bed beneath me moved ever so slightly. I got into a crouch, ready to spring off it and run if I needed to.

"Li Grand Zombi," my mother said again, stepping

forward. In the blackness I could only make out the paleness of her taut face, the darkness of her hair and eyes. I couldn't even be sure that she had eyes. "The Great Serpent."

"What do you want from me?" I asked, but my words came out in a shaking whisper, the air from my breath freezing into a cloud.

"It travels between both worlds, from the Kalunga to here, through the layers, through the Veil, just like me," she continued. Her voice had grown lower and lower with each word she spoke until it was something entirely inhuman. "Together, we will bring you back."

From the corner of my eye I could see the shiny black head of the python appear over the edge of the mattress, its long forked tongue slithering in and out.

I dared to look the woman in the eye as she came closer still. I dared to eke out the words, "You are not my mother. I don't know who you are."

She smiled, black teeth. "I was your mother. Then she died. But I am a part of you."

The mattress began to sink under the python's weight as it undulated across the bed. Now if I were to make a run for it, I'd have to jump over its body.

"How long did you have possession of her?" I asked the creature that wasn't my mother.

She shook her head. "I was always there. I am in you." She took another jagged step until she was at the foot of the bed. I could have sworn the shape of her head was expanding, that protrusions were rising out of her temples, a growing monster in the dark. Every single cell in my body told me to look away, to get away while I could. This wasn't my mother. This wasn't any one thing. This was evil incarnate and it had come for me. She extended an arm out to me and instead of pale, wrinkled skin, I could see short, dense fur. Her fingernails were now talons. "Come with us. Come to where you belong."

This couldn't be happening. This couldn't be happening. This couldn't be happening. This all had to be in my head, in my sick fucking head full of my sick fucking problems. I wasn't on medication. I didn't have that wall between reality and the world beyond. Nothing was being kept out anymore.

I shut my eyes, closing them so tight I saw red stars and dots behind them, and though about what Maryse had told me. *The energies shared and exchanged can cause ripples, holes in the fabric of the Veil, and where there are holes, bad things can get out.*

There were two bad things in the room with me, two bad things that had gotten out. Me and Perry together had produced so much pleasure and love and comfort and bliss, and all the while our radiance was letting the bad things in. The universe had to balance things, didn't it? How dare it just let two long-suffering people be happy for once.

I kept my eyes shut and chanted to myself, "You aren't real, you're in my head, you're not real, you're in my head," but the truth was I didn't know if I believed that anymore. For all I knew, everything could be real from here on out.

Even so, it was like my chanting, my concentration, had caused the energy in the room to shift. It felt like the room had grown still. It felt like the weight on the mattress had lifted. I couldn't hear the snake's tongue or breathing. I couldn't hear the rustle of my mother's nightgown. I heard only my heart, threatening to explode, my lungs wheezing from exertion.

I sucked in my breath for strength and prepared to open my eyes, hoping I'd see an empty room as it was before. I willed for the nightmare to be over, to be alone, to be safe, to see nothing at all.

I opened my eyes.

She was *right there*.

My mother's demon face, inches from mine. She had no eyes, just cavernous black holes, and skin that scaled like a lizard's. Her mouth was stuck open, a tiny red snake coming out of it in place of her tongue. Though her face was frozen in vile horror, she was laughing and screaming just inches away from me, sounds from another time and another place, sounds that reached through my ears and pierced my very human soul. There was nothing else inside me except fear and terror like I'd never known before.

The snake in her mouth came out for me, slowly, two yellow slits for eyes. It said, "I always wanted a grandson."

And that's when I finally screamed. I screamed bloody murder and tried to gather the strength to run out of the room.

In seconds, the door busted open and the light went on. It was a wild-eyed Maximus, staring at me in panic.

"What happened?" he asked, just in time to see the end of Li Grand Zombi's tail slither into the bathroom like a tapered black slug. The demonic entity of my mother had already disappeared with the light.

"Holy fuck!" he exclaimed, once he spotted the snake. He didn't run away though, he marched in, peering at the snake as the black tail completely disappeared around the bathroom door. He looked at me, motioning for me to stay put and asked, "Are you okay?'

"Do I look okay?" I asked, my body rapidly growing cold and starting to shake. "Go after it, but be careful."

He looked around for something sturdy and picked up an old lady-type vase, as if he was going to knock out the python by throwing ceramics on its head. This wasn't a caper film.

Armed with it, he went inside the bathroom and flicked on the lights. I heard him say, "Huh," and heard the opening and closing of cabinets and the toilet seat before he came back out.

"There's nothing in there," he said, putting the vase back down on the end table.

"But you did see the snake."

"I wish I hadn't." He suppressed a shiver. "What was it doing? What happened? I thought I heard voices in here, and just as I was about to fall back asleep, I heard you scream like...Jesus, Dex..."

I bit my lip while I debated sharing just how crazy I was. I decided to ask Maximus to hand me my cigarettes, then climbed back into bed and lit one. I explained what happened with the snake and my mother, what she said, what she looked like, and then went back to the first times I'd seen her in the mirror back in BC.

"It's getting worse," he remarked, and motioned for me to give him a cigarette too.

"Bunch of moochers," I muttered, but still lit one for him.

"So now do you see, even just a little, how the tears between the worlds could become worse when you and Perry are together? Just standing beside each other your energies attract amazing things, mainly malevolent things. Now...well, since you guys started screwing each other on a daily basis, that energy has multiplied. Your chemistry dissolves through walls and windows. You make a gate-keeper job much harder."

I ignored the screaming pain my chest. That urge to find Perry in her room and make the sweet love to her that I was so damn addicted to. It figured we would make and break worlds by our coupling, because damn, when I was deep in thrusts of our souls and hearts and bodies, it felt like something so much more.

It was going to fucking ruin me to never have that again.

"You're doing good, Dex," Maximus said, reading my face. "Maybe a little harsher than I'd be, but I guess Perry is the type of woman to try and fight for you anyway."

"Please," I croaked, the cigarette shaking in my hand. "I can't hear this anymore."

Maximus changed the subject. "So tell me about your mother. Why do you think it wasn't her? What was she?"

I shook my head sharply, not ready to go down that road at this time of night. "Something else I'd rather not talk about. Tell *me* something. Tell me about Rose."

His features froze, his skin turning pale so that every scattering of freckles stood out. Ah ha. Now here was the thing that Maximus didn't want to talk about. I didn't care though. If I had to deal with Perry and my dead mother, he was going to talk about Rose. There was a story there and I had to hear all of it. I was going to go Barbara Walters on his ginger ass whether he liked it or not.

I stared at him, prodding him with my eyes. He stared right back then sighed. He pulled up a chair to the side of the bed and sat down on it. It was only then that I realized he slept in a plaid pajama set, like a lumberjack Hugh Hefner. Figured.

"Rose..." He began, then puffed hard on the cigarette. "Rose was my next chance. After I screwed things up with you, I had to make good."

"Why? What happens otherwise, does someone come after you? Jacob PD?"

"In a way. We aren't really governed by anyone in particular, it's just kind of instinctual."

"So no one Jacobs the Jacobs?" I smirked.

"No. Not really. There is a network through the Veil; you'll get images, see people you're supposed to help. If you don't help them, the images become more vivid. You start to hear voices and you get this gut instinct that just tells you what to do. When I...when I decided I couldn't guide you in any way, I expected to get backlash from it. Maybe I'd get sick or something until I found you again. But I didn't...later I met another Jacob who explained the exception. I asked how he knew that—he just smiled and said he knew and that's all. So obviously I wasn't as in tune with my purpose as I thought, or...I don't know. Maybe I was forsaken."

We were getting off the topic of Rose, but I had to ask, "So where were you born, really?"

"I wasn't born."

"Okay, jackass. So when did you remember coming into existence? You must have had parents..."

He shook his head. "No parents. I just woke up one day in Louisiana, in a small apartment in Baton Rouge, in almost the same body I have right now. I knew who I was, what my purpose was, and I took it from there. It sounds crazy, and now that I know your world, it *is* crazy. But that's the only way I can explain it. Whoever I was before, I don't know. How long has this body been around? I don't know that either. But I do know I will die one day and this body will die with me. That's the one thing that hasn't changed."

This was just too fucking weird. Fucked up sprinkles on a slice of psycho shit cake. "Back to Rose..."

He cringed. "I tried to ignore Rose for as long as I could. After I left you, I went around the USA exploring for a bit. It was amazing, to just be living and not have any duties. I started to think that if I was forsaken or forgotten, that it would be okay. I'd be happy with that. I could live a free life like everyone else. But then the images started coming. I'd see Rose in my dreams, and hoooo-boy, I'd see her whole life flash before my eyes. Her as a young girl working on a farm, dancing with boys at high school parties, serving people at a bar. Then I started seeing the images in broad daylight, over and over again, and the Veil started ripping open and I knew that if I just walked through it, I'd be right there with her. That I had to show her the gifts she had, the gifts I could sense were starting to manifest. She had been seeing demons in the dark, things out of the corners of her eyes. Sometimes she'd be staring at a spot right before her, and I could see that demon as it made its way through the Veil and right to her feet. She knew something wasn't right, but she couldn't really see it. If only she knew what she could do to drive the demon back into the Veil. But she didn't. I had to teach her that."

"It travels between both worlds, from the Kalunga to here, through the layers, through the Veil, just like me," I said absently.

"What?"

"What my mother said to me, about the snake she called Li Grand Zombi."

He nodded. "Some things get through. And some people, like Rose, they have the ability to put them back."

"And now we're getting dangerously close to *Buffy the Vampire Slayer* territory," I said.

His lips jerked up in a quick smile. "Not quite. For one, we're missing a Giles."

"I guess you could be Giles now. You're getting old."

He glared at me. "I am. But it's still not funny."

"Back to Rose…"

"Back to Rose. So one day I just bit the bullet and stepped through, right into Nameless. I introduced myself to her and asked if they needed help. The universe makes things happen for us. I knew I'd get the job, like I've gotten most jobs."

"Like you did with Jimmy," I mused miserably.

"No, that was just good old-fashioned bribery," he admitted sheepishly. "I'm no longer a Jacob. I may have some supernatural....uh, aftertaste...but the rules don't apply to me anymore. I have to make things happen. The universe screws me over like it screws over everyone else." He sighed, sensing I was going to ask him to continue. "So I got the job and I began working with Rose, hoping she'd be a lot easier than you. And she was, at first. I reckon she almost knew I was coming, the way she just accepted things. I was working with her for at least a year before I got her tipsy one night and told her the truth. I took her to the Veil once, knowing she'd have more strength when she got back."

"Physical?" I asked, thinking about my own strength after I was sent in.

"A little bit physical, but mainly mental. When she came back out, she could see everything. It opened her mind. I helped her use that power to start sending demons back through when she saw them. She was able to. It takes a lot of thought and concentration from her but she can do it. Maybe not all the demons, but the ones she sees herself. Rose wasn't born here to save the world. She's just a helper, like so many others."

"Like me?" I asked.

"Dex, I didn't know what you were then and I still don't really know now."

"Some Giles you are," I grumbled. I stubbed the

cigarette on a bunch of change that had scattered across the bedside table. "But let's get down to what really happened. As fascinating as all this stuff is, it's still way over my head, and I don't think I'd even really understand this new... fucked up world...even if you drilled it into me day after day. So let's get to the thing you don't want to talk about. Let's talk about Rose. Why you left her. And when you became immortal." I was tempted to put air quotes around "immortal" but I knew all this shit actually was real.

He rubbed at his jaw, his stubble making a scratchy noise on his calloused fingers. "After Rose began to get the hang of things, I started getting flashes of someone else's life. Another girl. Young. But I didn't want to go. I'd fallen in love with Rose. We lived together. We spent all our time together. But the images wouldn't stop. I finally started seeing Mambo Maryse, hoping she could explain what was going on and what I could do about it. She said short of going rogue, there was nothing I could do. It was my duty and I had to move on.

Of course, I couldn't accept that. I couldn't just leave Rose, I loved Rose. I mean I *loved* her, Dex. More than anything in this world. You know what that's like."

I felt like my soul was being sliced open, piece by piece. I swallowed thickly and nodded.

He smiled sympathetically and continued, "So I looked into the whole going rogue thing. I told Rose about it and she agreed. It was the only way we could be together. Aside from the fact that I would forever be pulled to help someone else, there was the matter of what she and I did...together. You catch my drift? Just like with you and Perry, the more we were together, the more rifts opened. The more demons she'd have to put back. The more haunted she became. It was a lose-lose situation anyway. So I did it. I loved her enough to give up my immortality. To be able to die, to grow old. I gave it all up for her."

I sucked back on my lip, almost afraid for him to continue. "And?"

"And everything was fine, for about a year. And then we broke up."

"Why?"

He shrugged. "Nothing abnormal. She wanted to stay in New Orleans and work in the bar. I wanted to explore the world. She wanted kids one day. I wasn't sure what I wanted. She wanted to live a normal life—I was a constant reminder that her life was anything but normal."

"But you fought for her," I said. "You must have, if you loved her that much."

"I did. I did what I could. In the end, Rose called it off. She walked away. There was nothing I could do. I gave up immortality for her and she ended up breaking up with me anyway. How's that for the universe screwing you over? If that wasn't the perfect initiation into how fucked up this world can be, I don't know what is."

Fuck me. That was some heavy shit. No wonder the tension between the two of them was so damn loaded.

"How can you live with that...knowing what you gave up, to be able to live forever?"

He got out of his chair and stretched his arms above his head. "We all have to make sacrifices, Dex. To me, Rose was worth it."

"Is she still worth it?" I asked.

He smiled sadly. "I'll let you know. I think it's time for me to get some sleep. I thought we'd get some of the atmosphere shots tomorrow then start looking into flights home."

I nodded, my mind bombarded by questions and the competing need to sleep.

"Are you gonna be okay in here?" he asked, pausing by the door. "I can stay if you want me to. Hold your hand."

"Get the fuck out, ginger balls," I told him. But I managed to smile.

The door closed behind him and I was grateful that he left the light on. I lay back and tried to keep my eyes open for as long as I could, every sound making me jump in my skin, until the sounds no longer mattered and the questions went unanswered and my heart took a brief pause from bleeding. I was out.

16

"More coffee?" Maximus asked me, about to pour from the French press. Funny how life goes. Now I was eating breakfast with him, chatting over how much the Crescent City had changed over the years, while Perry was nowhere to be found.

Well, that wasn't true. She had stopped by Maximus's room in the morning before I woke up and told him she was going out on her own during the day and would text him later if he wanted to shoot a few scenes or do some voice-over work. The fact that she didn't speak to me at all, that she was out there avoiding me, that she was struggling with all the horrible shit I said to her last night, reopened that wound, rubbing salt right in it.

I nudged the coffee cup over to him, trying to bury my feelings deep down. The last thing I wanted was Maximus feeling sorry for me. I hated the fact that he knew what was going on, that he was the one who initiated it. You'd think that would have made me want to relate to him more, but all it did was make me resent him.

Of course, the situation between him and Rose was

devastating as anything, but as the terrors of the night faded away, I was left with my own hurt, my own hole I'd begun to dug, and someone else's sob story wasn't going to make me feel any better about myself. Besides, I kept thinking that if Maximus had truly loved her, he would have found a way to keep her. Didn't love truly conquer all? Although it certainly wasn't conquering shit for me.

I was just about to push my plate away and head back upstairs to the room when Rose appeared in the breakfast room doorway.

I smiled at her and gestured to Maximus. "He's almost done. He sure does eat a lot."

She didn't smile (not that I expected her to). "Actually, Dex, I'm here to see you. Do you mind coming for a walk with me?"

Maximus and I exchanged a quick look. I didn't know what Rose wanted, but if it was a private talk between the two of us, it couldn't be good. Private talks were bad news these days. I had a feeling she wanted to rip me a new one over the way I treated Perry, and as much as I deserved it, I really wasn't in the mood to feel worse about the situation.

"I'm not going to bite," she added, and then she smiled. I didn't trust her at all.

I looked down at Maximus. "If I'm not back in an hour..."

He rolled his eyes and went back to finishing his toast.

I tried to give Rose a carefree grin but failed. I was inexplicably nervous and followed her out of the B&B and onto Royal Street.

It was warm out, not as humid as yesterday, and the sun was just starting to push aside the low clouds. The air smelt damp and slightly like hot garbage, something I'd gotten used to.

I looked up and down the street. "Well, where to?"

"Wanna get the best Bloody Marys in town?" she asked.

"Is the Pope Catholic, and does he wear a funny hat and drive around in a Popemobile and live in Vatican City and—"

She raised her hand. "I get it, Dex."

We walked down Royal Street for a bit in silence.

"I hope you're not taking me to your bar, because I'm sorry, you don't put enough horseradish in your Bloody Marys. Ever try a Caesar? Now that's something you guys should be doing."

"No, it's not my bar," she said, and we took a left down a street until we ended up near a bustling restaurant by the river where a three-piece band was lazily playing in the shade.

We placed our order with the waiter and I asked her how Ambrosia was doing.

"She's fine," she said. "She got some shots for some diseases even though she was telling the doctor that she could concoct her own herbal solution. But you know western medicine. If you can't buy it from a pharmaceutical company, it doesn't work."

I nodded politely, waiting for her to jump on me about how horrible a person I was.

She cleared her throat. "Max called me this morning. He told me everything."

I winced, the sun coming out in full-strength and blinding me. "I see."

"I am so sorry," she told me, leaning forward. Even with the sun's glare in my eyes, I could see the sadness in her face, her grey-blue eyes mirroring my own. She really was a very pretty girl, her delicate doll-like features could have snared any man. I could see why Maximus had been so crazy about her, even more so when I remembered that she hadn't always been so hard.

"It's okay," I told her, smiling at the waiter when he brought us the Bloody Marys.

"It's not okay," she said with quiet anger. "How could it be okay? I can see how much you two love each other."

Oh, fucking ouch. That was an arrow to the chest. I tried to regain my breath and said, "I love her. She doesn't know how she feels about me."

"She loves you," she said simply. "Even if she won't admit it to herself, she does."

"And she told you this?"

"No, she hasn't. She doesn't have to. I just know."

"Well, Maximus never told me you were psychic," I said, and took a sip of the Bloody Mary. Salty, spicy, sweet—it was perfect. "Wow, that has been the best one so far."

Rose ignored me. "You're pretending like you can't do anything about it."

I looked at her sharply. "I can't do anything about it. Don't you fucking think I would if I could?"

She sat back in the seat and crossed her arms, examining her fingernails. "You're taking the easy road out. You're just giving up."

"I am not!" I yelled and pounded my fist on the table. The cutlery jumped. People turned and looked. I tried to rein it in.

She looked at me carefully. "Dex. I was stupid. I gave up. I thought I couldn't live a life with Max because he'd remind me that I wasn't normal. Then I lived a life without Max and realized it was much, much worse. Max kept me normal. He kept me sane. He loved me. And I loved him just as much. I fooled myself into thinking I was being noble and making a sacrifice so that I could have a better life. It didn't work that way. I should have held on to him. I should have compromised. I should have made it work. The alternative has torn me apart."

I sucked in a sharp breath through my teeth. She didn't understand; it wasn't the same. "If I go with Perry, she may die. If she ever gets pregnant, it could kill her."

She shrugged. "So then adopt if you want children."

"That's not the point," I said, glaring at her glibness. "The two of us together, we create fucking holes in the universe. We'll make things worse for each other and for other people."

She tilted her chin down. "I saw more demons and more ghosts when I was with Max. I'd rather live my whole life with them everywhere I turn than live this one without him in it."

"There would be so many consequences," I added.

"And what about the consequences of you not being together? This isn't your decision alone, Dex. If you want to really be selfless and noble here, you'll have to tell her. Acting like an asshole isn't going to explain anything. Your Perry, she's been through a lot with you. She deserves more than this."

"If she knew...what if she'd want to get pregnant, just to prove a point?"

"Is that really what she'd do?" she asked carefully. "Or is that just what other people are afraid of?"

I mulled on that, sitting back in my seat. I took a long suck of the Bloody Mary, hoping the vodka would go to work a little faster.

"Don't let other people tell you how well you know someone," she added. "Don't let other people, no matter who they are, decide what happens to your life and hers.

You will live a lifetime of regret if you let others influence your decisions. Believe me."

I eyed her. "So then, who influenced yours?"

She looked down at her hands. "Maryse."

Now it was starting to make sense. Why she broke up with him. Why she walked away.

"Then why don't you and Max try and make it work now? You're here. He's here. You still love him, don't you?"

She smiled softly but it never reached her eyes. "Some risks get scarier as you get older. The less you have to lose, the less you want to try."

"So there's no hope."

"Sugar, we'd be dead *without* hope."

I sighed, feeling like we'd just gone around in a circle.

"What a bunch of fucked up, lovelorn, ghost-seeing shit-burgers we are," I said.

"Don't forget crazy," she added.

"That is forever and always a given, sweetie."

She sipped on her drink, her nose scrunching up at the clump of horseradish I saw get sucked up her straw. I started thinking it was nice that Rose pulled me aside to discuss my love life without trying to make me feel shitty, that she was so concerned about Perry and I to do so.

Then I could see the uncomfortable look on her face, even when the horseradish was long gone, and I knew that wasn't the real reason why she took me all the way out here to have a drink. There was something else.

"What is it?" I asked wryly.

"It's Maryse, actually," she admitted. "I'm worried about her. She feels like the whole zombie thing, that they'd be going after her next. That she's being targeted and will end up a sacrifice."

I hated to sound callous, but in the grand scheme of my personal situation, I could only say, "So?"

"So, I believe her. I think that whoever is raising the dead, they are doing it to show off, to show how much power they have. But they can't keep it up forever. They're going to need more and more power, and the only way to do that is through sacrifice. Chickens and snakes, they won't work in the long run. The person will start going after people with power, people like Maryse."

"Isn't she already hexed anyway?" I pointed out, remembering the creepy poppet in her lair with the nail driven through it.

"I think she is, but I think her weakness is being done remotely. They aren't cursing her to take power from her, they're cursing her so she can't get involved, so she can't fight back. They will want her in the end. And I think the end is near."

"Very dramatic."

"We're talking about the living dead here, Dex. It's going to be dramatic."

"So what are you going to do?" I asked. *Because we're all getting the fuck out of here*, I continued in my head.

"What can I do? This is the occult, a different type of supernatural. I'm not magical like they are. I can't do hoodoo or hexes or raise the dead. I can't do anything."

"Shouldn't you at least be keeping an eye on Maryse then? Surely you could have told me all this shit over the phone. Or better, by email."

She shook her head. "Ambrosia is with her now. The doctor's sent her home."

"Already?"

"I told you, she has her own ways of getting better."

She probably just flashed the doctors her gorgeous smile and that was it, I thought, feeling weird about it. I eyed Rose, who was staring at the live band. *We play for tips*, their cardboard sign said.

"Do you...do you trust...Ambrosia?" I asked, even though my words had trouble getting past my lips. Damn, was I drunk already?

"Of course I do," she said absently, her attention still on the band.

"I was under the impression that you didn't really like her."

"Ambrosia Paris?" Rose asked in an odd voice. She turned around to face me, a wide smile on her lips. It was so out of place on Rose, it looked kind of creepy. "Everyone loves Ambrosia. How could they not? I do. And I know you do and Maximus does and Perry does."

Okay, so Rose wasn't as perceptive as I once thought. To be safe, I reached into my pocket and started rubbing the now greasy Van Van oil bottle on my fingers.

"Listen," Rose went on. "I was wondering if maybe you'd help me get to the bottom of this. All of you. At least make an attempt before y'all go. I've got a few guns in my truck now. Why don't the four of us go to Treme tonight and see if we can find any zombies. If we can find them, we might be able to find the ritual scene. If we find the scene, we might find the person responsible."

"That sounds like a *terrible* idea."

She looked at me with pleading eyes. "Come on, Dex. I know this is driving you crazy too."

"Actually, I have other things to worry about."

"But maybe you're only worrying because you're being forced to. Maybe you're not thinking clearly because of what's going on around us. Don't you feel it? That feeling things are being controlled around us, like there's a heaviness in the air we're breathing?"

"I think that's called humidity."

"And then there are your dreams on top of everything."

I looked at her sharply while my heart skipped a bit. "My dreams?"

"Maximus told me. And he told me he saw it too. Li Grand Zombi. Dex, if you see that again, you're in a bad place. You're lucky that didn't try and drag you to the Kalunga with it."

"Kalunga," I said. "That's the word my mother used."

"It's Kongonese. And it means the Veil. Where your mother, where these spirits are coming from. This isn't a coincidence. Whoever is creating these zombies, they are fucking with us, pardon my French. They are conjuring up these spirits for us, to terrify us, maybe destroy us. Maybe to get us weak enough for a sacrifice."

"But I saw my mother before I got here."

"And now she's getting a little extra help to step through. Next time, you might not be so lucky."

I rubbed at my forehead and glared at my Bloody Mary. Stupid reality was still here, loud and clear.

"Please, Dex," she asked. And then I had to ask myself why she wanted to do this so badly and how much I actually trusted Rose.

I gave her a noncommittal smile. "Let's go see what the others say."

∼

"Fuck no," Perry said, shaking her head vehemently. It was the first time I'd seen her all day, and I hadn't even said hello before Rose bombarded her and Maximus in the lobby as they flipped through magazines, waiting for us.

Maximus seemed on the fence. "It's risky, even if we don't find anything. You know how bad the neighborhoods are. The chances of us getting carjacked are extremely high."

"And that's why we have guns," Rose said brightly.

I looked over my shoulder at the receptionist who was pretending not to listen to us. She was doing a bang-up job, rubbing oil into the leaves of her plastic houseplant.

"Okay, I'll go," Maximus said, obviously wanting to make Rose happy. But that wouldn't do if Perry wasn't coming.

"You guys are crazy," Perry muttered. I was staring at her, begging her to meet my eyes, but she looked everywhere else except my direction.

"Wait a minute," I said, stepping into the middle of the room and raising my hands. "I'm not leaving Perry here by herself."

"I'll be fine," she muttered. "Why do you care anyway?"

"Really?" I asked, feeling like I was about to get sucked into something I couldn't get out of.

Maximus picked up on it and quickly said, "Then I'll stay with Perry. You and Rose go together."

Rose and I eyed each other. She looked a lot happier than I knew I did.

"Uh, thank you Maximus," I told him. Perry sighed but I could tell she was relieved. I wanted to know if I was the only one who'd seen crazy shit in the last twenty-four hours. I wanted to ask her what she was so afraid of. I wanted to talk to her, to hold her, touch her, love her. Last night was the first night I'd slept away from her in weeks and it was already killing me inside, feeling like a million years had already passed between us. I couldn't let it be like this.

I looked to Rose. "So when should we leave?"

"Well, I'll go back to my place and get some stuff together. I'll pick you up around 5PM, just before darkness falls."

"Should I bring anything?" I asked.

"Just your sanity," she said. "And your camera, just in case."

I watched as Rose left the lobby, and when I turned around, Perry had gotten up and was making her way across the lobby to her room.

Maximus caught me staring and grabbed my arm. "Let her be, she'll be fine."

"I know. But I won't." I ripped my arm out of his grasp and went down the hall after her. She was almost in her room, the door just closing, until I stuck my foot out and wedged it in the space between.

"Perry, please," I said.

She glared at me from the door, trying to close it shut. "Go away."

"I won't. And you know I can break this door down if I have to."

"Then I'll yell for help."

"Why? Who is going to help you? Help, help, my boyfriend is trying to talk to me?"

"Dex," she warned.

"I just want to talk to you. Give me two minutes of your time. I promise. Then I'll leave. Or you can scream."

She thought about it, her eyes displaying a wealth of emotions that I was itching to get to the bottom of. And while she thought, while she was looking away, I took in the rest of her—her lips that she was rubbing against each other in worry, the delicate definition of her collarbone as it stood out above her square-necked tank top, the curve of her breasts, her little waist that was hidden somewhere in the breezy folds of clothing. I wanted nothing more than to kiss her hard as fuck, throw her on the bed, and devour her from head to toe. Tell her I loved her, that I'd always love her, and I wasn't about to give up on us. I'd tell her the truth, I'd tell her everything. I'd share my burden with her and decide on our future together.

But she looked back at me and I knew it wouldn't happen. I couldn't say a thing.

"I'm sorry, Dex. I can't."

The wall was back up. She took her heart back. Maybe I never even had it to begin with.

In a daze, I removed my foot from the door and she closed it in my face. I stood there outside of it, listening, hoping I could hear more, that she'd come out and see me again and let me explain. But I too was afraid to talk, too afraid to hear the answer.

"Dex," I heard Maximus whisper from down the hall. I turned and looked. He was waiting at the stairs, looking pretty pleasant considering the circumstances. I had to wonder if he was enjoying this, that Perry and I were as miserable now as he and Rose were. If this all came down to one-upmanship in the end, if we were doing it even now. I had to wonder what Maximus and Perry talked about in the lobby while Rose and I were gone. I bet it wasn't anything close to the truth.

I wiggled my jaw, trying to disperse some of the anger that wanted to come out. Now wasn't the time. If he said something to her to make her hate me even more, I'd find out about it. I couldn't even like that damned ginger for more than a day.

I walked toward him, balling my hands into fists.

"What is it, fire pubes?"

He grimaced. "Dex, grow up."

"Oh I can see it's worked out real well for you."

He muttered something to himself that sounded like "back to crazy" and then headed up the stairs. "I just want to make sure you're taking the right equipment with you. I'll be staying behind so I can't help you once you're out there."

And now I was wondering if Maximus was staying behind because he really was worried about Perry, or because he just wanted to plant more lies in her ears about why she and I weren't meant to be.

I missed the days when I wasn't so paranoid. I missed a lot of things.

"Dex?"

"Hmmm," I grunted.

He stopped outside his room and put his hand on my shoulder. "Thank you for going with Rose. I know this is important to her."

I grunted again. "I hope I can trust her."

He took his hand away and frowned at me. "Rose?"

"Yeah. Considering I'm heading into one of the worst neighborhoods in the city, let alone the country, with a nutso Southern girl carrying a bunch of guns, who wants to hunt down some zombies, yeah I really hope I can trust her. Well, can I?"

He nodded grimly. "I'd trust her with my life. I'm sure she'd be no different with yours."

Great.

17

"You know, I appreciate how fast we're racing around here, but I think if you want to see some zombies, you're going to have to drive just a tiny bit slower," I said to Rose. "It's not like zombies are known for being Olympic sprinters."

We'd been driving around Treme and some other inner city ghetto that Rose had dubbed "No Man's Land" for about an hour. Despite her guns in the crew cab, she was playing it extremely safe, which meant driving fast and running every single stop sign or red light. She said the minute we slowed down or stopped was the minute we were car-jacked, which I thought might be a slight exaggeration. That was until I think we witnessed a robbery at a 7-Eleven and a drug deal dispute that spilled out onto the road, guns blazing, and I realized that it was good that Rose was erring on the side of caution.

Still, if she really thought we were going to find any zombies, we'd need to go a bit slower.

"Fine," she said, but didn't let up on the gas. "I'm not getting a bad vibe here anyway."

"You're not? Because the minute I see people waving guns in public, I know the vibe ain't good."

She glared at me, her eyes flashing orange and grey in the passing streetlights, her hair taking on the color of a creamsicle. "Supernatural vibe. Don't you ever pick up on that?"

"I did earlier in the week," I admitted. "Guess I just haven't been paying attention lately."

"Well, I reckon whatever we're looking for we would have picked up on already. Let's just head back to the Quarter."

I exhaled in relief. That sounded like a plan. Each minute we were away, I felt like Perry was being taken further and further from me. It had taken so much to get her to open up as much as she did, to let herself be vulnerable with me, and now I was afraid that door was closing and I'd never get that chance again. Yes, it was all of my doing but I couldn't help but go over what Rose had said earlier, that it wasn't over unless I let it be.

"Thinking about Perry?" Rose asked after a few minutes.

I stared at the window, at the darkness that did all but swallow the abandoned vehicles, the splintering houses, the people who watched the street with angry eyes waiting for an excuse to let the world know how pissed off they were at the shit hands they were dealt.

"I'm always thinking about her," I said.

"Dex," she began, maybe another reminder that love was worth fighting for, maybe another condolence. But it sounded like her words were getting strangled in her throat. I turned to look at her, concerned. She was staring straight ahead of her, eyes wide, mouth open in surprise.

In our hurry to get back to the Quarter, she had pulled the truck down a long, dark street where low cars weren't loitering and people weren't yelling. I guess hoping to bypass the worst area and cut through to one of the main drags.

But this street wasn't as harmless or as abandoned as it looked. At the very end of it, near the lights and bustling traffic of the main thoroughfares, there was a mob of people standing in the middle of the road. There looked to be about twenty or thirty of them, but they were too far away to make out any individual features. At the moment they just seemed to be standing there, swaying back and forth on their feet. A group of people waiting for something.

"Neighborhood watch meeting?" I asked, though I was getting this particularly unsettling feeling, like my scalp was prickling.

"I don't think so, sugar," Rose said uneasily and slowed the truck down. "I reckon we better turn around."

"Good idea," I said. She checked in the rear view mirror to make sure no one was behind us, and was about to turn the wheel when suddenly the truck sputtered and rolled to a stop, halfway across the shoddily-painted dividing lane.

"The hell?" she cried out, slamming down on the gas. The pedal flopped under her weight. The truck had completely died, lights dimming down to nothing. She frantically tried the ignition, but the key wouldn't even turn. "Shit, sorry, but shit, shit, shit!"

My heart had finagled its way out of my chest and up to my throat. I kept my eyes on the mob in front of us, watching them as closely as I could. At the moment they were too far away to be a threat, whoever they were and whatever they were doing. But if the truck didn't start soon, we were going to get noticed. And if we got noticed by this mob in one of the New Orleans' ghettos, I had a feeling things were going to get real ugly.

"What's wrong with it?" I asked her, afraid to look away, afraid that if I did, the people would somehow notice. At least the headlights were off now. "Does this always happen when you're in immediate danger?"

"I don't know!" She began pounding her hand on the wheel in anger. "I don't know, it's never done this. It's just dead. Shit!"

"Okay," I said slowly. So far the group of people were staying put, maybe not even facing our direction. Perhaps luck was on our side. "Do you know anything about cars?"

She gave me a disgusted look and quickly opened the door, hopping out of her seat and going for the hood. I jumped out too, the air cooler now and slightly damp. Though the houses on either side of the street were derelict and abandoned, I felt like a million eyes were watching me. That uneasy feeling on the back of my head slowly extended down my neck, down my spine, tickling my ass and balls.

"Do you have any experience at this?" Rose asked as she popped the rusty hood. I winced at the jagged noise she was creating and looked again to see if the crowd of people had noticed. They were still standing there, not moving, swaying like reeds in a light breeze.

"I have no idea how to fix it, if that's what you're asking," I told her. "But a similar thing happened to me in New Mexico once."

"Yeah, and?"

"I think it was the work of a few evil shamans." I quickly glanced at her. The realization spread across her face. Of course this wasn't her dependable truck just randomly malfunctioning. This was the work of a Bokor. Which meant...

Her eyes flew to the crowd at the end of the street. "I *really* hope those are your average shoot-em-up thugs."

As if they'd heard her, the crowd began to move. It took us a few seconds, squinting at their dark forms against the blackened street, to figure out if they were coming toward us or not. They were coming toward us. And quite fast. They weren't Olympic sprinters, but they might pace well in a marathon.

"Get in the car," Rose said quietly. "Now."

She slammed down the hood and we jumped in the front seats as she tried the ignition again and slammed her foot down on the gas, pumping it. Like before, there was nothing. And now the mob of people was only a few yards away.

"Are those zombies or real people?" I cried out. "Zombies or real people?"

"I don't know," she whimpered. But I knew she did. Now that they were closer, I could make out their shapes and faces. Their expressions. They were mainly bigger-framed black men, though there were a few white derelicts sprinkled in there, the types with crazy tattoos on their faces, stained wife beaters and meth-crazed eyes. People that no one would care about if they went missing or ended up dead. People who would have people spitting on their graves. Expendable members of society.

They all looked absolutely insane. They faces held no humanity. They were drooling, with snapping teeth and outstretched arms. Just like the zombies of your nightmares. Only these were much, much worse. Because this group moved in tandem, in unison, like a flock of evil birds, and they could be quick when they wanted to be. They had already started to run.

I could see Rose was about to abandon ship and make a

run for it, but that would have been certain death as well. I grabbed her arm to hold her, and panicking, said, "Let me try the car."

I put my hand on the key, and concentrating as much as I could, hoping that somewhere inside of me I could fight back against what was being done to me, to us, that if I had this power it could be used for *something*, I turned it.

The car started with a roar. The lights went on.

And Slayer's "Dead Skin Mask" came blaring out of the speakers, as if we were listening to that song at high volume just before the truck died.

Rose let out a whoop of joy and immediately slammed the car into reverse, hitting the gas hard. We lurched forward in our seats, my hands crammed against the dashboard to prevent my head from going through the glass, and Rose whipped it around so we were going in the opposite direction.

Right into another car.

It clipped the front of the truck, Rose's side, and then we spun around in a three-sixty before we slammed into the side of telephone pole. My head knocked against Rose's, and then the door and everything went a sickly shade of red.

Slayer shut off.

I thought I was out for maybe a few seconds. My head hurt in two places, where I hit Rose and where I hit the window. I winced and looked up, the window totally cracked. I touch my temple and looked at my hand. My fingers were covered in sticky blood. What had happened?

I carefully turned my head to see if Rose was okay, wincing through the pain, trying not to vomit. She was gone. The seat next to me was empty. There was blood on the cracked windshield but her door was closed. It was like she just calmly got out of the car and left me here.

I tried to call her name, but my mouth felt like it was filled with sawdust. I needed to focus. What happened? The car. A car hit us.

Oh my fuck, the zombies.

I straightened up, grinding my teeth at the immense pressure in my head, at the wooziness, and forced my vision to line up. The mob was gone from the street and I couldn't see the car we hit. Maybe they'd driven off. I tried to look through the cracks on the window to see if there was damage on the road but something else caught my eye.

I was wrong about the crowd of zombie people being gone. I didn't know how long I was out—long enough for Rose and everyone else to disappear. But that wasn't true.

Up ahead on the road. There was someone walking—no *running*—toward me. I panicked, adrenaline pushing through the fatigue and taking over, and I was about to jump out of the car when the dark figure suddenly dodged to the left, disappearing into a mound of high bushes.

Fuck this noise. I had to find Rose. I had to get out of here. I moved over to the driver's seat and was about to turn the ignition when I realized the keys were missing. I frantically searched the ground, the seat, the middle. There was nothing.

"Fuck!" I screamed, wanting to bang my head against the wheel, knowing it would probably make me lose consciousness.

"Think, Foray, think," I muttered to myself, forcing my brain to catch up. My eyes darted nervously to the road and back, feeling like I could be attacked at any minute by whatever had run into the bushes. At this point I was hoping it was just some neighborhood derelict because I would gladly hand over the guns, the cameras, whatever money I had if that was the case. I'd smile at them and kiss their feet. I could be their bitch, I'd make it work. It would be far better than having to face the walking dead.

I had two choices, really. I could either make a run for it or I could hotwire it. It was an old truck; it shouldn't take all that long.

I leaned down, and with an impatient fist, broke through the panel beneath the wheel and pulled out the wiring. I fished out the flashlight from the center console and stuck it in my mouth and did my best. Blue wires to blue wires, twist. Check.

Once I did that, I readjusted my angle, trying to see better, when I heard a god awful moan from beneath me. As in beneath the floorboards, coming from the ground. Suddenly the whole truck shifted, as if someone or something was trying to lift it up. It tilted to the left then to the right.

The flashlight fell out of my mouth and I put both hands on the dash, trying to steady myself. The movement stopped, the truck settling, but the groan was still there. I wasn't alone. There was something or someone underneath the car.

I sucked in my breath, trying to regain control, to keep myself from freaking out. It was barely working. I could either run or keep hotwiring and hope I dragged this thing away with me. And there wasn't time to really weigh either choice.

I kept trying to hotwire. I picked up the flashlight and ignored the moans and groans right beneath my feet, a mix of human agony and mechanical failure. Come on, come on, come on.

When I got those wires twisted, I felt like maybe the end was in sight. That I just needed a few more seconds and a bit of luck. Well, luck was on vacation that night. I raised my head for just one second to see what the outside situation looked like, and in that second, everything changed.

For one, through the cracked windshield I could see a darkened figure coming down the street, cloaked entirely in black. Whoever it was walked with purpose and also with ease. They were seductive, confident, and smooth. It was the walk of a woman who knew what she wanted and knew she was about to get it.

It was then that I suddenly couldn't move. I had leaned back against the seat when I saw the figure, and now I was frozen in place, the flashlight dropping out of my mouth again, and I couldn't do a thing about it. My limbs wouldn't lift, my head wouldn't turn. I was lucky my mouth was closed but I couldn't even open it to scream.

Suddenly the glove compartment started shaking like something was inside and trying to get out. It rattled, and I was torn between watching that and watching the figure move toward me. She was still obscured by the distance, the darkness and the fractures in the glass. But it didn't matter. I could already tell who it was. And for once I wasn't enamored by her.

For once I saw things very clearly, very deeply.

Ambrosia.

Somewhere she laughed, maybe it was out on the street, or in the truck, or in my head.

The glove compartment popped open with a hiss, a sound that sunk into my spine. The large black head of a python came out, its long, skinny tongue flicking like the Devil's pitchfork. It slowly emerged, pushing forward, its shiny scales undulating. Its head hung there for a moment, seeking, searching, before it pushed itself out of the glove compartment and dropped to the passenger seat. It curled up momentarily as the rest of its mammoth body continued to flow out of the tiny space. It was somehow bigger than the one in my room last night, at least fifteen feet long and two feet thick at its middle, and yet I knew it was the same beast, the same entity. Li Grand Zombi. It had come back for me.

I could have easily closed my eyes and just given up. My nerves were so shot, so frayed, that any sudden movement from the python would have put me into cardiac arrest. I knew that. I knew that if I was lucky, I would be found the next day, maybe days later, apparently dead from the effects of a car crash.

But I couldn't just give up. I was tired of doing that. I wanted to fight.

Ambrosia stepped forward, closer now so that I could see her coldly beautiful face, her wicked eyes. I wondered how I could have been so foolish to fall for her. The way I acted around her when Perry, my fucking Perry was there, the things I'd said. I'd acted like a douche of the highest order, a horny asshole, the worst of the worst. This woman had controlled all of it, and for all my supposed willpower, I had let her. I had let myself succumb to her advances, perhaps not all of them, but enough to make me a walking idiot in her wake. I should have known better—I should have been a better man. Now I knew, now I felt her power pulling at me, trying to glamour me, compel me. She got as far as my body, able to hold it in place. But she couldn't get in my mind anymore. I had seen the truth.

The snake began to rise upward so its head and beady eyes were at my level. I wasn't even sure if pythons could move like cobras, but this one was. It looked ready to strike.

"Declan," Ambrosia said, her lips moving as she came into view. "I was told that was your full name."

I couldn't have had a snappy comeback if I wanted to. Only my eyes were mobile. I wanted to ask her why she was doing it, but I had a feeling I knew why. I wanted to ask where Rose was but I had a feeling I didn't want to know.

Ambrosia stopped walking, her cloak flapping behind her, and raised her hands straight up to the sky, crying out something in a language that borrowed a lot from French but contained a whole bunch of words I didn't understand.

Suddenly, the darkness on the sides of the streets that I had assumed was foliage or structural remains began to move amidst dots of flickering light. It was the zombies, and they were walking forward, stepping out into the street, holding candles in their steady hands. There must have been forty of them, much more than I had counted earlier. It was the same mob, still moving in unison, their scarred faces glowing from the candlelight, their eyes glinting dully. A mass of people who had died and were brought back just to do this one woman's bidding. Her power was terrifying, and once again I felt for Perry, the only person who had suspected her from the beginning.

There was no time for my self-inflicted pity party, no time to think about where I went wrong and what the repercussions would be. The python hissed something that sounded like *Devil* and lowered its head. I prepared for the strike, for its teeth to wrap around my skin, but then I remembered how pythons killed. Not from their bite. From their muscles choking the last living breath out of you. Ambrosia was the one who was poisoning me—the snake would just finish me off. Li Grand Zombi and she were working in tandem.

The snake began to slither across my lap, and I heard a scuffle in the seat behind me. My eyes flew to the mirror, even though I knew I shouldn't have looked, and there was my mother.

"My son," she said, a fleshless skeleton hand coming

forward and resting on my shoulder. "Come meet your potential."

I looked ahead, my heart slowing down, my lungs closing up. Ambrosia smiled and blew a kiss at me. All the lights from the candles around her went out. Everything went dark.

A snake tongue slithered across my hand.

18

"Row, row, row your boat, gently down the stream..."

Somewhere in the distance, someone was singing. I was on a small, white boat, peeling paint coming off the sides, flaking onto my feet.

I was alone.

Everything was grey. The sky with its heavy mass of low clouds, clouds that looked too wide and too heavy for it to hold up. The water that lapped along the side of the boat, the dark shapes that swam underneath the steel water, even the flowers that hung from the nearby trees, rising out of the swamp, were absent of any color.

"Merrily, merrily, merrily, merrily," the voice went on, pleasant and clear.

I looked around me. There was no sign of where I'd come from, no hint of where I was going. It was like I was in a grey globe, floating in a giant circle. I didn't even have oars.

There was a splash in the water alongside the boat and I looked over. There was a long, thick serpent wriggling in the waves. Its head was the head of my mother, pale grey skin, dark grey eyes. Fangs for teeth.

She started rising out of the water, that awful smile, that scaly black body.

She opened her mouth and sang in a deep, demonic voice, "Life is but a dream."

Then she lunged for me, her mouth snapping.

But she didn't get me. She couldn't reach.

I stared right into my mother's soulless eyes and recognized the expression in them. The fear. The failure.

She dropped straight back into the water as if she'd been struck.

I looked up. There was another rowboat in the distance, moving away from me, toward the horizon. A woman sat in it, too far away for me to see. She was sitting still, her body small and frail, and the only thing I could make out were glinting eyes.

She floated away until she was a dot, until she totally disappeared, swallowed up by the grey waves and sky.

～

WHEN I CAME TO, I was already screaming. The pain was everywhere.

I opened my eyes and saw Ambrosia standing in front of me, a sharp and bloody knife in her hands. I looked down. I was tied down to a chair, totally naked except for my boxer briefs. My bare chest bore a long, deep cut down the middle of it. Red blood dripped from my collarbone, down between my pecs, to just below my ribs. That explained the excruciating pain. I blinked hard and fast at the scene, trying to get my breath. I was in the middle of a darkened room, a circle of salt and candles burning all around me. It looked like the interior of a small cabin, all dark wood and splintering floors. Between a few cracks, I could see the gleam of water wavering underneath. A house on stilts. This must have been Ambrosia's lair.

It wasn't just the two of us in the room. At first I thought the shadows were watching me, that I was imagining eyes amongst the black. But then I could see the figures of zombies—her slaves—coming through, standing around against the walls, waiting, and biding their time.

And in one corner of the room was Rose. She was also tied to a chair, stripped to her bra and underwear. She had the same marking as me, a slash made down her middle, though she also had one that ran horizontal, completing a cross. I suppose that was next on the torture agenda. She had another symbol drawn on the tops of her feet, the blood coagulating into dark droplets. Her head had flopped to the side, her frizzy white-blonde hair covering her face. I couldn't tell if she was breathing or not. I couldn't tell if she was alive or dead.

I licked my dry lips and tried to talk. It took a few seconds before I could form words. "What have you done to her?"

Ambrosia passed the knife from one hand to the other. "Considering I just made you bleed and I'm still standing here with a knife, you should be more concerned about yourself, Declan Foray." Her eyes went over to Rose and back to me. She smiled. "But for all intents and purposes, Rose is dead. Just like you'll be once I'm done with you."

With deliberation, she stepped forward and placed one hand on my shoulder, holding herself steady, and raised the knife. I tried to squirm and headbutt her, tried to break free of the ties, but I couldn't. My muscles strained, sweat covered my brow, but the ropes only dug more into my flesh.

She worked fast. With one agonizing swipe, she drew the blade across my chest.

I bit my lip, trying to hide my scream. The fresh cut bled profusely, just underneath my tattoo, as if *And With Madness Comes the Light* was underlined in red.

"Trying to be brave are we?" she said with amusement. "Dawlin', you have no idea what you're in for, do you? This is just the beginning of the ritual. Once I start removing pieces of you, you won't be so brave anymore. You'll have to scream, even if I remove a piece of your tongue."

I tried to not let my eyes widen at that part about "removing pieces" but it was hard not to. With any other person, I would have called her bluff, but I knew Ambrosia had it in her.

"You're one ugly bitch, you know that?" I snarled at her.

Her face jerked back momentarily before she appeared smooth and calm again. "So I guess I can't compel you anymore, can I? Well, that will change when I'm done with you. All your precious willpower will be out the window. You do know what's out the window here, don't you? Many, many alligators. Swimming rats. Snakes."

My mind flashed back to being in the boat amid the grey, the Beetlejuice version of my mother. Had that been the Thin Veil?

"You intrigue me Declan," she said. She crouched down with the knife and began carving intricate patterns on the top of my foot. The pain was blinding. "Your energy is unlike anything I've ever seen, anyone I've ever met. I knew the moment I met you, that I needed you, I needed it."

"It?" I grunted as she went to the next foot.

"Yes, it. Your essence. What makes you, you. Your mother told me some wonderful things."

I was so disgusted, so angry, that I could barely feel the

pain as the blade dug slowly into my foot, scraping along the bone. "What do you know about my mother?"

"I know she was easy to conjure. I know she's been trying to reach you. I know what she wants with you."

"What?" I seethed.

She looked up at me and smiled. "That's for her to say. I wouldn't want to step on any toes. Speaking of toes..." Her gaze went to my feet. "I wonder if you'd miss yours."

"What do you want with my toes?"

She stared at them for a moment before shrugging. "Nothing actually, they don't hold much. Though they're pretty large for your height." She smiled at me. "I already have my sacrifices worked out for me."

She crouched and began drawing the blade from my ankle bone up my inner calf and thigh, hard enough to draw blood. She paused, the blade dangerously close to my balls, and I sucked in my breath, daring myself not to move.

Quick as a wink, she swiftly took the blade back down and did the same up the inside of my other leg. Then she cupped my balls in her hand and squeezed them lightly.

She leaned in and whispered into my ear, her hair smelling sickly sweet. "If I were a lesser woman, I'd cut off your balls and make good use of them. The amount of power and testosterone you carry is enough to fuel a small city."

I winced as she squeezed them even harder. "It's too bad you weren't weak enough to give me a good time, because I would have given you the best time. You can't even get hard."

I narrowed my eyes at her and hoped she could hear the venom in my words. "There's only one woman I'll get hard for."

She rolled her eyes, her lip curling slightly. "Oh, of course. This Perry. Well, I hope you had fun with her while it lasted, because when this is all over, you'll be no different than the men over there. You'll be mine, you'll do as I say, and any memories of this life will be gone."

I watched as she straightened up and walked around the circles of candles, the flames licking at her ankles. The eyes of the dazed men in the shadows followed her every move.

"Why are you doing this?" I asked, my voice dry and hoarse. If I was going to die here, I might as well get some answers. "What's the point?"

She stopped and glared at me. "What is the point? I thought that was pretty obvious. People underestimate me, they always have. They don't even believe that I've descended from Voodoo royalty. The Voodoo Queen's blood runs through me! But everyone thinks I'm a sham, thinks I'm nothing but a stupid, delusional girl."

She was definitely delusional.

"Only Maryse took me under her wing. She was the only one who believed in me."

"And then you got her shunned."

Ambrosia pursed her lips. "Well, yes. She didn't want to have anything to do with the dark arts. But the dark arts is where all the power is. It is what Voodoo is. All these years it's become white-washed and weak. All the real traditions, the rituals, the real power had been stripped. It's become commercialized. I want to take that power back, back to who started it, to those who deserve it, those who can make the world whimper."

"The Mambo wouldn't have let you do that."

"No, you're right. And she didn't." She walked over to a door and opened it. I heard the squawking of a few chickens, and she emerged with a black one in her hands. "I've been putting hexes on her from the very beginning. Nothing large, just enough to wipe her memory, to make her comply to me. Like you, I could never really make her do what I wanted, but I got enough out of her. I got her to teach me a lot of things that she never would have otherwise. I practiced and practiced and practiced until I knew I was ready."

She walked to the middle of the circle and quickly sliced off the chicken's head. It fell to the ground with a wet thunk, the eyes still blinking, the beak still moving. I hoped that was its nerves backfiring, that the poor fucker wasn't still alive.

She held the headless body in her hands like it was still alive, blood spurting out from the neck.

I swallowed thickly, my eyes drawn back to the chicken head. It was staring at me. "If you're all about tradition, if you think the culture has gotten white-washed, then why are you going after black people? They're your own."

"To make a point," she said angrily, and I saw that façade of hers slip again. "Aren't you listening? Look at my brothers and sisters in this city. We made this city, and now we're being kept in these neighborhoods to kill each other. Nobody cares. The police don't. The city doesn't. The country doesn't. We thought that after Katrina the focus would be on us and our crime and our poverty and what was really going on. But it didn't last. It's back to shit again. No one even cares if black people are dropping left and right like flies. If anything, they're happy. They only care when they reappear and start attacking white people."

I couldn't fathom her reasoning. Her point was lost. She was mad, and mad with power. I wanted to buy more time by asking more questions, but I didn't know what I'd end up doing with the time I got. "But you're turning them into slaves, just like they once were. Doesn't that strike you as wrong at all, or just a little ironic?"

She glared at me. "Everyone has to make sacrifices. You're one of them."

She jerked the chicken at me and the blood went spraying onto my body, covering me with hot rivulets from head to toe. She came forward and glared down at me.

"I tried everything with you, Declan. I tried to give you the easy way out. If you'd been weaker, this would have been over with before it got painful. I tried the candles, the oils, the poppets. Everything. The only way I'll ever have complete control of you is if I take parts of you away. You'll be weaker, and I'll be stronger. It worked with Maryse, it will work with you."

She reached out to my face with a bloody hand and I tried to jerk away. "What happened to Maryse?"

"She's dead," she said. "And the real kind of dead. She was too frail to serve me as a slave, though *that* would have been wonderfully ironic. She's underneath the house right now, a snack for the alligators."

Her fingers traced my cheekbone. "You really are a handsome man," she whispered soothingly. "Perfect cheekbones. Perfect lips. The darkest eyes. Everything about you is perfect. Except for your ear."

I froze. Her fingers moved up to my ear and began stroking the lobe, her skin sticking to mine from the chicken blood.

"What about my ear?" I asked, my voice shaking.

"It's a shame I'll have to take part of it. Though I'm going to guess you're not much of a listener anyway."

She took out the blade and aimed it at my ear.

No. Fucking. Way.

I started bucking in my seat, trying to find a point of concentration, trying to get my strength back to break through whatever motherfucking spell this bitchy witch put

on me. It was almost working too; though my feet felt para-
lyzed, I could feel the restraints around my arms coming
loose.

Ambrosia tried to get the knife close, but I kept moving.
I ended up with a large gash along my jaw and she started
swearing in French. Suddenly, she stood up straight and
raised her hands in the air. The shadows began to move and
five of her slaves came at me. They held my head in place. I
stared up at them, looking into their dull eyes, pleading for
some recognition, for some humanity to be left. There was
nothing in them at all. My hope was fading.

"I'd try and stay still if I were you," Ambrosia warned
me. "Unless you want me taking out your eye instead."

I closed my eyes, not wanting that. I reached out in my
mind to Perry, hoping that somehow she could hear me. I
listened, and hoped I could hear her. There was nothing but
the labored breathing of the zombie slaves, their foul stench
of death.

Ambrosia took the knife and very slowly, to prolong the
pain and agony that seized every part of me, she cut away
the very top edge of my left ear.

I screamed and screamed until my throat felt ripped, my
lungs raw. Warm liquid rushed down into my ear canal,
trickling down my neck.

She moved away, proudly showing me the piece of my
ear. She reached into her dark blouse, pulled out a small
bag she was wearing around her neck, and put the piece of
ear inside. She grinned at me. "The things I can now do
with this, the person I'll become."

I could barely talk through the pain. My ear stung and
throbbed, so hot and so fiercely. "You're pure evil."

She shrugged and wiggled her lips. "You know, when
people keep telling you that you're bad and that your beliefs

are bad and everything you do is bad...well, eventually you just become bad. Why not? Why not give them what they want and then make them wish they never wanted it."

I looked over at Rose, at her lifeless body. Ambrosia caught my eye and went over to her. She grabbed her by her hair and yanked her head up. Rose had an X carved in her forehead, her eyes were open and unseeing.

"Rose and I never got along," Ambrosia said to me, as if she were confiding with a girlfriend over drinks. "I didn't like how Maryse pandered to her, to someone so...ordinary. But, she does have some attributes that gave me a little bit of mojo. And it was really fun trying to compel her. She led you right to me and she didn't even know it."

"What are you doing with her?" I was starting to feel woozy from the pain and had trouble keeping my head up straight.

"I told you. Same thing I'm doing to you. I already gave her a dose of the poison. Comes from the pufferfish. Does a fine job of tricking your body into thinking it's dead, so fine that even doctors can't tell. You saw what happened to poor old Tuffy G. Then I'll bury her for a while...There's a tiny mound out back that used to be an ant hill. I can only stick her about three feet in or so before the water floods the coffin but it should work for the sake of the ritual. I'll do a few rites, dig her up after a few hours, give her the datura. Then she's all mine to do my bidding. That is unless I accidently give her too much. That's the problem with the elixir. If you don't give enough, the person still has a bit of free will, albeit terrible hallucinations and memory loss. If you give too much, you'll lose them completely and forever. They go mad, so mad that even I can't control them. I learned the hard way with Eric Smithe. I just wanted him to attack someone in the parking lot, act like a real zombie, something that people would really fear and talk about. I wanted this to start becoming front page news. Then he turned on me and bit me."

I'd stopped listening. The room was starting to spin a bit and I was dangerously close to passing out. I couldn't tell if it was the loss of blood and stress on my heart, or if she had really taken something from me after all of this bloodplay.

She let go of Rose's head and came over to me, bringing a small vial out of her pocket. "The trick with you will be figuring out how much to give. I can't be sure how this will work on you since you've been so resistant to me. But considering I have most of your essence now, I think if I accidently leave you brain-dead, it wouldn't be the worst thing that could happen. Your body will still be fun to use for a short time, whether you've gone mad or not."

She nodded at the zombie slaves who were still standing around me and they went for my head again. They held it in place, while two of them pried their large hands into my mouth, one holding the top jaw, the other holding the bottom.

"When you wake up, you'll only know me. You'll only remember me. I will raise you from the ground, save you from the dirt, and you will do my worst for me. You won't have Perry. You won't have your friends. You'll have no memory of who you are. I pray, for your sake, that you do what you're told and that no one you love will ever see you in your new state of being."

I tried to move, even though I knew it was useless. I tried to push my tongue forward, to prevent anything from going down my throat. But it was futile. Ambrosia came over and poured the liquid down my throat, a vile, thick poison, and I choked on it.

They stepped away and I immediately tried to vomit, to

throw it back up. But things were already happening. My throat began to close. My fingers, toes, arms, legs, everything became rigid like I was being held by millions of imaginary hands. In my chest, my heart thumped loudly, then became slower and slower, losing its rhythm, its speed, its sound. The air stopped reaching into the depths of my lungs, becoming more and more shallow.

My brain started its final descent, slowing shutting down the circuits. I was losing the capacity for thought. So, this was the death of Dex Foray. This was the end of the man I was.

I realized it didn't mean anything without Perry by my side. She was my reason for living. She was the reason I'd come alive in the first place.

It's a shame, I thought for the last time, *I realized that truth far too late.*

19

It was the noise above me that woke me up. My consciousness came on like a dimmer switch, slowly introducing my brain to the new reality.

I was happy to recognize that it was my own brain. It didn't mean I felt 100%. In fact, my thoughts felt slow and stunted and I felt the drugs coursing through me, trying to bring my vitals down to a dangerous level. But I was still Dex.

And I was being buried alive.

It was black as tar and the noise that had woke me was the sound of dirt being thrown on top of the narrow coffin I was in. I could also hear Ambrosia chanting to herself, sounding faraway and muffled.

And now's when you panic, I told myself. I tried to move, but my limbs weren't having any of it, the poison still in control of that part of my system, reluctant to let go.

The dirt kept coming, quicker and quicker. I had a feeling that Ambrosia was having her minions do the burial services, and even though she said she was only burying me three feet underneath the ground, that three feet was enough to eventually asphyxiate a person. I could tell they were getting close to being done too. The fresh dirt that was being thrown on top wasn't as loud as before.

I started breathing harder in my panic and tried to slow my breath. I needed to conserve air in here and I needed to think. The minute she dug me out would be the minute she'd try and administer the datura, the mind-control drugs. The stuff that turned you into a mindless slave, or a batshit crazy lunatic. I'd seen enough in the mental hospital to know that a batshit crazy lunatic wasn't as fun as it seemed, even if it meant I'd try and take a bite out of her. When I saw her, there'd be little to stop me from ripping her fucking head off and pissing on it.

Aside from her slaves, of course. I didn't know how strong I was, I just knew that I was conscious when I wasn't supposed to be. I was supposed to be in a state of near-death until after she'd administered the mind-control drug. She was expecting to open the coffin, hoping to find me alive but helpless, and that would be that. I finally had something on her—my own fucking free will again, and I knew she wouldn't see it coming.

The dirt and chanting continued until I couldn't hear either anymore. The ground vibrated slightly with short bursts—they must have been pounding their shovels into the dirt. So much elaboration for a silly ritual, as if anything she was doing would appease the Voodoo Gods.

I needed a plan and I needed one fast. Her devotion to tradition was the only thing that was buying me time and saving me from my imminent slavery. But it was hard to make plans when you were trapped in a musty-smelling box, no bigger than your body, with the air slowly running out. My only plan was to get out of the fucking ground, but I could barely move my arms. If it were any other circumstance, I could have probably pulled a Hulk Dex maneuver and punched my way out of the grave. It actually would have been pretty awesome. But I was still weak, and I was losing time.

And maybe a little bit of my sanity. It was one thing to find yourself buried underground—fully alive and conscious with three feet of hard-packed dirt between the surface and you. It was another thing to realize you weren't alone in the coffin.

The area beneath my bare feet, what I thought was the damp, gross sides of the box, just *moved*.

There was something beneath my feet, moving very slowly, like it was just waking up. Scales brushing against my soles.

Oh fuckity fuck fuck.

I knew exactly who I'd been buried alive with.

Her partner in crime, Li Grand Zombi.

The python continued to coil around at my feet, seeming to go in circles. I cursed myself for being 5'9" and having the extra space at the end of the coffin, although I suppose the alternative would have been to have the snake packed on top of me like sardines.

Now I had to think faster but the presence of the great serpent did nothing to get me into gear. All it did was put my already strained heart into overdrive, turn my tired brain into mush. I thought I'd run out of things to fear already, but it turns out there was a lot more.

I could only hope that it didn't have the head of my mother this time.

Ignore the snake, it's just sleeping, ignore the snake, I thought to myself. I hoped Rose was faring better than I was.

I had been so happy to be myself again, to be alive, but now the alternative didn't seem so bad.

The snake didn't care what I was thinking. Perhaps it was feeding on my fear. I could feel it pressing its body up against my feet, pushing at them until my knees shot up a few inches and rammed into the top of the coffin. I'm sure I would have noticed it hurt, but all I could feel was the snake's tongue skittering along the cut on my inner thigh, perhaps licking where the blood was. It headed up my legs and I immediately put my hands down over my junk, remembering what Ambrosia had said.

The python paid my hands no attention. It came up over them, over my pelvis, heading for my stomach. It paused there momentarily and I could hear it breathing, the sounds amplified in the darkness. It was watching me, sensing me, deciding what to do next. I wondered how much of the snake was just an animal acting on animal instincts and how much was someone else, a demonic spirit from the other world.

I was still trying to wonder that when the giant serpent resumed its movement. It came up all the way to my head and started coiling itself around my head and throat, forcing its body underneath me and the box, and looping back around again. It did this, winding around me, until it held me from head to toe.

And then it began to slowly, systematically, squeeze me to death.

My hands flailed, trying to pry it off of me, but there was no use. It was far too strong, its body made to choke the life out of its prey, to break their bones. My ribs began to crack.

Dex! I heard Perry's voice in my head. *Dex! I'm here, I'm here!*

At least I thought it was in my head. It was hard to tell when I was losing consciousness again.

The snake stopped squeezing for a few moments, as if it had heard Perry as well. Then came the scraping sound of a shovel going into dirt, muffled and distant, but it was there.

"Dex!" I heard her voice again, this time it wasn't in my head. Oh god, please let that be her, please let that be her.

I opened my mouth to yell. As if on cue, the snake began constricting again, choking the words from me.

The sound above the coffin intensified. I knew she was there, I knew she was coming to save me. I didn't know how, but there she was. I just hoped I could hold on long enough. I could feel myself turning blue, my lungs burning for air they couldn't get.

I also hoped that Ambrosia wasn't within earshot, because things would get ugly for Perry, very fast. Unless my baby had the upper hand and already kicked that bitch's ass.

Suddenly the coffin lid was hit, struck by the shovel and I heard Perry gasp, clear as day. The top of the box began to move, cracks of dim light coming in followed by dirt that fell on my body.

I looked straight up at her as she removed the lid. Though it was probably the middle of the night and dark as sin, I could see the glow of a flashlight nearby. After being in that box, everything outside of it was much clearer.

I saw her beautiful, sweet eyes staring at me, threatening to spill over with tears, so much longing in them, her dark, wet hair spilling around her. Then her eyes flashed with horror once she realized what she was staring at: a giant black python wrapped around me, trying to take my last breath.

"Oh God, Dex, no!" she cried out. Her tiny hands flew to the snake, trying to pull it off of me to no avail. The snake squeezed harder. If I could have gasped, I would have at the pain of my lower rib breaking.

This couldn't be the way I was going to go, after all of this, to die in front of Perry's eyes. I tried hard to hold on, to stay awake, to stay alive but everything was in her hands. I was helpless. Only she had the ability to save me, to save me from death, from myself, from everything.

I love you, I thought.

She smiled as if she heard it, tears streaming down her face and falling onto me. Then she straightened up, grabbed the shovel, and said, "If this hurts you, I'm really, really sorry."

She raised the shovel in the air, looking like a divine warrior princess, perhaps of the gardening variety, and brought it down.

I shut my eyes and the edge of the shovel pummeled into the snake, pressing hard into me but not breaking my skin. I opened my eyes to see her bringing the shovel back out of the snake, guts and blood dripping from the edge of it, raining down on me. The snake was still holding on, not fully severed, but it had loosened enough that I could get a small amount of air into my lungs.

Perry raised the shovel again, and from the crazy determination in her eyes, that kind of determination I only ever saw in her, I knew she was going to finish him. I just hoped she could do it without making me a part of the snake kabob.

She brought the shovel down sharply, and with a sick squelching sound the snake suddenly released me. I gasped loudly for air, trying to pull it off my neck. Perry stared at the severed snaked for a few triumphant moments before she dropped to her knees and reached down into my grave to pull the upper half of the snake off of my neck. Then she reached beneath my shoulders, as far as her fingers could go, and slowly pulled me so I was sitting up. The python's dead body dropped to my waist, freeing me.

"Dex," she whimpered, taking my face in her hands and peering into my eyes. I wanted to tell her so many things, but air wasn't my friend yet. My throat and lungs were too bruised and raw. The only thing I could do was lean up as far as I could and kiss her, just a brush of our lips, but enough. Just to remind me that this was why I was alive.

It also reminded me that she was kneeling on the ground, soaking wet somehow, and I was sitting upright in a coffin, half-naked, a severed black python wrapped around me. It was then that she looked down at me and gasped. Her frightened eyes went from the markings on my chest, legs and feet, to the gash on my jaw, to the place where the top tip of my ear used to be.

"What the fuck happened to you?" she whispered, terrified. "Where is your ear?"

"I'll explain once we get out of here," I said hoarsely, finally finding my words. With her help, I got unsteadily to my feet and climbed out of the box. I knew I looked quite the sight, now covered in dirt and snake guts. At least the mix was deterring the mosquitos for the time being. "How did you find me?"

"It's a long story," she said. "I came with Maximus but I... I don't know what happened. I lost him. The zombies, they're out there. They tipped our boat. I swam...I don't know what happened to him. I...I think maybe I heard him drowning. I'm sorry." She was near tears again and I put my arms around her and held her to me, grunting quietly through the pain of the cuts and my broken rib.

"You did good, kiddo," I told her, whispering into the top of her head. "You did good."

She sniffled and then pulled away. "I just had a feeling I knew where you were. I could sense you."

"What about Rose?"

She shook her head. "I don't sense her. What happened?"

I chewed on my lip. "She's buried somewhere here too."

"Then we have to dig her up, she might die we if we don't."

"I think she's already dead."

"No," she said determinedly. "It doesn't mean we shouldn't try. If I gave up hope on you, I wouldn't be here now."

I looked over her shoulder, at the shape of Ambrosia's small cabin in the distance. There was a light flickering in one of the windows, but I couldn't see or hear anything else. Perry was right. We had to try.

"Okay," I said. I tried to bend over to pick up the flashlight, but the pain was too great. She quickly got it for me and I shot her a grateful smile as I took her hand in mine. It definitely wasn't the time to get sappy and we definitely had a lot to talk about and we *definitely* didn't know where we stood as a couple, but I wanted to take the moment and hang on to it. At this point, I wasn't sure if it would be our last.

She nodded at the flashlight. "Come on, let's get Rose. Then we'll find Maximus and get out of here."

For once I wished the big red giant really was immortal. I hoped Ambrosia's minions hadn't found him, though the bayou was still quiet aside from the occasional splash or bird cry. No gnashing of the teeth to be heard.

I shone the light into the area around my shallow grave. It did look like it had been an ant hill at one point, and then had probably been turned into a compost heap. Though it was maybe only twenty square feet and wildly uneven, it looked like it was the only land around. Everything else that my flashlight caught beyond the mound shimmered like water.

"Over there," Perry whispered, pointing to her left. I shone the light over and we quickly crept forward. The ground had been disturbed recently, but it looked more like something had been dug up rather than buried. We looked over. It was a grave alright, but it was empty.

"She must have buried her way before me," I said. "She already has her."

"Well what can we do?"

I looked back at the cabin. Rose was in there. But was it too late? And was it worth the risk of trying? The two of us versus a heap of mind-controlled zombies wasn't exactly a fair fight.

Suddenly there was movement from the water and I knew the undead were rising slowly out of the swamp, as if they'd been there all along, waiting like alligators. I hoped that at least a few lucky gators got a meal out of them.

Perry whirled around toward the sluicing noise and I shone the flashlight on them, their eyes shining with madness. Yup. The undead.

I was about to tell Perry to run, to take us back to her boat, when I felt a presence behind me. Automatically, I made my body go slack, as if Perry had just dug me out and I was a bit brain-dead still.

"Where do you think you're going?" Ambrosia said, her hand resting on my shoulder. "I figured the poison would wear off faster with you." She looked over at Perry, who was frozen in a mix of hate and fear as the zombies came closer and closer. "So you thought you'd come and try to save him.

Well, I'm sorry dawlin', he can't be saved. And now, neither can you."

I was grabbed from behind by six strong hands and ripped backward just in time to see a bunch of Ambrosia's slaves lay their hands on Perry.

I yelled out for her before I was yanked forward and dragged through the dirt to her cabin. The ground disappeared and we had to slog through water to get to the entrance. They threw me up the stairs and up onto the rickety porch. No wonder Ambrosia practiced her magic out here, no one would ever suspect a thing. No one would even hear you scream.

I was shoved back into the cabin where I fell onto the floor covered with feathers, candle wax, and blood. The chicken's body was gone, nailed to the wall with a knife. They immediately picked me up again and hauled me to one end of the main sacrificial room, whirling me around to face the door. Perry was brought in after me, Ambrosia holding onto one arm, her nails digging in, while another slave held the other. I fought to get free while she fought to get free, trying to get to each other. Our eyes said it all.

There was a groan coming from another small room and we both craned our necks to look. Rose was stumbling out of it, covered in dirt and blood, long, white hair in her face. It was obvious that we were too late. Rose had already lost her mind and free will. She was already under Ambrosia's control. There was no more Rose.

"I haven't tried anything on her yet," Ambrosia explained, watching with clinical amusement as Rose staggered across the room, seeming to have no clear place to go. "You can both witness the dawning of the new Rose, the extent of my power."

She started chanting loudly in her Voodoo speak, Perry

wincing since it was right in her ear. She then yelled, "Rose, this man means you harm."

For a minute, I thought Ambrosia was pointing at me, but it was a lean, handsome zombie-man to my right. Well, he would have been handsome if he hadn't looked stoned out of his gourd.

"Rose," Ambrosia continued, "I am your master, I am your protector. Destroy this man. Bite him, kill him. Tear him from limb to limb." Then she started chanting again, her eyes rolling back in her head, as if she was calling some dark force to do her bidding.

I eyed a few oily candles in the corner of the room, all burning brightly. I wondered if Rose's name was on one of them and if hers was the only name. I wondered if this zombie shit was actually going to work. To see them as the walking, yet recently deceased, was one thing. To see one *become* a zombie, someone that you knew, was another.

Rose had paused in the middle of the cabin, in between Perry and me, in the circle of candles that had melted down to wax. It was almost like she was listening.

Then she turned very slowly to face the man, the man who still had a firm grip on my right arm. This could go nowhere or this could get ugly. I didn't want to see Rose this way, this hardened girl with her aching heart for her lost love. This wasn't her.

But this Rose started to come forward, walking jerkily like the drugs were creating spasms. She kept coming and between the strands of her blonde hair, I could see her eyes. Blue-grey and crazed.

Rose stopped a couple of feet away, swaying back and forth as if she needed an extra push. Ambrosia yelled something at her, fire in her evil eyes, and Rose moved again.

She reached out for the man, wrapping both of her

hands around his forearm, and bit him. She took a literal bite out of him, her mouth coming away dripping with blood and muscles and tendons. I nearly shit myself and had to look away from the sight, from this Rose that was no longer human. Across the room, Perry sounded like she was about to vomit.

Ambrosia clapped gleefully. "I knew it."

Rose still stood there, like a robot, the man's stringy flesh handing from her mouth until Ambrosia screeched another word and Rose lunged at the man again, this time her mouth going for his chest.

All this time, I was wondering if the zombie was just going to stand there and take it. He was still holding onto me. Didn't he understand pain? What was happening?

He answered that fairly quickly. With one huge swipe of his mutilated arm, he grunted with rage and threw Rose backward until she slammed against the nearest wall. The candelabras shook overhead. Rose collapsed like a rag doll to the floor.

I watched her for a few moments until I saw she was breathing, then I glanced at Ambrosia. A look of surprise was on her face. Apparently, this was something she hadn't planned for.

"Well, that was interesting," she noted. "I should pit them against each other more often. Their basic instinct to survive...survives."

"You are a sick fucking bitch," I snarled at her. "It's not your choice to play God."

She smiled coldly, her eyes narrowing. I saw her nails dig further into Perry's pale arm and I immediately regretted saying anything. "If I don't play God with the power I am given, than why am I given the power?"

"You stole their power," Perry sneered.

Ambrosia immediately elbowed her in the face, Perry dropping to her knees as she screamed out in pain. I tried to get to her, to break free, but the men around me were fast.

Ambrosia kicked at Perry's side and said to the slaves nearest her, "Take her over there, hold her open."

I did not know what the fuck that meant but I had a feeling I was going to find out. The men took Perry to the farthest wall and held her back against it, one man pulling one way with her arm, the other man pulling the other. Blood trickled out from her nose, but her attention was just on me, only on me. Her blue eyes cut me deep.

"Now it's your turn, Declan," Ambrosia said. My nostrils flared. I made a move to run, to jerk out of their grasp, but they held me in place, even the man with a chunk of his arm missing.

Ambrosia picked up a candle from the floor, lit it, and started coming toward me with it. She began to chant, low and gravely sounds. Everything she said sounded like death.

She paused right in front of me, the candlelight flickering in her face. For once, I saw how ugly she really was. Her smile was crooked, her hair was rough and split, her skin light, but ashy. Her eyes danced with wicked joy, glinted with the absence of her soul. All her beauty was masked by the fact that I knew who she really was.

"Even though Perry dug you up, the ritual is still in process," she told me. "You were dead and now you've risen. Now you will become my own."

From behind the candle, she lifted a syringe. Before I knew what was happening, she stabbed it into my neck, plunging the drug deep into my veins.

Perry screamed, the sound immediately amplified by whatever new drugs were surging through my body. The room swirled and twisted on itself, the candles turned into a kaleidoscope of lights.

Perry was still across the room, terrified, a lamb to be slaughtered. I was supposed to slaughter her.

But I couldn't. Because the datura or whatever Ambrosia injected into me, didn't work. I was high as fuck, and tripping out hardcore, but I was still me.

And I could tell the witch was watching me carefully. She probably even gave me an extra dose of it since the original paralysis poison didn't stay in my system long enough. If she caught on that it didn't work as well as she'd hoped, she'd either pump me full of drugs until I was brain-dead, or she'd flat-out kill me. And Perry too.

I couldn't let that happen. So I did what I attempted to do earlier. I let my mind go slack. I let my muscles droop. I played up the fact that I was on some wild and scary drug trip. I channeled my inner teenager, on those nights I did too many mushrooms and smoked too much pot.

I pretended to be a zombie. I pretended to be hers.

"Declan, can you hear me?" Ambrosia asked, peering at me. I ignored the annoying use of my full name, and stared straight ahead at an imaginary spot on the wall. She waved her hand in front of my face and I had to think whether I should respond to it or not. What did zombies do? I took a risk and slowly, jaggedly, turned my head her way. My eyes looked to a spot on her forehead.

I could see her expression changing, frowning, suspicious.

"Declan are you ready to do my bidding?"

I decided to not show anything. I kept staring, dumb-faced, swaying slightly. It was only then that I heard Perry whimpering. She was believing it, all of it. She had no idea.

I had to ignore that. I couldn't screw up now. I had to

play this up for as long as I could, until I was sure that Perry and I could escape. While I stared dully at Ambrosia, my mind tried to recall what the room looked like and if there were any weapons anywhere. There was just the knife, I remembered seeing it sticking out of the wall when I came in, skewering the dead chicken to it.

Ambrosia studied me for a bit longer and then started her chanting, her commanding words vibrating off the walls. She waved the candle around then delicately placed it on the floor. She walked over to a bookshelf and pulled off a large jar of oil, bringing it over to me. It smelt disgustingly sweet, just like her—baby powder and bitch.

She placed that on the ground too, and started dipping her hands in it. Then she rubbed the oil all over my face and neck, down my chest, arms, and legs. Even my crotch. She rubbed that area a little too long, but what I'd said earlier held true. I'd only be hard for Perry.

When she was done, she stepped back to admire her handiwork. From what I could tell, all she did was rub me in a vat of stinky almond oil. To her, it was probably the finishing touches in her ritual for mind-control, and though I had no doubt that she did have power, that she could bend dark forces to her will, it wasn't working with me.

I should have been relieved at that. But then she came closer, a cloy smile on her lips, and I knew it wasn't over yet. My allegiance wasn't sealed.

"Declan," she said seductively, putting her arms around my neck. Suddenly I had images of the stereotypical Voodoo ceremonies: blood orgies and naked, dancing, writhing bodies and animal sacrifices. If she was asking me to fuck her, right here, right now, I didn't know if I could do it.

She leaned into my ear, the one that was still whole, and whispered, "Kiss me like you mean it."

And so I did. I had to. I kissed her hard, kissed her long. Her tongue snaked against mine, hard and greedy. She was absent of everything I loved about Perry—her warmth, her softness, her vulnerability.

I heard Perry gasp, knowing she was watching this, but I had to keep going as long as Ambrosia commanded me to.

Finally she pulled away, her breath heavy, and I had to hold back a grimace. My face had to be blank, neutral, stupid. I felt like I'd just kissed a snake.

"Now," she said slowly, "we'll see what else you can do." She started to undo her blouse until her bare breasts were showing. She shrugged off her cloak to the ground, the blouse falling away afterward. She was completely nude from the waist up.

Oh shit. Oh no. No, no. No, this wasn't good. This I couldn't do, I couldn't do this to her, with *her*, and I couldn't do this to Perry. I was trying to save our lives, but I had my limits. This was it. This would be something neither of us could walk away from. But if I didn't comply, we wouldn't be walking anyway.

She came forward and brushed her nipples against my chest. "If you're truly my follower, you will do as I say, when I say it."

I steadied my breath, trying not to freak out. I could feel the pain radiating off of Perry as she prepared for what she knew was going to happen. Ambrosia was going to make screw her, a display of her control.

"Stop it!" Perry cried out in agony. It broke my heart, but it made Ambrosia turn her head. "Stop it! If you're going to kill me, then just kill me. I don't need to see him like this, not like this."

Ambrosia cocked her head and then eyed me up and down. "Perhaps I am being a little too cruel to your girlfriend, Declan. I can always use you later, when she's gone. And speaking of..."

She flashed her smile at Perry. "I think your wish is my command this time. I will kill you. Well, Declan will. Won't you?"

Though I wanted to breathe out the biggest sigh of relief over the fact that we just dodged a naked bullet, I stared forward, trying not to blink, to think, to give any sign of myself. Ambrosia stepped away, still shirtless, and picked up her candle. She began chanting.

I knew it was time. I had to think fast.

"Declan, go kill Perry. Eat her, finish her, destroy her."

This was it.

I brought my eyes over to Perry who shook there, still held between the two slaves. She really thought this was it, that I was going to eat her alive, and not I the way she liked.

I staggered toward her, walking unsteadily but full of faked menace. Once I was out of the range of Ambrosia, once I knew she couldn't read my eyes, I made sure that Perry *could*.

I was just feet away, coming toward her with my mouth open, hands bared, trying to convey to her everything I could with just a look. Everything I held, everything that was me was in my eyes. I hoped she knew who she was looking at.

I didn't have to worry for long. Perry immediately recognized me, the terror disappearing from her face, her shoulders relaxing.

But that wasn't good.

I heard Ambrosia make an irritated sound behind me. She saw Perry's reaction. She already knew.

"Get him! Kill them!" She screamed.

I quickly lunged past Perry, to the knife stuck on the

wall, and ripped it out of the chicken. Without even thinking, without even looking, I spun around and flung the knife across the room.

It landed square in Ambrosia's bare chest.

The whole room seemed to dim with power, the lights and candles all flickering. It took me a few seconds to realize what had happened, that I threw a fucking knife at her and that I actually hit the target. The knifed bobbed out of her chest like she was a piece of meat at a butcher. She wheezed again, sputtering blood, put her hand around the handle, and feebly tried to pull it out.

She couldn't. She gasped her last dying breath then collapsed to the floor, blood pooling around her.

There wasn't much time to think about it. We could only act. I grabbed Perry and pulled her out of the zombies' grasp. I guess Ambrosia's death had stunned them and I hoped they were stunned enough that they'd be totally harmless.

But Perry and I only got as far as the door when we realized that they were still following her very last order.

To kill us.

The eight or so men in the room started running for us just as we leaped down the stairs, landing in the murky water. We didn't have flashlights, we didn't have weapons, we had nothing.

"Where did you park the boat?" I yelled as we slogged through the water, colder now than it had been before.

"I don't know, I can't see!" she cried out. It was pitch black everywhere, the moon hidden by passing grey clouds.

We didn't have time to stand around and spot it. I could hear them following us, the porch creaking under their weight, the steps breaking beneath them. I didn't want to turn around and look. I grabbed Perry's hand and pulled her forward, deep into the bayou.

The water pulled back at us, thick with roots and weeds. Trees leaned over, trying to catch us by surprise. But we kept going, even though we could see the foliage coming further and further apart, the waterways taking over the landscape. As we splashed through, the water rose, first to our mid-thighs, then to our asses, then to our waists.

"You okay, baby?" I asked her, my grip tight around her forearm now.

She made a grunt, her way of telling me to shut up and just keep going. I knew that about her now, how we communicated when we were trying to escape from certain death. What Rose, dear Rose, had told me earlier came into my head again. She'd rather choose a life of more ghosts and demons than one without Maximus by her side. I'd have to say the same. The dead, the evil, the wicked, they would come after Perry and me whether we were together or not. But if we were together, fuck, at least we had each other.

I wanted to tell her that, but the middle of the swamp wasn't the best place to do it. Or was it?

"Listen, Perry," I said. Then the bottom beneath her feet dropped and her head went under. My head went under next.

We flopped to the surface in surprise, the brackish water coming into my throat. I coughed it out and looked around trying to keep her close to me. We could swim, but I had a feeling they could too. And if it wasn't the zombies who'd get us, whom we could still hear splashing, hot on our trail, it would be the alligators. I was already imagining their rough tails brushing against my feet.

"The trees," Perry said, jerking her head in their direction. The action made her go under again and I pulled her to me.

"Stay with me. Stay with me," I said, spitting out the water, keeping my arm tight around her waist. "Remember what we had to do on D'Arcy Island?"

She coughed, but managed to nod. Over her shoulder, in the distance, I could see dark shapes coming closer.

"Grab hold of my neck and hold on tight," I said. "I'll bring us to that tree. We can at least get out of the water."

She brought her arms around me, her legs wrapped around my waist, like she was piggybacking. I swam forward as quickly as I could.

"Are you sure you can handle me?" she asked.

I nodded. "No problem, baby."

But there was a problem. Back in D'Arcy Island I struggled but I got the job done. I wasn't much better now. My strength was still subdued thanks to the drugs Ambrosia gave me. My imagination was getting the better of me, the psychoactives kicking into high gear, and my limbs felt like lead. I couldn't let her know that though, I'd just have to push through the strain.

We had almost made it to the nearest tree when my heart and lungs just decided to give up. It happened suddenly, both organs seizing up and putting me in a stranglehold. I don't know if it was the strain of the events, the brutality my body had already endured, or the psychosis, but it was like I decided I'd died one too many times today.

My head went under, then Perry's, my toes straining to find ground but finding none. She let go and swam to the surface. I kept sinking until she pulled me up enough to get air.

"Please, Dex," she sputtered through the water. "Please, we're almost there."

I tried to use my arms, to doggy paddle forward, if not just tread water, and keep afloat. But they failed after a few attempts. Soon I was sinking under again.

Perry yanked me up one more time and I swore it would be our last. The zombies were closer now, I could hear their grunts, the water churning beneath their limbs. They obviously weren't affected, but I was.

"I won't let you die on me!" she yelled, her face coming up to mine. The moon chose that moment to poke its head out from behind the clouds. It illuminated the darkness of the water, the milky paleness of her skin, the fragility of her eyes. Oh God, I was lucky to have loved her. So, so lucky.

"Dex!" she yelled again, my eyes closing. "You are not leaving me! I cannot go on without you. You are my future, you are my everything!" She started crying and kissing my face. My head sunk under.

But she wouldn't give up. She linked her arm under mine and pulled me along as far as she could.

My head fought for surface, fought for air, but every last strength in me was gone. I took in water. She stopped pulling me. The water churned beneath my feet, and I could see hungry eyes glowing in the dark.

In the distance, the roar of the zombies became greater. It shook the water, muddy vibrations, until I knew that even if I wasn't drowning, she would die here with me. Together. It should have made me feel better not to have to go alone. But all I wanted was for both of us to live. With each other. Until we were old and grey.

The world was turning black and my lungs were now all water. My life flashed before my eyes, and most of it was of Perry. For her short duration in my life, she changed the way I knew how to live. And love.

We're saved, her voice cut in. *We're going to be okay.*

I didn't know if that was her parting goodbye or what that was. In a way I did feel saved. I felt peace for knowing her.

Then the water got choppier, my limbs bobbing around, and the roar of the zombies filled my ears to the core. Something hard grazed the top of my head. The current tried to pull me away, but big, strong hands came down and planted a firm grip under my armpits.

I was yanked to the surface, my lungs gasping hard for air, but only taking in more water. I was still drowning.

"Shit," someone murmured and I was pulled backward, my spine being scraped along something hard. I barely felt a thing.

Suddenly I was on my back, staring up at the moon and the two people peering over me.

"You're going to have to give him CPR," Maximus said to Perry as I continued to sputter.

Even in the moonlight, I could see her glare at him. She brought me upright and started pounding on my back, a rather crude version of mouth to mouth but it worked. The water flowed out of my lungs and onto the metallic flooring. I moved my head to look around. We were on a air boat driven by Maximus and in the opposite corner from me was a white-haired mound of limbs: Rose. Nearby the zombies were swimming for us, almost within reaching distance.

I couldn't speak so I just pointed.

"I'm on it," Maximus said. Just as the closest zombie latched his hand onto the side of the boat, we lurched forward and zoomed out of the way, leaving the zombie, the death, and the bayou behind.

We whirred away into the night.

"Are you missing part of your ear?" Maximus asked incredulously after a few moments.

And that was the last thing I heard. Once again, my body wanted to give up, my limbs becoming heavy, my mind shutting down like a tired old machine. Luckily I knew I wasn't going to drown this time. I knew I was in good hands. I keeled over right onto the boat and made a note to thank Maximus when I woke up.

20

I was back on the goddamn row boat again. Back in the world of grey and monotony, of silky swamp water and huddled trees.

But I wasn't alone.

My mother was on the boat with me, sitting at the end, a shawl wrapped around her. Her eyes were focused on the water, like I wasn't even there. For once she didn't look vaguely demonic. She looked as I remembered as a boy— a pretty woman with a lot of pain in her dark eyes.

It was weird being so close to her. I was still afraid, just as I had been when she was alive, never knowing what she was going to say or do to me. I didn't know where we were, though I was going to assume I was inside the Thin Veil, and I didn't know what rules applied. Was I dead? Was this my life now? Was she taking me somewhere in the row boat, someplace I'd never return from?

She began to sing "Row, Row, Row Your Boat" again, her clear voice sending icy fingers down my spine. She sang the whole song, her voice carrying out over the water and coming back to her in harmony. I remembered that about her, that sometimes she would sing to me, when I wasn't being terrorized of course. Only now did I realize that *she's* where I got my singing abilities from.

"Declan, you have to go to sleep now," she said kindly, still looking at the water.

I shivered at the uneasiness in the thick, grey air, at the blank look on her face. Should I say something to her? I didn't want to draw attention to myself. She could strike fear in me like no one else could, even when she looked normal.

"Michael is in bed, he's going to sleep, why can't you? Why are you always so afraid, Declan? Did Michael say something to you? Is it me?"

I swallowed hard and looked over the side of the boat, to see what she could be looking at. There was nothing but water glinting under a sun I couldn't see.

A sad smile came across her lips and she lowered her hand into the water, just brushing the surface. I had to imagine there was some younger version of myself in there, talking back.

"I'm sorry for what happened yesterday. Sometimes... sometimes I am not myself. I think it's getting worse. But I still love you very much. You must know that, my son. I will always love you."

I felt a lump get stuck in my throat. I nearly choked. My eyes were wet for some reason.

She went on, tears coming to her eyes too. "Please remember that. Remember this. Remember the good days when you look back. You were very much wanted by both me and your father. We will always be your parents. We raised you, it didn't. You are our child and no one else's."

I had to say something. I had to know.

"What happened to you?" I asked her, my voice breaking.

She smiled again, still looking at the water. "Sometimes something very good can come from something very bad."

"Was Michael the same?" My older brother had always been the overachiever, the sane one, the good son.

She didn't say anything. Her face contorted in pain.

"Mother, is Michael the same as me?"

She closed her eyes and a tear rolled down. "I don't even know your brother sometimes."

What the fuck did that mean?

"Mom..."

"Be strong, no matter what happens to me. No matter what happens to your father. Be good. I know you have that in you, even if he doesn't."

"Who!" I yelled at her, the boat rocking beneath me as I stood up, trying to get her attention. "Who isn't good? My father? Michael?"

She finally turned to look at me. Her eyes were now empty sockets.

"Go to sleep, Declan."

And so I did.

∼

"He's coming around," a woman with a heavy Louisiana accent said. "I'll see if I can find her."

I didn't recognize the voice of the person speaking and was met with a spinning head and the strong urge to vomit, all before I even opened my eyes.

Please let me not be on a boat, please let me not be on a boat, I thought to myself. *Also, no coffins please.*

"Hey buddy," I heard a familiar voice say. A heavy hand was placed on my arm.

I carefully opened my eyes, blinking hard at the stream

of light that was coming in through a window. My eyes moved over to Maximus who was leaning over me, his red hair gleaming from the sunlight like some ginger halo.

"Oh god, am I in hell?" I asked, my throat feeling like it had been scraped with sandpaper. "Where am I?" Panic suddenly shot through me like an arrow and I made a feeble attempt to sit up, even though every single part of me hurt. "Where's Perry?"

"She's fine," he said, pushing me back down into the bed. "The nurse went to go get her. She was so worried about you she wouldn't sleep until they gave her a sleeping pill. I think she's passed out in the waiting room somewhere. And if you can't already tell, yes you are in a hospital."

I groaned and tried to reach up to my ear. There was a lot of gauze wrapped around it and my head. "Fuck me, what happened?"

"You don't remember?" Maximus asked, pulling up a chair and sitting down.

My mind went back over the events. No, unfortunately I remembered everything until he pulled me onto the air boat.

"I remember you rescuing us. How long have I been out for?"

"Two days," he said.

"What?!" I exclaimed. "Why...what's wrong with me?"

He smirked. "Well aside from the fact that your body was carved up, you had a broken rib from a python, according to Perry anyway, your ear's been Van Gogh'd, and you had a concussion from the car accident, your blood was pumped full of two poisons. The doctors are amazed you're even alive considering how much you had in your system. I hate to sound trite, but it's kind of a miracle."

But I wasn't the only one this was done to. I looked at him. "What about Rose?"

I already knew it was bad news. He dropped his eyes to the floor. "Rose is alive."

"How alive?"

He sighed and ran his hand through his hair. "She's...the drugs did some damage to her. They don't know if it's reversible. She's in there somewhere though, I can see it. At the moment though, she can't really talk or do anything. She can't even go to the bathroom by herself."

My heart jerked. "I'm so sorry, man."

He eyed me. "No insult?"

I gave him a melancholy smile. "I'll give you a free pass, for now."

He bit his lip and nodded. "Well, that's the way life goes sometimes, doesn't it?" He cleared his throat.

Ugh. I hated feeling so terrible for the big guy. I wasn't built for this. "So how did you find us? Perry said it was a long story and then there were zombies and she never had a chance to explain."

He seemed happy to be off the subject of Rose. "You were gone quite a while, long enough that we were getting worried. Even Perry. We tried your phones but they kept ringing, no one picked up. I went down and asked the receptionist if we could borrow her car and go look for you guys and that was all set up when I got a phone call from Maryse."

"Mambo Number Five?" I asked but then remembered what Ambrosia had said happened to Maryse and immediately felt bad for making a joke.

"She said she felt we were in danger and that Ambrosia was coming for her. I told her where you guys were, what you were doing, and that you weren't answering the phone.

She said Ambrosia probably already had you. We had to get out to her place. We'd then have to take her boat from there. She gave some pretty rudimentary directions: drive boat three miles northeast, turn back in at a stump with a heron's nest on top, head down inlet, past the rotting fishing boat. All of this with a fucking flashlight. I'm amazed we even found Ambrosia's place, actually. Then the call dropped and we never heard from Maryse again. We borrowed the receptionist's car and took straight off after you."

"What happened to Rose's truck?"

"I called the cops and let them know. They eventually called me and said they found it abandoned and in a serious accident. Couldn't find the other car at fault. Your camera equipment was stolen out of the back seat, probably from some street punks. They did find your phone though." He fished it out of his pocket and displayed it. "Must have fallen out of the seat when you hit...whatever you hit. Was it car?"

I nodded. "I think so, anyway."

"Did you get any footage shot?"

I shook my head. "To be honest, I was too chickenshit to be filming in that neighborhood. We were just about to come home. Rose made a wrong turn on the wrong street. The truck just died and suddenly there was a zombie mob. But here's the thing, when I tried to start the car, it *worked*." I stared at Maximus carefully as if he could give me an explanation to that.

He shrugged. "I couldn't tell you why."

"Well as long as you don't call me special again."

He gave me a dry look. "You're sitting here and talking to me when you shouldn't be Dex, I think that's pretty special." He reached into his pocket and pulled out a piece of rumpled paper. "When we got to Maryse's she was gone, so was Ambrosia's air boat. But she left this behind."

He handed it to me. I eyed him suspiciously. "Holding back police evidence now, are we?"

I looked at the paper and I read it out loud, "Tell Rose that I'm sorry. It wasn't my place to interfere. Everyone should be allowed to make their own mistakes."

"Do you think that maybe Maryse was involved with Ambrosia's plan somehow?" he asked.

I shook my head, wincing at the headache it brought on. My ear throbbed sharply. "No. I know she wasn't. This is something else." Maximus never knew what Maryse had done, that she'd discouraged Rose from staying with him after he'd gone Rogue. I didn't know if it was my place to tell him that either, not now when his heart was a mess and Rose was an invalid. But since when did I ever play it safe?

"What it means," I went on, "was that she told Rose not to hold on to you. She told her it would be better for both of you if you weren't together. That she shouldn't take the risk."

His mouth dropped slightly. "How...?"

"Rose told me. She said she regretted it every day, letting someone else influence her decision. She said she'd rather live her days with ghosts and demons with you by her side than the alternative. You would have been worth the risk. It's true."

He sucked in his breath and looked to the window, his eyes becoming glossy. Oh shit. Don't tell me I was making the ginger fucker cry now?

I watched him, wide-eyed and uncomfortable, unsure of what to do or what else to say.

Finally he said, "Thanks, buddy," in a choked voice and got to his feet. He looked to me and smiled. "I needed to hear that."

"Am I interrupting something?" a quiet voice said from the door. My heart skipped in leaps and bounds. I swiveled my head so fast that the room spun but I did not fucking care.

Perry was standing in the doorway, rubbing her hands up and down her arms. Her hair was pulled back in a messy ponytail that she'd obviously slept in. She was wearing jeans, chucks and a Faith No More shirt she'd cut into a tank top. Her face didn't have a lick of makeup on it and I knew she hadn't slept in days. But she was still the most beautiful woman I'd ever seen. And, no matter what, I was still the luckiest son-of-a-bitch in the world.

"No," Maximus said quickly, looking between the two of us. "I was just on my way out."

He squeezed past Perry and left the room, closing the door behind him.

She stood there for a moment, watching me, the distance between us seeming far too large and heavy. I smiled. That's all it took.

She came rushing over, big blue eyes welling up, and threw her arms around me, burying her face in my neck. I didn't even feel any pain. I closed my eyes, my grin taking over my face, and wrapped my arms around her, not caring that it was pulling on my IV drip. I held her as tight as I could, with what strength I had.

Perry sobbed away, trying to speak but not being able to.

"Shhhh, it's okay," I soothed her, stroking the back of her head, her silken hair feeling like heaven under my worn fingers.

I held her like that for as long as I could, just relishing the weight of her in my arms, her heart beating against mine. I decided I was lucky enough to be given a second chance with her, I wasn't going to screw it up. It didn't matter if us being together opened more doors to other worlds, I didn't care if her pregnancy could ruin us. I wasn't going to let her go on the advice of others. What Rose said to me was true, I just hurting too much to listen to it. It hurt to know that I had just given up when the going got rough, that I didn't have enough hope in me to forge through. To risk it all.

There was always another way. I didn't know what Perry was feeling but I knew how I was feeling. I knew her heart was worth all the ugliness we'd have to endure. I wasn't going to give her up on chance. It threw a wrench into what I really wanted—a baby with her, a lifetime together, but there was always another way.

"I'm so sorry, Dex," she cried, pulling away so she could look at me. I gently ran my thumbs under her eyes, wiping away her tears. "I'm so sorry."

"Baby, I'm sorry," I told her, holding her face in my hands now. "I said things I shouldn't have because I got scared."

"I know it was Ambrosia."

"I know. It doesn't matter. I'm sorry I doubted you to begin with. I should have believed you."

"I said some horrible things."

"*I* said some horrible things. Baby, I wish I could take them back."

She sniffed and looked away. "Me too. But I'm glad you said them. Because I *am* young, Dex. You're like nine years older than me and it scares me, you know? You have all this experience with the world, with sex, with relationships—everything. I feel like I've barely lived. This ain't easy to say but...I worry about us. I worry that I'm going to screw it all up because I don't know what I'm doing. This is so new to me."

"Perry, it's okay." Her honesty was breaking my heart.

She shook her head. "It's not okay. Dex, I am so goddamn afraid, you have no idea."

I kissed her forehead softly and whispered, "I have some idea."

"No," she said. She leaned in closer, our noses touching, her eyes searching mine. Oh god, I was so close to just ripping the IV out of my arm and taking her right there on the hospital bed, severed ear and all.

She went on, her voice warbling, "No, I've been holding back, Dex. I've been too scared to even let myself feel anything deeper than my skin. Do you know how I knew I was close to losing you last night?"

"The Mambo called up Maximus."

"No." She licked her lips. I wanted to lick them too, but I felt she was about to tell me something important. "I mean, she did. But I was in my room. I was pacing back and forth, so fucking worried about you. I sat down on my bed and just tried to think, to calm myself down. I had one of your cigarettes you know, so I lit it up—I didn't care, they let you smoke everywhere here. And then I saw Pippa."

I frowned. "Really?"

"Yeah. Really. It was her, just as always. Standing at the end of the bed. Gave me a fucking heart attack but...you know, it was good to see her. It was nice. I...I feel like she's the only one in my family who really cares...and who really understands." She rubbed her lips together and sniffed. My baby kept breaking me. "She didn't say much. She just said...that I shouldn't worry. That there is only good from love. That our hearts are magnets. That we couldn't stay apart for long."

Our hearts are magnets. I'd heard Perry's thoughts say that before. I'd always liked the sound of that.

"And as corny as that all sounds, I think she's right," she

added.

I nodded and pulled her to me again. Pippa may have been a mortal like us but, like us, she knew a thing or two about love and loss. I'd take her advice any day.

"Dex," Perry said into my neck, her wet lips brushing my skin, sending shockwaves through the rest of my body. She pulled her head back and kissed me, hard and soft and deep all at the same time. I couldn't have been floating higher.

She brushed back my hair, careful to avoid the damaged part of my head. There were so many things in her eyes, so much fear and so much hope.

Perry took a deep breath and put her hands on either side of my face. She kissed me again, looked me dead in the eye and said, "Dex Foray. I love you."

Her words took a while to sink in, like the finest drugs, like the start of that trip you never want to end.

She smiled despite herself, despite the look of shock that I knew was on my face and continued, "I love you, I've loved you from the very start. And...sometimes I think I can't possibly love you more. And then I do. You fill me up and break my own heart open, you know? It just creates more room. There is no limit. I love you, I love you, I love you and I'll die saying it because I was born to feel it. I am in love with you, you wonderful, funny, handsome man."

I might have been floating on air earlier, but this...this was grounding me. This was pulling me down, dark and deep and oh so fucking good. This was holding me in place, letting her words wash over me, the sincerity—the love—in her eyes, the passion in her touch. This was something real. This was what I wanted to be buried in, this truth.

I thought my smile would split my head in two. I felt breathless, my heart racing triumphantly. I felt grounded, weightless, alive and otherworldly. I felt her skin, electric between my hands. I pulled her to me and kissed her, kissed her so damn hard even as I started to laugh with joy.

"Baby," I managed to say when I held it together long enough, "Baby, I love you, more than ever, more than anything in the fucking world. You are my world. And all I've ever wanted is for me to be yours."

She kissed me. I kissed her. She traced my skin, I traced hers. Every single nerve in my body was alive. And to say I was hard as concrete would have been an understatement.

I pressed my fingers into her face. "Baby, the first chance I get, I'm going to fuck the shit out of you," I growled.

She smiled coyly, her eyes twinkling. "I think it's called making love now."

"Then I'm fucking making love the shit out of you." I kissed her hard again, pulling her closer against my body, knowing the hospital gown I was in was tissue thin and did nothing to hide my arousal. I'd never wanted her so bad. I wanted more than anything to seal this, to make this real, make it physical.

There was a knock at the door.

Of fucking course.

A chubby-faced nurse poked her head in. She frowned at the sight of Perry practically lying on top of me and gave us a forced smile.

"I'm sorry, the doctor will have to see him soon," she said, then shut the door with a grunt of disgust.

Perry grinned, bright as sunshine, and straightened up. "I can take the hint."

"She looks a bit like the nurse on *Fawlty Towers*," I noted, remembering an episode we'd watched recently.

She climbed off of me and looked up and down my body. "Except you have more than an ingrown toenail. Dex, you know what happened to your ear right?"

I gulped. "I vaguely recall Ambrosia slicing it off."

"The doctors tried to reattach it. They discovered it on Ambrosia when they found her body. But it was too late. Actually your body heals extremely fast, Dex. Almost all your cuts are healed. They can't really explain it."

No, but we could. I grimaced. "So I'm real ugly now, is that what you're saying?"

"Well they said your ear should be more or less like normal when it fully heals. You'll just be missing a little tip."

"But the tip is the best part," I groaned.

"Be glad she didn't go after your dick then."

"*You* should be glad she didn't," I said, then relaxed back, feeling suddenly exhausted. "Oh well, I guess it was about time I had a flaw."

Her mouth twitched up. "Right."

I looked at her in earnest, remembering Ambrosia, what I had done. "Am I in any trouble? For, you know?"

"No. I explained everything to the police. Self-defense through and through. She's dead and they're pretty happy about it. The attacks had been getting out of hand lately and contrary to what Ambrosia thought, they *were* trying to do something about it. I feel like it still might be swept under the rug and explained as bath salts...whatever keeps the public happy."

"Miss Palomino," the nurse said from the door. "I'm sorry."

Perry looked at me, cheeks beaming, and kissed me quickly on the lips before she trotted out of the room.

The doctor came in soon after, pretty much telling me the same thing Perry had told me. Amazing immune system, ear will almost be normal, surprised I was still alive, blah blah blah.

But I wasn't the only one who'd come alive. Perry did when told me she loved me.

She loved me.

She loved me.

∾

I WAS in the hospital for another night for observation. The nurse started limiting visitor contact for fear of overexertion, so I didn't see Perry or Maximus much until I was ready to leave.

I slipped on my clothes, careful not to hurt my rib or tear all my stiches. I was almost fully healed, the cut underneath my tattoo just a ruddy, faded line, but I didn't want to push my luck.

"You ready to go?" Maximus asked having opened the door a crack and stuck his head in.

I shot him a look over my shoulder and went back to pulling on my shirt. "Can't a man get dressed in private anymore? Thought you would have gotten a good enough look at my junk when I was in the swamp the other day. Though, I hope you accounted for shrinkage."

He didn't say anything to that, not even a snort of disgust, so I turned around and looked at him. He looked forlorn and serious, face wane.

"What is it?" I asked.

"I'm not going with you," he said.

"What?"

He sighed and shut the door behind him, leaning against it. "I know I promised I'd do the show with you and Perry, I know Jimmy was counting on it. But I can't go. I have to stay here. I'm sorry."

I nodded, understanding. "Rose."

He chewed on his lip thoughtfully. "Yeah. She's doing a bit better now. She can talk and kind of care for herself. She doesn't remember me though. She doesn't remember any of us. She doesn't know what she is."

"Shit."

"Doctors said amnesia is a side effect, that I should be happy that she's at least improving. Dex, she has no one but me now. Maryse has now been proclaimed dead. She doesn't have any family. She doesn't have anyone to look after her."

I straightened my shirt out and looked him in the eye. "Maximus, you go do what you have to do. Perry and I will figure things out on our own. We'll be okay."

I picked up my duffel bag that they'd brought to the hospital for me and made my way over to the door. I stood a foot away from the flannel-coated, red-headed giant and it struck me with surprising emotion that this might be the last time I'd see the douchecanoe again.

"Take care, man," I said gruffly, holding out my hand.

He grasped it, squeezing tight enough to break a normal man's hand. When I thought it was time for him to let go, he pulled me to him slightly and peered down at me.

"Dex, I know I can't stop you two. And I know it's not my place anymore to tell you otherwise. I don't want to do to you what Maryse did to Rose and me. You love her and she loves you and I reckon maybe that's just enough to even things out. You take care of Perry, ya hear? And take care of yourself."

Fuck. I needed to get out of the room before I started having my period.

I gave him a curt nod. "See ya, Maximus."

I left the room and walked down the hall. Perry was waiting for me.

21

"Baby, please, I'm going to come," I moaned, thrusting into her, afraid to slow my pace.

Perry kissed me deeply, her pulse racing in her lips and whispered, "Just go slower."

I threw my head back and tried to steady myself. "I'll try but if I blow my load early, it's all your fault."

"You're so romantic."

Fuck romance. This was serious business. My balls were so blue, they were navy. "Baby, it's been forever since I've been inside of you."

"It's been five days," she said. "And your rib is still hurting you, I can tell." I grunted and decided to shut her up by pulling out of her and flipping her around on her stomach, spreading her legs with my knees.

"Fine, you want slow, you got it," I said gruffly into her ear. I pulled back a bit on her hair because I knew she loved it and I liked to pretend I was riding her like a cowboy. My wild mustang steed.

I licked my fingers and started running them from her lower back, down the crack of her ass, past her wet hole, all the way to her clit. And back again. Slowly. So slowly. Just as she asked.

She tensed under my touch. I knew I was pushing boundaries with her, but what was the use of boundaries if they weren't there to be pushed?

I leaned forward on her, making sure she felt the weight of me. "Is that slow enough for you?"

She groaned, her breath coming shorter and harder. Her ass moved in rhythm against my fingers and I rubbed her clit with silky pressure. If I was going to come like hell in a handbasket, then she was going to as well and way before I did.

I kept at it until she started squirming under my fingers and did what I loved most, begged me to put myself inside her. I partially obliged. Even though my swollen balls were begging for release, I wet my tip against her folds and stroked it up and down, following where my fingers had been. She started moaning louder, her legs spreading further. Perfection.

I finally gave her what she wanted, what we both needed. I thrust myself inside her, keeping myself pressed against her back, wanting to stay as close as possible. The bliss was unimaginable.

"Can you feel me?" I murmured, feeling myself slowly losing control. Five days had felt like a lifetime.

"I feel you," she gasped. "All of you."

I pounded into her, quickening my pace again, pushing myself and her to the edge. This was how I loved her. I loved her so much. I wanted her to feel my love, every single inch of it.

We came loud and hard and fast and I don't know if it was the endorphins I was high on or something other-wordly, but the bedroom really did seem to shimmy and shake, sparkle and warp, all outside of my view. Maybe we were creating tears in the fabric of the world. Or maybe, maybe we were just creating something new. Something wonderful.

Fuck, she was amazing. *This* was amazing.

I rolled over onto my back, my hand resting on her wonderful ass. "That was long overdue," I said, once I caught my breath.

"I can see it was," she mused, still panting. "I hope you're ready to go again tonight because we have a lot of lost ground to cover. Your cuts are all healed now, and apparently your rib is no excuse."

I let out a small laugh and grinned to myself. "Give me five minutes, baby, and you'll be the one begging me to stop."

She giggled, so fucking cute, and snuggled up to me. "I love you," she said, tracing the bridge of my nose with her finger.

"I love you, too."

More than ever.

$\sim$

EVEN THOUGH WE'D just got back, it hadn't taken long for Perry and I to get back into the swing of things. Now that everything was out in the open and we were luxuriating in our feelings for each other (at least I was —she couldn't tell me she loved me enough), we had our "normal" lives to plan.

Obviously Perry's home was my home and my hone was hers. We knew we were going to have to have a meeting with Jimmy soon and we weren't sure if we could count on having EIT as a job in the future. But we made a pact to each other that we would think about all the alternatives, to keep trying, to never give up. I offered to take care of Perry no matter what happened, but she was still determined to earn her own wages and I'd support her no matter what she chose, whether it was still working as a host at Shownet or bartending at a bar down the street.

The other thing she had to deal with was her family. She couldn't avoid them forever and though New Orleans put us under a great strain, I could still see how her severed ties with her family was really bothering her.

"Why don't I take us down to Portland next weekend?" I asked Perry. We were both lying lengthwise on the couch, half-naked as we'd been a lot lately, and watching *Fawlty Towers* again. Fat Rabbit was on the floor and eyeing us with doggy disdain. He was the only reason why I wasn't getting a blow job at the moment—we all found it too strange with a dog in the room.

She tensed up and I didn't know if it was because I had just started to put my hand down her pants. She swatted at my hand and gave me a dirty look. "You can't turn me on and talk about my parents at the same time."

I sighed and removed my hand. Fair enough. "So, what do you say?"

She exhaled sharply through her nose and mulled it over for quite some time. Finally she said, "Not next weekend. But soon. Maybe in April. Or May."

"Perry you can't avoid them forever. What about Ada?"

"I text her every day. I called this morning."

"You know what I mean. She needs your support. She needs to see you. Remember what you went through when you were a little fifteen?"

She nodded. I tried slipping my fingers down her stomach but she was too quick for me and hit me again.

I kissed the back of her head. "Whatever you choose, just know I'll be with you if you need me. I'd never let you do this on your own. I know how tough families can be."

"But they don't really like you, Dex."

And I didn't really like them. "True. But that's just right now. I'm your boyfriend. I love you. You love me. Maybe over time, they will change their tune. And if they don't, so what? You're with me and that's all that matters."

We lapsed into silence for a few moments, watching Basil slap Manuel around.

"Dex," she said softly.

"Mmmhmmm."

"Have you been having dreams about your mom again?"

I swallowed hard. "No," I told her honestly. "I haven't." The last thing I saw of her was when I had that vision of us in the boat, when she told me she loved me, the cryptic things she said about Michael.

"You seemed to be dreaming about her last night."

This was news to me. "Oh?"

"It wasn't necessarily bad. You were just calling out for her. You sounded...upset. Like sad."

I held her closer to me. "I don't remember."

"I don't blame you. You've been through so much. I don't know what New Orleans did to us but...god Dex, I'm going to be having nightmares for weeks to come, I know it. Finding you buried in that coffin..." she trailed off and let out a sob, shaking slightly.

"Hey, baby," I murmured into her neck. "We made it. I'm alive. You're alive. We're here. We're home. We're home."

I held her like that until the end of the show when my cell rang.

I peered at it. A New Orleans area code.

"Hello?" I asked.

"Dex," Maximus's drawl came through the air, thicker now that he was with his adopted brethren.

"Maximus," I said. "How's life? How is Rose?"

A pause. "She's better. She still doesn't know who I am, not really, but I've got an apartment set-up for us in the Quarter and I hope to move her in there soon. I've got some of her managers handling Nameless for us, so at least that will stick around for her in case she regains her memory soon."

"Well that's great," I told him. "You can still go drink your face off for free."

Perry rolled over to face me. "Tell him I say hi."

"Perry says hi," I told him. "She also says you're ugly."

"Shut up," she said, hitting me again.

"So violent," I mouthed at her.

"You need to get a room," Maximus said.

"We have one, you're the one intruding."

Silence. He cleared his throat.

"Have you told her about me?" he asked. "I mean, what I am?"

My eyes nervously flitted over to Perry who was back to watching the DVD. "No," I said carefully. "I haven't. I was planning on it one day, when things calm down a bit here."

"Good. I reckon she should know the truth. About everything."

He was meaning the baby thing too, the holes in the Thin Veil. I had no plans to tell her *that* part, not for a long time. There were some things she just didn't need to know. Not yet.

"Well, listen," I started.

"Yeah, I should get going. Just wanted to see how you were holding up."

"Almost fully healed. Back to full fucking capacity."

"Now, I'm not sure if you mean the capacity to fuck or... you know what? I don't want to know."

"No, I don't think you do."

"Have you spoken to Jimmy yet...I haven't called him."

"We'll be dealing with him soon. You just take of Rose. Give her our love, okay."

"Will do."

I was about to hang up the phone but quickly said, "Bye, ginger balls" at the last minute. Things were going back to normal.

∼

IT TURNS out that even though Maximus left us under noble circumstances, that didn't mean that Jimmy saw it that way. In fact, Jimmy was right pissed off (though that was no surprise).

"I don't fucking believe it," he muttered into his hands. Perry and I were sitting across the table from him in his office. We'd decided we had to tear ourselves away from our marathon sex session to finally have the meeting and fill Jimmy in on what happened. I hadn't given him the footage yet, wanting to torture him a bit with Maximus's sudden departure from the Experiment in Terror team.

"Well, that's the truth," I said matter-of-factly. "He's staying in New Orleans to look after his sick ex-girlfriend. Kind of fucking noble, if you ask me."

"No one is fucking asking you, Dex," he grunted, face still buried.

Perry and I exchanged a look. She didn't even want to come to the office, saying we could just tell him over the phone, or at least I could go in by myself. I knew she was afraid of him, but I wanted to prove that we really were a team. And to be honest, I wanted to prove more than that.

But first things first.

"So, this is great," he went on caustically. "All this sponsorship and we once again have nothing to show for it. Do you have any idea what this means? They won't want to deal with Shownet again."

"Who are the sponsors, anyway?" I asked out of curiosity.

He sighed, his breath fluttering the papers on his desk. "Enerbomb. An energy drink company."

I snorted. "Well nothing says ghost-hunting like having a fucking cardiac arrest. Are you sure Jack Daniels wasn't interested?"

He looked up at me sharply. I'd never seen his eyes so viper-like. His glasses should have been fogging up. "Is this the time to make jokes, Dex? You've ruined the show. You've ruined me."

"Don't be so dramatic," I said pulling out the USB stick from my pocket and sliding it across the table. "Here. This is what we shot. You can show your Red Balls sponsors that."

He picked it up like it was a wriggling insect.

I nodded at it. "Go ahead, take a look. We'll sit here and wait."

Jimmy shot me a wary look but did as I suggested. He put the USB into his laptop and went through it. Maximus had already picked out all the shots before we left NOLA, so it was easy putting it all together. It wasn't everything, just cropped shots of the exterior of the house intersected with NOLA stock footage and Perry's narration, then everything we'd shot in the interior, ending with the zombie coming after Perry. We ended it in a fade to black, fudging the truth a little and saying that Perry was attacked and then the zombie "ghost" just disappeared in front of our eyes. It was a little bit better than saying he was a real person who jumped out the window to his death for the second time. RIP, Tuffy G.

When he was done, he looked over at us in awe. Well, maybe "awe" was a slight exaggeration. But he looked more impressed than he did ten minutes ago.

He took off his glasses and rubbed at his eyes. "So," he said slowly, "are you telling me that you finally got something amazing and the person who's responsible for it is now gone?"

I grinned, knowing he would say that. "No. Because Perry and I have always had the power to make this amazing. I hate to say this but Maximus was good, he actually was, but it wasn't him that made this work. It was the extra help. It was the extra camera. Just having someone else there. Perry and I, we're too busy staying alive, we can't be worrying about everything. An extra person on our team would make everything run a lot smoother. All the shows will be like the one we just showed you and your sponsors will be cracked out and happy."

He squinted at me, not trusting a word I was saying. "Okay. So if you're right about this, then who would the third person be?"

Perry spoke up, "Let us work on that tonight and get back to you about it."

He directed his disbelieving gaze to her and to her credit she didn't shrink in her seat as she usually did.

"What?" she added. "We have someone in mind, we just don't want to say anything until it's official."

He grunted something. I took that moment to push the envelope further and I put my arm around Perry.

"Don't worry about Jimmy, baby, it always takes him a while to come around."

I smiled as I bit my lip and relaxed in my seat, enjoying the sight of his eyes widening as he put everything together.

"What the hell is this?" he asked.

I shrugged. "What is what?"

"You two are an item now?"

Perry and I exchanged a smile.

"Oh right, this," I said. "Forgot you didn't know."

He was flabbergasted and pissed off, a very Jimmy-esque combo. "I didn't know? Look, I don't care who you're with, Dex, but you do remember what happened with *Wine Babes*."

"I left when it became boring and monotonous."

"Well...I don't know about that..." he said, taken aback.

"And didn't Rebecca just quit?" In fact, Rebecca just told us that this morning when she came by to see how were holding up. The break up with Emily was one of the factors to *Wine Babes* demise, she just couldn't handle it, but working with Jenn had got to be too much, too. I couldn't blame her one bit. I'd been there. "Actually, at this moment, doesn't *Wine Babes* not exist anymore?"

He grunted, eyes studying the papers in front of him. "What's your point, Dex?"

"Everything happens for a reason," I said, getting to my feet. "*Experiment in Terror* might be the show to bring Shownet out of the ground."

He looked at me sharply. I remembered what Seb and Dean had told me the other week, that even they had gotten the talking to about dwindling hits and numbers and their stoner show cost nothing to make. Perry and I had discussed that no matter what Jimmy said, we'd be okay. That we'd go out on our own and do our own thing and make our own damn show if that's what we wanted to do. But even though Jimmy was a giant pain in the ass and the biggest thorn in my side (now that Maximus was in Louisiana, anyway), Shownet was where I got my start, it's what brought Perry and I together, and if I could save the show and possibly save the site, then that's what we'd do. It would almost be damn near poetic.

And I wanted to make sure it was on my terms. Mine and Perry's relationship would never come into question. Our motives for filming a show or not filming a show wouldn't either. We wanted to hold the reins this time. We wanted all the control and considering the risks we took for the show, I'd say we deserved it.

Of course, Jimmy didn't look like he believed a word I was saying. It didn't matter. Tonight we'd have our answer.

~

"To threesomes," I said, raising my jug of beer in the air.

We were sitting in a tapas bar in Pioneer Square, the rain falling steadily outside. Rebecca and Perry were across from me, my two favorite women, and we were making a toast. Not to my boyish sexual fantasies but to our future.

Our plan was in effect. We had just asked Rebecca to become the third member of *Experiment in Terror* and she'd gleefully accepted. Now that Maximus was staying behind in NOLA and taking care of Rose, we realized that it really was worth it to have someone else on the team with us. Someone to organize shit and film when we needed an extra hand. She wouldn't be on camera, even though Perry asked her to, but she'd make sure everything was running smoothly. And we knew Jimmy loved Rebecca and wanted to use her in any way he could. With *Wine Babes* kaput, he'd be happy to know that Rebecca was still with the Shownet team.

Meanwhile, Jenn could go fuck herself. But that was neither here nor there.

"To threesomes," Rebecca and Perry said in unison and the three of us clinked our mugs together. We chugged it down and then waved over the waitress for another round.

Rebecca dabbed at her red lips with a napkin. "So where is our first adventure?"

"It ain't Napa Valley, baby," I told her. "So you can forget the wine and macaroni and cheese."

She grinned. "Good. I was so sick of that bloody shit. I never want to drink another glass of wine again. A pint of ale is all there is for me, now and for good."

"All these years in the states, and you still speak funny," I teased her, sitting back in the booth. The bar was crowded, everyone having a good time, and it felt fucking good to have my favorite people around me. Cold and wet outside, dry and warm inside. A perfect Seattle night.

"Ha ha," Rebecca said, shooting me her patented dirty look, made more vicious by her thick eyeliner.

Perry smiled. "We don't know where we're going yet. But that's something you can look into. Start searching around the web to see if there are some paranormal hotspots or new hauntings. No matter how implausible it sounds, flag it and we can all look into it together. Go from there."

I squeezed her knee under the table. I loved seeing her take charge. It was about time.

A Foo Fighters song came on in the bar and Rebecca got up. "Care to dance with me, Dex?" she asked, batting her eyes. She looked to Perry. "You're next, by the way."

Perry grinned and sipped back her beer. She swatted at

my ass as Rebecca pulled me to the floor. "You better not turn her straight," she warned me.

"Baby," I said raising my arms out to the side of me, "if I haven't made her want cock at this point, you know she's muff for life."

Perry laughed and rolled her eyes while Rebecca hissed, "Dex!" in my ear, continuing to pull me backward until I was surrounded by a bunch of collegiate drunk idiots trying to both dance and rock out to Dave Grohl.

I scoffed at them. "You think this is rock?"

"Dex," Rebecca warned again. "You can't dance to anything heavier than this."

"I dunno," I said, taking her hands in mine as if we were preparing to waltz. "I think I can dance to anything. It's why God gave me feet."

"Please don't tell me what else God gave you," she groaned.

I laughed. "You know me too well."

She smiled but her eyes had turned serious. "I do. So when are you going to do it?"

I gasped in mock surprise. "My dear Rebecca, did you lure me to the dance-floor under false pretences?"

"Of course," she said. She nodded subtly to a blonde chick waiting at the bar. "If I wanted to dance with someone properly, I would have asked that woman over there."

"She's nice. Big boobs, full ass. You and I have similar tastes."

She grunted. "Come on, Dex, I'm serious."

"So am I."

She kicked my leg. Her pointy shoes should come with a hazardous warning.

"Hey, ow," I scowled at her. "I was recently a human carving board, remember?'"

"Hey, Dex. When are you going to do it?" she asked again.

It was my fault. I'd been stupid enough to let Rebecca in on my secret. I was regretting it now, but I had really needed her opinion.

"I don't know," I told her honestly, my eyes drifting over to Perry who was drinking at the table, looking comfortable and happy. "Not for a while. I'll know when the time is right."

Rebecca grinned and squeezed my hands. "I'm so excited. You're going to get married!"

"Shut it," I warned her, giving her a biting look. "I haven't asked yet and she hasn't accepted."

"But you bought the ring today, didn't you?"

I nodded. It was burning a hole in my fucking pocket as we spoke. After Perry and I had gone to see Jimmy, we went back to the apartment. I excused myself saying that I had to go get my car insurance renewed (which was true) and that I'd be right back. I ended up going to this jeweler just outside of town, one that specialized in vintage baubles. The generic diamond bullshit wasn't fit for my Perry. I didn't want chicks asking her how many carats it was or how much I paid. I had the money—it was just no one's business.

The ring was from the sixties, made of white gold, and honestly couldn't be more perfect. Naturally there were a few diamonds, but they acted as accents and flanked a center stone thingy of red and yellow. Ruby and yellow topaz—my birthstone and hers.

I wanted to show it to Rebecca in person, but I was too terrified to take it out in public, so the best she got was a quick photo from my phone after I purchased it from the overjoyed Croatian man. I erased the photo right after and when I got back to the house, Perry made me go on a walk with her and Fat Rabbit. Right after that Rebecca wanted to do drinks so we could discuss our business proposition. I didn't have the time to take it out of my pocket and hide it somewhere, so there it was. At least it was in the tiny change pocket in my jeans, a place I could barely fit my fingers.

"I hope I'm a bridesmaid," Rebecca said. "Oh, you're going to have an amazing wedding. I can't wait to start planning this. The bridesmaid dresses have to be amazing, I know this perfect tailor in Bellevue who could do it."

And then Rebecca was babbling and babbling about the wedding. I didn't hear a thing until the song ended. I shot her an apologetic smile and marched straight to Perry, holding my hand out to her.

"Care to dance, m'lady?" I asked.

Perry smiled sweetly and put her dainty hand in mine. I closed my fingers over it and choked back on a sudden lump in my throat. Soon. Soon I would be on my knees doing this.

Asking for her hand in marriage.

She got up and I brought her to the dance floor, pulling her body close to mine. I don't even know what song was playing. It didn't matter.

All that mattered was us.

Me and the future Mrs. Dex Foray.

THE END

WHAT'S NEXT?

Thank you so much for reading Come Alive, book #7 in the Experiment in Terror series.

If you want to connect with me, you can always find me on Instagram (where I post travel photos, fashion, teasers, etc, IG IS MY LIFE and the easiest place to find me online)

-> or in my Facebook Group (we're a fun bunch and would love to have you join)

-> Otherwise, feel free to signup for my mailing list (it comes once a month) and Bookbub alerts!

UP NEXT...oh folks, we are getting closer to the conclusion of the series. EEK! Ashes to Ashes - book #8 - is out and ready for your consumption and answering burning questions such as:

- Is Dex going to propose?
- How will Rebecca fit with the team?
- Is this the scariest book yet (yes. It is).

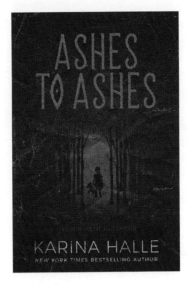

ACKNOWLEDGMENTS

Thank you: My amazing Scott MacKenzie and our dear Bruce – I love you both. The crazy awesome authors of Fight Club, the ladies (and Rob) of Halle's Harlots. My parents, for being awesome (like cleaning my house, walking my dog and putting together my elliptical machine kind of awesome) and for letting me use their boat as an office. Kelly St-Laurent, Megan Simpson, Emily Franke, Megan Ward and Kara Malinczak – you all really stepped up to the plate with this one. EIT fans, everywhere, this book's for you.

ALSO BY KARINA HALLE

Contemporary Romances

Love, in English

Love, in Spanish

Where Sea Meets Sky (from Atria Books)

Racing the Sun (from Atria Books)

The Pact

The Offer

The Play

Winter Wishes

The Lie

The Debt

Smut

Heat Wave

Before I Ever Met You

After All

Rocked Up

Wild Card (North Ridge #1)

Maverick (North Ridge #2)

Hot Shot (North Ridge #3)

Bad at Love

The Swedish Prince

The Wild Heir

A Nordic King

Nothing Personal

My Life in Shambles

Discretion

Disarm

Disavow

The Royal Rogue

The Forbidden Man

Romantic Suspense Novels by Karina Halle

Sins and Needles (The Artists Trilogy #1)

On Every Street (An Artists Trilogy Novella #0.5)

Shooting Scars (The Artists Trilogy #2)

Bold Tricks (The Artists Trilogy #3)

Dirty Angels (Dirty Angels #1)

Dirty Deeds (Dirty Angels #2)

Dirty Promises (Dirty Angels #3)

Black Hearts (Sins Duet #1)

Dirty Souls (Sins Duet #2)

Horror Romance

Darkhouse (EIT #1)

Red Fox (EIT #2)

The Benson (EIT #2.5)

Dead Sky Morning (EIT #3)

Lying Season (EIT #4)

On Demon Wings (EIT #5)

Old Blood (EIT #5.5)

The Dex-Files (EIT #5.7)

Into the Hollow (EIT #6)

And With Madness Comes the Light (EIT #6.5)

Come Alive (EIT #7)

Ashes to Ashes (EIT #8)

Dust to Dust (EIT #9)

The Devil's Duology

Donners of the Dead

Veiled

ABOUT THE AUTHOR

Karina Halle, a former screenwriter, travel writer and music journalist, is the *New York Times*, *Wall Street Journal*, and *USA Today* bestselling author of *The Pact*, *A Nordic King*, and *Sins & Needles*, as well as over fifty other wild and romantic reads. She, her husband, and their adopted pit bull live in a rain forest on an island off British Columbia, where they operate a B&B that's perfect for writers' retreats. In the winter, you can often find them in California or on their beloved island of Kauai, soaking up as much sun (and getting as much inspiration) as possible. For more information, visit

www.authorkarinahalle.com